Lucien leaned toward her and kissed her chastely, but Theia *wasn't* here for that. She'd had enough of chastity.

She moved her other hand to Lucien's neck, thumb against the rough stubble at his jawline, and kept him from pulling away as she deepened the kiss. He wasn't difficult to persuade. He also tasted of mint. Theia laughed softly against his lips, and Lucien drew back slightly, a puzzled smile on his face.

"What's funny?"

"You brushed your teeth before I got here. You heard me coming, and you brushed your teeth."

He smiled, a hint of color to his cheeks that wasn't reflected firelight. "Maybe I just like clean teeth."

Theia shrugged off the borrowed robe. "Be quiet," she murmured and climbed over his lap...

Jane Kindred is the author of the Demons of Elysium series of M/M erotic fantasy romance, the Looking Glass Gods dark fantasy tetralogy and the gothic paranormal romance *The Lost Coast*. Jane spent her formative years ruining her eyes reading romance novels in the Tucson sun and watching *Star Trek* marathons in the dark. She now writes to the sound of San Francisco foghorns while two cats slowly but surely edge her off the side of the bed.

Books by Jane Kindred

Harlequin Nocturne

Sisters in Sin

Waking the Serpent
Bewitching the Dragon
The Dragon's Hunt
Seducing the Dark Prince

SEDUCING THE DARK PRINCE

———

JANE KINDRED

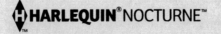

Recycling programs
for this product may
not exist in your area.

ISBN-13: 978-1-335-62953-1

Seducing the Dark Prince

Printed in U.S.A.

Dear Reader:

They say the devil is in the details. The "devil," in this case, happens to be the hero of this story. Lucien Smok isn't a conventional Prince of Darkness. He fights his nature, resisting his fate. But in the world of the Carlisle sisters, fate is everything.

Crafting the details of what kind of devil Lucien would be wasn't easy. As the quintessential serpent among the serpent/dragon shifters in my alternate Sedona, he has a lot to live up to. Which, for Lucien, turns out to be the crux of his problem—living up to other people's expectations.

I also had my heroine, Theia Dawn, to worry about. In the first three books in the series, the sisters have awakened, bewitched and redeemed the immortal souls of their lovers. With their Lilith blood, they've been the tempters of the serpent in the garden instead of the tempted. So it makes sense that Theia—whose name means goddess—would be the temptress of the ultimate snake. She's always been the good one, the quiet one...the one who was so busy taking care of everyone else's feelings that she forgot to devote time to her own. In Lucien, she'll discover what she's been missing.

Wishing you unexpected magic,

Jane Kindred

Chapter 1

Like the ethereal substance his last name evoked, Lucien Smok was breathtaking—literally. The moment Theia saw him across the temple reception hall, the air rushed from her lungs as though it had been sucked into a vacuum. Pale blue eyes like pieces of ice locked on hers from beneath long lashes, dark brows in an ivory face lifted in amusement above them as if he was well aware of the effect he was having on her.

She'd seen him before somewhere. In a dream or a dark premonition. Beneath the reception hall's Baroque quadratura-painted ceiling—invoking the blessing of the gods of Olympus—he reminded her of a painting by Waterhouse, Narcissus winking just for a moment at the viewer before returning to his reflection.

But beautiful or not, this wasn't some breathless lust at first sight. She really couldn't breathe.

Theia clutched at her throat and tried to make a sound, but nothing came out. Her lungs were locked in a spasm, convulsively trying to take in air against some obstruction.

Her dark-haired Narcissus crossed the reception hall in two swift strides and embraced her from behind, arms wrapped around her waist and hands clasped tight beneath her breasts, a gesture of intimacy. Vertigo swam over her, making her feel as though she were floating within herself, a lighter-than-air balloon encased in a human frame, bobbing against its edges.

He hugged her forcefully, jolting her against him, almost off the ground—once, twice, thrice.

Another spasm of her diaphragm forced what remained

of the air in her lungs through her windpipe and dislodged the champagne grape she'd swallowed wrong. Such a small thing to cause so much trouble.

Air rushed in so quickly that she choked on it, gasping and coughing until tears ran down her cheeks.

"All right now?" The soft voice at her ear brought her fully back to herself. His hold around her hadn't loosened and was decidedly more intimate than it had been when he'd been performing the Heimlich on her.

Theia realized she'd relaxed into his embrace, her arms sliding around his, and she let go with a jolt and bolted from his grasp. Though the moment had seemed epic and prolonged, none of the other guests were paying any attention.

His smile was one-sided—a slight leftward lift that combined amusement, smugness and a hint of offense. "You're welcome."

"Sorry. I didn't mean to… I mean, thanks. I appreciate the—"

"Don't strain yourself, darling. It's okay. I'm used to this reaction."

Theia's embarrassment dissipated, and she narrowed her eyes, wrapping her arms around herself. "What reaction?"

"Women going weak in the knees and tongue-tied around me. I expect it's being this close to money." His voice had the lazy, sardonic drawl of James Spader's bad boy Steff in *Pretty in Pink*. "Does that to some women, I understand."

"Wow. I take it back. You're a complete ass."

"Not the first time I've heard that, either." He held out his hand. "Lucien Smok, heir to the Smok Biotech fortune and your hero today."

Theia kept her hands tucked under her arms. "Gosh, how fortunate for me. And I've heard of you."

"Of course you have. Hence the reaction." His hand

dropped casually to his side. "Are you going to reciprocate?"

Theia blinked at him. "What?"

"Your name. Not going to give it to me? Then let me guess." Before she could react, Lucien had drawn her left arm from where she'd tucked it, his fingers stroking the crescent moon and descending cross tattooed on her inner forearm. The slow, sensual touch sent a shiver down her spine. "The mark of Lilith. You must be a Carlisle. I'm going to guess Theia." He let her go, and Theia wobbled a bit from having planted her feet so firmly to steel herself against him.

Heat bloomed in her cheeks. "How do you know that?"

"I cheated. I asked the groom."

"No, I mean Lilith. How do you know about Lilith?"

A fleeting look she couldn't interpret crossed his features. "I've studied astrology. I'm familiar with the symbol."

She was sure he'd meant something more than just the astrological symbol—a representation of the Black Moon Lilith, the elliptical focal point opposite the earth at lunar apogee. He'd associated it with the Carlisles. But Lucien didn't elaborate.

"Well, you're wrong," said Theia. "I'm not a Carlisle."

His brow furrowed, as though he didn't care much for being wrong. "Oh?"

"My name is Dawn. Theia Dawn. My sisters are Carlisles." She'd taken her middle name as her last after learning about the second family her father had kept hidden until his death. She didn't want the name that belonged to a cheater and a liar. But Theia didn't bother to explain any of this to Lucien Smok. Let him wonder. She turned on her heel and left him staring after her.

Gliding up beside her, her twin put her arm in Theia's. "Who was that?" Luckily, she'd taken Theia's right arm.

Theia wasn't about to let Rhea anywhere near that Lilith
tattoo, especially now that Lucien had touched it. Where
Theia occasionally had prophetic dreams and visions, Rhea
could cut right through the annoying interpretation of sym-
bolism with her "pictomancy" readings to see the future in
tattoo ink. And Theia absolutely did *not* want to know any
specifics about her future.

"Lucien Smok. His family owns the biotech firm that
recently partnered with Northern Arizona University. I
think he's a friend of Rafe's."

Rhea wrinkled her nose. "I wouldn't say friend. Phoebe
was telling me about the Smoks. Rafe's family knows them,
but she doesn't remember sending them an invitation. Some
uncle of Rafe's must have brought Lucien along."

Before Theia could speculate on what Lucien was doing
there, a commotion broke out at the front of Covent Temple's reception hall. A tall, Nordic hunk of beefcake was literally thumping his chest at the best man, who stood coolly
observing the former and looking perfectly at home in his
Armani tux, graying temples adding to his sophistication
against the rich hue of his skin.

"Looks like your man is fighting with Dev." Theia
nudged her sister. "Go get him, sweetie. We don't want Kur
getting out and eating the guests." Dev Gideon, their sister
Ione's boyfriend, had an unfortunate tendency to transform
into an ancient Sumerian dragon demon when provoked.

Rhea sighed. "Leo must have been celebrating a little
too enthusiastically." Like the thousand-year-old Viking he
was, Leo Ström was fond of a good, hearty drink.

Theia watched Rhea weave through the guests to get to
Leo, the shin-length red chiffon of her bridesmaid's dress
swinging and swishing gracefully. It was odd to see Rhea
in anything but pants. Not that Theia was much for dresses,
either.

She glanced down at her own, smoothing the fabric beneath the crisscross bodice. Only Phoebe could have gotten her and Rhea cleaned up this good. Well, Ione had, really. But Phoebe had chosen the fabric as part of her red rose-themed Beltane wedding—red, blush and white ribbon draped the room, woven around the support at the center of the hall like a Maypole and fanning out to form a latticed canopy.

Theia had to admit the dress looked fantastic with both her natural dark bob and Rhea's short, bleached-blond cut sculpted into points—the dead giveaway for those who had trouble telling them apart. Rhea had curled her points at the tips for the occasion, adding a dab of cherry-red dye. She'd added some of it to the points of Theia's bob, too. It was more difficult to see against the dark color, but Theia preferred subtlety.

With Ione officiating as high priestess in her longer, dusty-rose version of the dress, the twins' red had made Phoebe stand out. She'd been absolutely gorgeous in a fairy-tale bone-white off-the-shoulder sweetheart gown with beaded lace and a vintage mantilla from Rafe's own grandmother.

Theia glanced around, realizing she hadn't seen Phoebe in a while. Or Rafe. God, you'd think they could wait a few hours for the honeymoon.

Her glance fell once more on Lucien Smok, flirting with one of the younger members of Ione's coven. An unfamiliar irritation prickled along Theia's skin as his hand rested on Margot's shoulder while he leaned close, Margot laughing at something he'd said. Theia shook off the sensation. *No. Absolutely not.* This couldn't be jealousy, because she had absolutely zero interest in Lucien Smok. Or the heart-stopping contrast of his pale eyes with his nearly jet-black, effortlessly messy hair.

He caught her watching him and winked.

Theia looked away deliberately, her eyes on Rhea lead-ing Leo away from the open bar. It was always amusing to see Rhea, her form slight beside him, managing the Chieftain of the Wild Hunt. Having spent the last thousand years under the control of a Valkyrie, he seemed perfectly content to let a woman take charge despite his outward bluster.

On the opposite end of the room, where the reception hall connected to the temple nave by a breezeway, the Sedona winds had apparently kicked up, and the doors blew open with a bang. Ione moved to shut them, her long, ironed-straight hair whipping about her head in a halo of setting-sun ombré, but paused and stood deathly still, staring at something on the other side of the doorway. Theia moved around the support column that blocked her view.

With the wind had come an uninvited guest—the necromancer who'd made more than one attempt on the lives of both bride and groom in recent months. Theia's jaw dropped open, and she sensed Rhea's shock echoing hers from across the room. Carter Hamilton was supposed to be rotting in prison.

His overly whitened smile flashed in his overly bronzed face as he stood bracing his hands between the double doors like Maleficent making an appearance at Sleeping Beauty's first birthday. "Am I too late to toast the happy couple?"

"How the hell are you here?" Ione's voice seemed icy calm as she faced her psychotic ex, but Theia knew she was barely keeping it together.

Carter's gaze acknowledged Dev as he appeared at Ione's side. "And there he is, like a good little cur, looking for a pat on the head."

A low rumble came out of Dev's throat—too low to be human.

Ione took Dev's hand. "Don't trouble, love. He isn't worth it."

Their newly minted brother-in-law emerged from the stairwell to the bell tower that was doubling as a dressing room, moving toward Carter in a way that ought to unnerve the other man. Even without the Quetzalcoatl tattoo visible at his shoulders beneath the white linen wedding shirt, Rafe Diamante was imposing. And the knowledge that Rafe possessed the necromantic power Carter had killed to try to get should have had the slighter man quaking in his boots. But Carter's smile persisted.

"You have no right to set foot on Covent property," Rafe warned.

Carter's gaze flicked over him. "Nor have you, my friend. I understand you've been formally expelled from the Covent for oath breaking."

"I'm not your friend. No one here is your friend."

Phoebe, descending the staircase behind Rafe, paused on the bottom step with one slipper-clad foot wavering over the floor, her face a white mask of shock. She'd been the one to put Carter in prison while she was still practicing law.

Ione's hand tightened around Dev's. "What do you want, Carter?"

"Just to see your faces when I tell you my good news. The conviction for the crimes you framed me for has been overturned. I'm a free man."

Cake and champagne churned in Theia's stomach.

Phoebe voiced her shock. "How is that possible?"

Carter's eyes settled on her, bitter amusement dancing in them. "So you don't deny you framed me."

"No one framed you," Rafe growled. "You murdered four people."

"Well, the state doesn't seem to agree. Nor does the Covent."

Preceded by a flourish of his hand in the air, a champagne flute materialized in Carter's fingers. "To the bride." Carter raised the glass toward Phoebe. "Who looks almost as lovely in white as she does in nothing at all. And I have the pictures to prove it."

A collective gasp rustled through the hall.

As Carter drank, Rafe charged him, the snake tattoo twisting and roiling beneath his shirt, but Carter's physical matter seemed to dissolve into smoke at Rafe's contact with him, leaving Rafe's fingers to close around a nonexistent collar. The bright grin was the last thing to go, like an evil Cheshire Cat.

Chapter 2

Ione was livid. "That was an astral projection. He's out of prison and accessing powerful magic. What the devil is going on?" She was staring at Dev, as if he ought to know.

"I don't know a thing about it, love, I promise. I haven't been privy to Covent business since I resigned my commission as assayer."

Rafe closed the adjoining doors forcefully and turned back to face the hall. "I, for one, am not going to waste a moment of my wedding day thinking about that insignificant, third-rate sorcerer. He wasn't really here, and that's precisely the way he should be treated." He stepped toward Phoebe and took her hand. "Care to dance, Mrs. Carlisle-Diamante?"

Phoebe smiled gamely. "I'd love to, Mr. Diamante-Carlisle."

The mariachi band Rafe had hired—its members all magical connections of the Diamante family—began to play, and Rafe led his wife out onto the floor.

Theia took a step toward Ione, intending to try to reassure her, but a hand on her shoulder made her turn.

"May I have this dance, Ms. Dawn?" Lucien's smile was mischievous. How did he manage to make an offer to dance sound dirty?

Before she could decline, he'd tucked her hand into his and slipped his arm around her waist, turning her toward the dance floor.

He pulled her closer as she started to draw back. "You wouldn't embarrass me in front of all these people by turning me down, would you?"

"I might."

"I've never been turned down before. It might damage my confidence. Could set me back years emotionally."

"Then I definitely should."

Lucien grinned. "But you won't."

"Won't I?"

"I fascinate you."

"Oh, for heaven's sake." Theia shoved away from him and stalked to the bar.

Like a persistent mosquito, he was buzzing at her side as she ordered her drink. "What if I blackmailed you? Would you dance with me then?"

Theia whirled on him. "Excuse me?"

"That was an odd little display from the groom. And I swear I saw the best man's eyes glow with their own fire. Not to mention the fact that someone just dematerialized right in front of us, and everyone is acting like nothing happened."

"Who the hell are you, anyway?" Theia narrowed her eyes. "Do you even know the Diamantes?"

"Of course I do. I'm exactly who I say I am. You can ask Rafael. Our families go back a long way. And there have been rumors about the Diamantes for just as long. Looks like today I've seen evidence that those rumors are true."

"Then maybe you should take up your concerns with *Rafe* himself, if you know him so well. I'm sure he'd find them very interesting."

"Ooh." Lucien gave a sexy little shiver that Theia tried not to physically respond to and failed. "It sounds like you're suggesting something untoward might befall me. Are you threatening me? I suppose you're one of them, too."

Theia's fists clenched at her sides. "One of what?"

Lucien leaned in intimately close. "Witches, of course."

Theia laughed. "That's what you're planning to blackmail me with? We're standing in the reception hall of the temple of the Sedona branch of the world's largest organized coven. It's not exactly a secret that there are witches here."

"But it is something of a secret that Rafe Diamante is a necromancer, isn't it? And that Dev Gideon is the host for a demon?"

It hardly seemed useful to argue the finer points of Rafe's incidental command of the dead or Dev's shared physicality with an enslaved dragon from the underworld. The fact was that Lucien's statement was irrefutable.

Theia hoped the look she was giving him was as murderous as she intended. "What do you want?"

Lucien's eyes widened and he let out a laugh of pure surprise. "Did you think I was seriously going to blackmail you? Sorry. I have a tendency to take a joke too far. I was just having a little fun with you."

"Oh, well, I'm *so* glad it was fun for you. Now you can fuck off."

"There *is* a little something I was hoping you could help me with, though."

Theia sighed, steeling herself for more innuendo.

"I understand you're working on your master's in molecular biology at NAU." That wasn't creepy-stalkery at all. "So?"

"I'm sure you've heard that Smok Biotech is undertaking a joint venture with the university microbiology lab."

Theia acknowledged this with an uninterested lift of her eyebrows, even though the new lab actually interested her a great deal. Smok was just the sort of corporation she didn't want the university to be associated with, a for-profit pharmaceutical giant. At the same time, it offered unprecedented funding opportunities for expanded research.

"I need someone I can trust to provide some oversight on a special project—someone who won't be fazed by...odd goings-on." Lucien flashed his crooked smile again, trying to charm her, but seemed to realize the smile wasn't working on her and let it fade. "To put it bluntly, someone familiar with the supernatural who also understands the science."

Theia crossed her arms and studied him. "And are you? Familiar with it?"

Something dark seemed to cloud his vision for a moment, but he shook it off and smiled. "Not quite as familiar with it as you are, I'm sure. You might say my family is magical adjacent. Our business intersects with the magical community. It's sort of a quid pro quo."

"Unless you're implying that I owe you for saving me from choking on a grape, there's no quo I could possibly want from you or your organization. I'm sorry, Mr. Smok, but I'm not interested."

Lucien met her gaze with a reproachful look. "Mr. Smok? Really?"

"Pretty much." Theia caught Rhea's eye across the room and moved away from the bar, but Lucien stepped in front of her once more.

"Talk to Rafe. Before you write me off completely, ask him about the mutually beneficial relationship the Smok family has had with the Diamantes for ages." He took a card from his shirt pocket, crimson with black lettering, and handed it to her.

Theia thought about refusing it, but that would just prolong the "dance." She snatched it out of his hand and walked swiftly away before he could say anything else, meeting Rhea halfway as she came to her twin's rescue.

"I saw your signal." Rhea glanced at Lucien still standing by the bar. He raised a glass of champagne toward them. "I wasn't sure you really wanted rescuing, though. He looks tasty."

"He's a creep, and I'm not interested. I'm more concerned about Carter's little magic show."

Rhea glowered. "Yeah, what was that? How the hell did Malibu Ken get out of prison?"

"I'm guessing one of his dirty friends in high places fixed it for him."

Lucien's words about quid pro quo and his family's relationship with the magical community came back to her. Both Rafe and Dev had spoken of connections that helped keep Covent business—and other supernatural events—from the public eye. Could that be the connection with the Smok family? Maybe she should talk to Rafe after all. Not because she had any intention of getting involved in Lucien's project, but because she and her sisters had a right to know who else knew about their business.

It wasn't until she was helping clean up after the reception ended that Theia found her opening. Phoebe and Rafe were about to leave for the Yucatán, and she wouldn't have another opportunity.

Theia stacked the folding chairs as Rafe collected them, his thick, dark waves tied back in a high, bobbed tail. "What do you know about Lucien Smok?"

Rafe paused in picking up a chair. "Was he bothering you? I saw him talking to you, but I figured you could handle him. I'd keep him at arm's length if I were you."

It wasn't quite the answer she'd expected. "So your family doesn't have some kind of simpatico relationship with the Smoks?"

Rafe's look was guarded. "I wouldn't call it simpatico, exactly, but there *is* a relationship. It goes back centuries. To the time of the founding of the Covent, in fact." The Diamantes had been founding members.

"You mean they're a Covent family?"

"No, not exactly." He handed her the folded chair. "There were no witches among the Smok family—that I know of. But I read a lot of Covent history in my father's records after his death. Information that isn't generally known."

It was unlike Rafe to be so cagey.

"What kind of information?"

Rhea's laugh rang out from the stairs as she came down with Phoebe after helping her change. Rafe set another chair on the stack and smiled at the sight of Phoebe in her usual bouncy ponytail, bangs across her forehead instead of swept back as they had been under the mantilla. "My father kept several volumes on Covent history and politics," he murmured, still smiling at Phoebe. "Ione has the keys to his house. Tell her I left some books for you in the library."

After seeing Phoebe and Rafe off with much ribbing and a fair amount of sisterly tears, Theia and Rhea flopped together onto the bench by the door, and Rhea kicked off her heels with a groan.

Theia removed hers more sedately. "Where's Leo?"

"I told him to go ride with the Hunt for a while and work off some of his buzz. It's weird. Alcohol doesn't usually affect him this much. He's got a pretty high tolerance."

"I thought the Wild Hunt only appeared between Halloween and Yule."

"It does, normally. But now that he's mortal, he's not bound by the Norns' rules and he can conjure the riders when he likes. There's always some sicko out there that needs a one-way ticket to Náströnd."

Theia poked at her décolletage. "It seems a little like playing God. How does he determine that someone is deserving of having their soul ripped out and escorted to hell?"

Rhea shrugged. "It's a scent or something. I don't ask too many questions. He gets all Gunnar the tenth-century Viking on me sometimes, like his soul is taking the reins even though he's no longer under the curse, and Gunnar can be a little…pompous."

"But you've ridden with him."

"Yeah."

"And you don't feel weird about it? About taking somebody out of the earthly plane?"

"And having one less pedophile or rapist walking the earth? Not so much."

Theia had to admit she didn't exactly hate the idea. As long as their guilt was certain.

When Ione and Dev came back from closing up the temple, Theia could see the tension on Ione's face. Carter had really gotten to her. She couldn't blame her. Carter Hamilton was like a nasty rash that just kept coming back. It hurt to see his manipulative bullshit affecting Ione like this.

As Ione picked up one of the plastic bins of supplies, Theia hopped up from the bench and grabbed another. "Do you need any help getting things back to the house?"

"No, I think we're good. Dev's already loaded up the car with the rest."

Theia followed her out with her bin. "By the way, Rafe mentioned something about getting the key to his dad's place from you. He wanted me to take a quick look in on it while I'm watching Phoebe's."

"His dad's place?" Ione set the bin on top of the others and loaded Theia's next to it. "I thought he was selling that."

"I assume he still is, but I guess nobody's been by regularly except the gardener, and he wanted me to take a look around."

Ione could always tell when one of them was bullshitting her, and the fact that she didn't push back on the request spoke volumes about her mental state.

She took a set of keys from her purse and handed them to Theia. "Just make sure you get them back to me."

As Ione got into the car, Dev took Theia aside. "She didn't want me to tell you this, but our unwanted guest pretty much ruined her plans for the reception." Dev glanced at Rhea leaning into the car to block Ione's view. "It was supposed to be ours as well."

Theia stared at him, confused. "Your what?"

"Reception. Don't react. She might snap if she realizes I'm telling you. But we drove up to Vegas a few weeks ago and tied the knot." He allowed himself a little grin while Theia suppressed the urge to squeal and jump up and down.

"You complete bastard. I can't believe you're telling me this now when I can't do anything."

"I suggested to Tweedledum that you and she could plan a little celebration for Ione later when she's cooled down."

"You're lucky you didn't say Tweedledee. Because Rhe is definitely Dum." Theia grinned but kept it subtle. "And you can count on us."

Rhea joined Theia as Dev and Ione drove away, waving like Stepford wives only to start jumping and squealing in unison the second the car was out of visual range.

"Can you believe the ovaries on that one?" Rhea laughed as they spun around. "Eloping and stealing Phoebe's thunder? Phoebe's going to be furious."

"I don't know how she kept it to herself all this time." Although Ione was certainly better equipped to keep a secret than the rest of them. Theia glanced at Rhea as the dance died down. "You'd better not tell me you and Leo are up to something similar."

"Me?" Rhea laughed. "Right. Like I'd get married." She winked, which wasn't reassuring. Everyone in the family was pairing off, and Theia was the odd one out. Rhea, as usual, could see what she was thinking. "Why don't you just let me read you again?"

"*No.* There's no reason to rehash what I already know."

"Which is what? That your love life is cursed? I think you're being way too literal about it. Just let me ask a more specific question."

The night was getting chilly now that the sun was down.

Theia pulled the shawl she'd borrowed from Ione around her shoulders, tucking her tattooed arm underneath it. "I'm good, thanks. So, takeout?"

Rhea sighed through her nose, her mouth in a thin line of annoyance, but shrugged her acquiescence. "Indian?"

Theia gave it a thumbs-up. "You order. I'll drive." She held out her hand for the keys.

"You're not driving Minnie Driver."

"Your car is not a person, and yes, I am. I saw how much champagne you had."

Rhea tossed her the keys and got in on the passenger side, patting the dash. "Don't listen to her, Minnie. You are too a person." She pulled up the delivery app on her phone and started making selections. "Whose house are we going to? Phoebe's or Rafe's?"

"Neither, actually." Theia ground the gears, and Rhea swore, gripping the seat. Theia ignored her, putting the car in gear properly. "Do you still have the address for Rafael Sr.'s place in your phone?"

Rhea glanced over at her. "The Ice Palace? Yeah, why?"

"There's something I need to pick up. We can pretend we're filthy rich, like Phoebe." She grinned without looking over.

"Ha. Phoebe, married to the richest man in town, and still keeping her little bungalow."

"I think she's still freaked out about those reporters outside Rafe's window filming him going spelunking in her *cave* that time."

"He *is* quite the cave diver. Oh, dammit."

"What?"

"We totally missed the opportunity for cave-diving puns. They're visiting cenotes on their honeymoon."

"Ah, damn. We're off our game."

Driving the labyrinthine route from Covent Temple back to the highway was much easier than driving in. A proximity glamour kept passersby from noticing the otherwise startling white byzantine spires against the sienna red hoodoos and hills of Sedona, and the disorientation spell on the road was an extra measure to confound those who might be purposefully looking for it.

Rhea's red and white Mini was a blast to drive up Highway 179 through the walls of rocks and around the curves threading through the pines on the way to the secluded community hidden in the hills. Theia drove an automatic hybrid, which didn't quite have the same kick.

"So what did you want to pick up, anyway?"

"Some papers Rafe's dad kept. He said there's some stuff about the original Covent and Madeleine Marchant I might want for my genealogy research." There was no point in giving Rhea ammo to tease her by letting know she was researching Lucien Smok.

"Don't we know all we need to about her?"

"Nothing is ever all you need to know about anything."

Rhea rolled her eyes. "Right. I forgot I was talking to Brainiac's daughter."

"So you're not at all curious about the origins of our Lilith blood."

"I just think you can overanalyze things. A little mystery in life is nice."

Mystery was exactly what Theia didn't want. She liked to know the whys and wherefores of things. Knowledge was power. And mystery... As far as Theia was concerned, mystery was danger.

Chapter 3

Lucien watched the revenant from the rooftop. Starlight lent a pale, unearthly glow to the proceedings as it swallowed up the dusk, leaving the red landscape sepia toned and casting flat, colorless shadows. The demon wore cowboy boots and a leather duster with a gambler-style cowboy hat, his horse tacked up in the Western style, but this was a Hunt wraith, an undead revenant of the Viking era who roamed the earth in search of dark souls. Less substantial wraiths rode beside him, their mounts, like themselves, phantoms. No one would notice them, even staring at them head-on. No one but a black-souled phantom like himself.

But the leader was different. He was no phantom but flesh and bone, unnaturally maintained, living tissue that ought to have perished centuries ago. And Lucien had seen him before. Just hours before—at the wedding of Rafael Diamante to Phoebe Carlisle.

Lucien followed the horse's trajectory, tracking the revenant with the scope on his crossbow. He'd slipped a little something into the Viking's drink to see if he could trigger him. The most it had done was to get him arguing with Dev Gideon, the eldest Carlisle sister's faithful companion. Rumor had it Dev was a shape-shifter, part man, part demon himself. The entire Carlisle family seemed to be magnets for unnatural beings. Not surprising, given their bloodline.

He wasn't sure what he'd expected when he'd decided to check out the Carlisle sisters for himself, but Theia's large, passionate eyes challenging him with far more moxie than her slight frame warranted was certainly not it. He hadn't expected someone witty and intelligent who took no shit. She hadn't fallen for his player persona. And she hadn't been impressed by his name—if anything, there'd been a little sneer on her face when she'd heard it—or acted impressed by his family's money. But maybe it was a different kind of power that impressed the Carlisle women. The kind that was infernal in origin. If only she knew.

Lucien turned in a slow arc to follow the horseman with his scope. Leo Ström's origins were what concerned him right now. How had he come to be the leader of the Wild Hunt? And what was the Hunt doing appearing on a lovely spring evening in Sedona, Arizona? Traditionally, it was said to appear around the winter solstice and was better suited to snowier climes.

They'd scented someone now, it seemed, and even from this distance, Lucien thought he heard their victory hoots as the phantom storm that followed them swallowed up their victim and they disappeared into the night, leaving it calm and warm.

He'd have to find out more about this Leo Ström. The man was involved with Theia's twin, Rhea, which could mean anything in terms of unnatural origin. It might even be Rhea's own magic animating him. It was unlikely she'd created the revenant herself, since the long dead were nearly impossible to give a convincing living appearance to, no matter how much magic the practitioner had. So perhaps she'd taken possession of a revenant created by some other unnatural power. And Lucien just happened to have access to information on any of a number of unnatural powers.

He stashed his gear and changed into something more appropriate. People might talk if he showed up at Polly's dressed like a cat burglar.

Polly was entertaining in her booth when Lucien walked in. Aware of her out of the corner of his eye, he made a point of not glancing in her direction, knowing it would drive her crazy. His ploy worked, and in less than five minutes, she'd ditched her patrons and sauntered over to the bar where he stood waiting for his drink.

"Well, look what the cat dragged in." She lifted her drawn-on nearly crimson brows with a little smirk as she leaned back against the bar beside him and raised her voice for the bartender's benefit. "Whatever he's having, it's on the house."

Lucien put down a twenty as the craft beer arrived. "That's sweet, but I've got it covered."

Polly pushed the bill across the slick wood toward the bartender. "That's a tip."

Lucien sipped his beer. "You're such a control freak."

"I like to treat my friends well."

"Oh, we're friends now?" Lucien turned to mimic her stance, elbows back against the bar.

Polly flipped her cherry-red hair over her shoulder, nails painted a dazzling sapphire blue. "Well, maybe frenemies."

"Seems fair."

"So what brings you back to my neck of the woods?"

"Edgar does." He always used his father's first name, never calling him Dad or Pop. "Smok Biotech is partnering with Northern Arizona University on a new venture. He sent me to supervise."

"That doesn't explain what you're doing in Sedona. NAU is in Flagstaff."

"I know where it is." Lucien took a swig of his beer. "Went to a wedding."

Polly's eyes sparkled with interest. "The Diamante wedding? Lucky you. Those invitations were highly coveted."

Lucien shrugged. "I didn't say I was invited."

Polly laughed. "Of course you weren't. So you crashed the quetzal's wedding and now you're slumming at my joint. Who are you after?"

"Who says I'm after anyone?"

Crimson waves swayed as she shook her head. "Darling, don't grift a grifter."

He finished his beer and set the bottle on the bar. "What do you know about the Wild Hunt?"

Polly pushed away from the bar and grabbed his hand, drawing him with her through the jostling patrons trying to get the bartender's attention. The joint was hopping tonight.

She led him to her booth, where the patrons she'd ditched were still waiting. "Meeting's over, boys. I'll get back to you when I hear anything."

The two pale twentysomething men with slicked-back blond hair shrugged and scooted out of the booth.

One of them frowned and hung back as she slid onto the seat. "Don't make us wait too long. The consequences may be dire."

"Stop being so dramatic, Kip."

Lucien sat on the bench. "*Kip?*"

Polly grinned. "Preppy vampires turned in the '80s. Eternally embarrassing." She gestured to one of her staff, presumably ordering a bottle of something. "So why do you want to know about the Hunt?

"Because I saw it tonight. And unless I've been doing way too much molly, it's May, not December."

"You saw it?"

"Why does that surprise you?"

The woman she'd signaled arrived with a bottle of wine and poured them each a glass, despite Lucien shaking his head.

"Generally, only someone who's a target of the Hunt is treated to that sight." Polly sipped her wine with a curious lift of her brow. "Have you been very naughty, Lucien?"

"No naughtier than usual. Why is the Hunt still in town at this time of year?"

"What makes you think I'd know?"

Lucien played with the rim of his glass. "Pols. You make it your business to know everything of interest—everything paranormal—that happens in the entire Southwest. Information *is* your business. Are you really going to make me pay for it? After what we've meant to each other?"

Polly laughed, her eyes twinkling in the wavering light of the candle on the table. "Don't push it, Hellboy."

"Ouch. Below the belt."

Beneath the table, the pointed toe of her shoe stroked the side of his leg. "Best location."

He moved his leg, and she uncrossed hers and crossed them the other way.

"But in the interest of our continued frenmity, I'll tell you what I've heard." She paused to top off her glass. "Last winter, the Hunt blew into town to deal with some riffraff, and the leader of the Hunt struck some kind of a deal that let him remain in the mortal realm indefinitely. Word is, it's because of—"

"Rhea Carlisle."

Polly tipped her glass toward him. "The quetzal's sister-in-law, yes. And today you crashed the quetzal's wedding. I take it Leo Ström is the reason."

"One of a couple of reasons." Lucien swirled the wine in his glass, thinking about Theia's large eyes. And the way she'd held on to his arms after he'd saved her from choking.

"And would another of those reasons be Rhea Carlisle's identical twin?"

Lucien glanced up, caught off guard. "Why in the world would you say that? I just met her today."

Polly shook her head knowingly. "Those Carlisle women have a way of getting under a man's skin. I'd be careful of that one if I were you. She's deceptively humdrum."

"What's that supposed to mean?"

"She's very *normal*." Polly said the word as though it were a terrible insult. "Very sweet. People think of her as the least talented of the bunch, but I wouldn't want to be anywhere near her with a secret I didn't want found out."

It was a warning he'd be wise to pay heed to.

"As for Ström, he used to come in here with a redhead years ago. A real redhead." She grinned and flipped her hair. "Not like me."

"And?"

"And apparently she's a rogue Valkyrie. A couple of regulars knew her—also Valkyries—and didn't care much for her."

That was the missing piece. The Valkyrie must have been the one to create the revenant. And somehow she'd made a deal with Rhea Carlisle.

Full of mango lassi and sweet Kashmiri naan, Rhea wasn't interested in reading an old man's treatises about the history of the Covent written in longhand. Which suited Theia just fine. Alone, she wouldn't have to hide what she was looking for. She drove Rhea back to her car before heading to Phoebe's place with Rafael Diamante Sr.'s archives.

Puddleglum, Phoebe's Siamese tabby, curled up with her in the guest bed while she pored over the materials, looking for anything about the Smok family. As she turned the pages, she noticed a peculiar effect when she lingered on an entry: the text on the page began to shift beneath her touch. Rafe hadn't mentioned anything about magically enhanced pages, but here it was. Like clicking a magical hyperlink to load a page of related content, touching a reference in the text made the copy on the page transform into the detailed document to which Diamante referred. When she lifted her finger off the page, it returned to the original journal entry.

Fascinated, Theia thumbed through an entry on the Smok family's history. But it wasn't about the Diamantes at all. It was an accounting of Madeleine Marchant's belongings, given to the nobleman who had been her benefactor—none other than one Philippe Smok, Vicomte de Briançon. And among those "belongings" were Madeleine's children: seven daughters, in fact. *Seven sisters.*

The Lilith blood allele—a hypothesis Theia had formulated when she and Rhea had first traced their genealogy—was passed down through recessive genes, only resulting in the Lilith phenotype when daughters were born to two carriers of the gene in Madeleine's direct line. And this always seemed to result in the birth of seven sisters with the gifts. But she hadn't realized that the first set of sisters were Madeleine's own daughters.

Puddleglum plopped down in the middle of the journal to announce that Theia was done reading. She hadn't realized how late it had gotten. Lying back on the bed and staring at the ceiling, she tried to work out what Lucien Smok's game might be. There was no way his appearance at Phoebe's wedding was a coincidence. Rafe was right. She should keep her distance. But if his family had a connection not just to the Covent but to Madeleine herself, then Lucien surely knew it and had sought them out deliberately. Theia had to find out what he was up to. Particularly with regard to Smok Biotech.

The arrival of the vision was the first indication that she'd actually fallen asleep.

It flew out of the night like a carrion bird, circling overhead, waiting for death, casting a heavy shadow on the creatures below: the crow. The wolf. The dragon. The flying thing drew closer, and now she was looking up at it, standing with her sisters. It was both a vulture and a reptile, a prehistoric lizard with wings—a pterodactyl, perhaps—its head birdlike, with glowing red eyes, bat-like wings stretching out from the lizard body.

In the distance, a rooster crowed, and the sound became

a screech in the thing's beak, a scream of laughter as it dived, talons outstretched.

The rooster crowed again. Light blazed through a crack in the blinds. Dawn light. The rooster was somewhere outside. Nice. Phoebe hadn't mentioned the built-in neighborhood alarm clock. Theia pulled the pillow over her head and rolled onto her side.

Before the cock crows twice. What was that from? Something in the Bible, she thought. New Testament. She hadn't been to church in years, but she remembered it now: Peter's denial of Christ. The cock outside had crowed twice. Not that unusual, probably. But why was that sticking in her head? Cock, not rooster. Theia giggled, knowing what Rhea would have to say about it.

Cock crows twice. The vision came back to her in a rush. It wasn't the Bible phrase she was thinking of, after all. The flying thing—it hadn't been a pterodactyl like she'd speculated in the dream. It was a cockatrice. And it was coming for them.

In middle school, she'd once gone with a friend to her church, an evangelical one. The preacher had spoken of some mad theory about human-animal hybrids and the evil plot of godless scientists who wanted to bring back such things as griffins, harpies and cockatrices. His theory claimed such creatures had roamed the earth before the Great Flood because of the sins of unnatural men who'd bred them, and God had wiped them out.

Theia had barely been able to contain her laughter, and her friend had been furious. Even at twelve, Theia understood enough science to know how idiotic such a theory was. Nobody was trying to splice genes across species to create monster hybrids, and even if they did try, it wouldn't work.

Except... Lucien Smok had said Smok Biotech's research at NAU was both scientific and supernatural. And what was more supernatural than mythical creatures that turned out to be real?

She certainly hadn't believed dragons were real until recently, when she'd seen two of them with her own eyes. Dev Gideon shared his form with the dragon Kur, and Rafe was a scion of Quetzalcoatl who sprouted iridescent feathered wings and snake flesh and commanded the dead. And she hadn't seen Leo shift, but according to Rhea's account of their time battling another ancient dragon in the Viking underworld, he could transform into a serpentine creature with the destructive energy of the mythological Jörmungandr— who maybe wasn't so mythological after all.

What if the Smok family's "magical-adjacent" connection was that they were bioengineering other such creatures?

Theia unhooked her arms from the pillow, and her eyes focused on the crimson business card on the nightstand. If she wanted to get to the bottom of this, she was going to have to take Lucien up on his offer.

Chapter 4

Lucien's phone vibrated in his jacket pocket. He'd been out on a job all day and had turned his ringer off. He took it out and glanced at it, surprised to see a voice mail notification from Theia Dawn. And annoyed that it seemed to make his heart beat faster.

Theia's message was brief: "We should talk."

Somebody else had talked, obviously. From the tone of her voice, he could tell she was better informed about the Smoks than she'd been yesterday. Lucien lay on his back on the Berber rug on the floor of his penthouse suite while he returned her call.

He grinned when she answered. "I knew you couldn't resist me."

"I can resist you just fine. It's your company I find intriguing." There was a pause as she apparently realized how her word choice sounded. "Your firm," she said quickly, followed by an adorable, mortified gasp.

He put her on speaker and crossed his arms behind his head. "So what can my...*firm*...do for you, Ms. Dawn?"

"I thought we were going to talk about what I can do for your..." She swore softly at herself in the background. It sent a little shiver down his spine to know how flustered she was when he wasn't even standing in front of her. "About the job. With Smok Biotech," she hastened to add. He wondered how flushed her skin was right now. With the chocolate-brown hair bobbed sharply at her chin and those little points of cherry red at the ends, it would make her eyes seem even larger.

"You want the job at the lab." He spoke lazily, imagining her large gray eyes blinking at him.

"If the offer's still open. And it depends on exactly what the job is."

"The offer is most definitely still open. Why don't we meet for dinner tonight to talk over the specifics?"

"Tonight?" Her voice went up slightly at the end, a little squeak of surprise.

Lucien smiled. "Is that a problem?"

"It's almost eight o'clock."

"Too close to your bedtime? I'm sure I can accommodate that."

"*No*, it's just—it's short notice. I wasn't planning on going out tonight. It would take me a little while to get ready."

"It's just a business dinner. You don't need to impress me."

"That's not what I meant." Her tone was clipped.

He loved getting under her skin. Lucien grinned at the thought. He'd like to get deep under it. Or inside it. In a manner of speaking. Lucien shook himself out of his little daydream. That wasn't going to do him any good.

"Why don't we meet at Cress at L'Auberge in an hour? Is that enough time?"

"Are they open that late?"

"They will be for me."

The last time he'd seen her, she'd been dressed as a bridesmaid in a bloodred chiffon dress that swung around her hips when she walked. Undeniably flattering, but he'd suspected it wasn't the sort of thing she normally wore. Neither was what she had on tonight—a conservative navy blue pencil skirt with a cream-colored blouse buttoned up far too high. It was an interesting look, perhaps something she thought a scientist would wear to a business dinner. The one departure from the conservative style was the pair of red crushed-velvet heels that drew attention to her fantastic legs.

"You really didn't have to dress up for me," he said as he pulled out her chair at their al fresco table above the babbling Oak Creek.

Theia sat almost suspiciously, like she wasn't sure what he was doing. "I didn't. I mean, this isn't for you. It just didn't seem like Cress was really a jeans and Tinker Bell T-shirt kind of place."

He smiled, picturing her in a Tinker Bell T-shirt. That seemed a lot more her style.

"It's whatever kind of place you want it to be, darling. Seriously. They know me here, and you may have noticed the place is empty."

Theia's eyes narrowed. "This doesn't impress me, you know."

"Of that I have absolutely no doubt." Lucien laid his napkin in his lap. "I hope you don't mind that I've ordered ahead. I should have asked if you had any food allergies, though. Is filet mignon all right?"

"No. I mean, yes, filet mignon is fine. No, I don't have any food allergies." She was gripping her water glass tightly.

"You don't have to be impressed, but there's no need to be so tense, either. Would it help if we dive straight into business?"

"*Yes.*" She'd answered almost before the words left his mouth. He was really enjoying how flustered he seemed to make her.

"Okay, so to start, I take it you spoke to your brother-in-law about us."

Theia took a sip of her water as if trying to buy time. "I got some information from him, yes."

"So you know what it is we do. Outside the lab, that is."

A questioning look appeared on her face for a moment before she masked it. "I do." She didn't. But she knew something. Something that was making her very nervous.

"As you know, there are two main divisions of Smok International: Smok Consulting and Smok Biotech. Let me explain how the consulting side of things intersects with the biotech business. Part of cleaning up other people's messes is dealing with what triggers those incidents in the first place."

Theia nodded, pretending to follow. The first course had arrived, and Lucien paused to try the bacon-wrapped lapin.

Theia's face lit up as she took a bite of hers. "Wow. This is fantastic."

"It doesn't suck," he agreed with a wink. "There are *some* perks to having too much money."

"Do you?" Theia took another bite, visibly relaxing. "Have too much?"

"Me personally?" Lucien shrugged. "I don't have any, as a matter of fact. This is all being expensed." He smiled at her dubious expression. "Still unimpressed? My inheritance is all held in trust, and it's dependent upon a few conditions I haven't met yet, so I get to represent my father's business, but everything I have belongs to him. Or to the company." He indicated the suit he was wearing. "This thing? Expensed." He flicked some mustard from his fork onto the jacket.

Theia laughed, the laughter obviously surprised out of her as she tried to cover her mouth, still full of rabbit. He liked seeing her laugh. It changed her whole face, like she'd let him in for a moment and let down her guard—something that was in place not just because she didn't trust him but a guardedness that seemed ingrained in her.

"You said something about triggers." Theia tried to go back to her frosty demeanor, moving beet curls around her plate. "What kind of triggers were you referring to?"

She was obviously trying to get him to explain more about what she was pretending she already knew. He figured he'd oblige.

"Your brother-in-law, for instance—Rafe Diamante. I noticed that the uninvited guest at his wedding reception— the *other* uninvited guest—triggered a partial transformation. Strong emotion is often a trigger for such things. Most shape-shifters learn to control when they shift. Or to adapt, if the trigger happens to be out of their control, such as a full moon."

"You seem to know an awful lot about Rafe."

"I know an awful lot about everybody, darling." He noticed her visible flinch at the familiarity, and he tried not to react. Part of being able to indulge in his extracurricular activities depended on making sure people saw him as a spoiled brat who'd never grown up. And part of him *was* a spoiled brat who'd never grown up, so it wasn't all that hard to pull off. "I know a lot about a lot of influential people with unusual problems, I should say."

The waiter arrived to take their starter plates and replaced them with calamari salad. Theia picked up a set of little tentacles, holding them up in the light.

"Not a fan of squid?"

"Hmm?" Theia had popped the calamari into her mouth, and she chewed for a moment before responding. "No, I love squid. I was just admiring it. I love it when they include the tentacles instead of just the rings. They're the best part." She took another bite, this time with her fork. "So these unusual problems." She paused to chew and swallow. "Shape-shifting." She'd lowered her voice on the word. "It's actually fairly new to me, so I'm not used to people talking about it so openly. Are there really a lot of them?"

"More than you'd suspect. The job of Smok's consulting arm is making sure no one does suspect. Sometimes it's literally cleanup—which I don't do." He showed her his hands—no calluses, manicured nails. "We have crews for that. People who don't mind getting their hands dirty and who can be counted on to be discreet. We had a crew out to your sister Dione's house a few months—"

"Ione," Theia interrupted him with her mouth still partially full.

"Sorry?"

She swallowed and wiped her lips with her napkin. "She goes by Ione. It drives her crazy when people pronounce her name wrong, like you just did, so she dropped the *D*." Theia paused, apparently only just registering what he'd said. "You were at her house?"

"Not me personally. Like I said, I'm not big on cleaning things. But we sent a crew at Rafe's request to do some repairs after a certain dragon demon stomped around in her living room. And I understand *his* trigger was, well, fairly intimate."

Theia reddened slightly. Dev's transformation was reportedly triggered by sex and blood.

"My point is that responding to unwanted supernatural activity, whatever the trigger, by cleaning up after the fact may be lucrative, but it's inefficient. At Smok Biotech, we develop technologies to suppress unwanted transformations. Among other things." He figured any more information would just overload her if she'd only recently learned that shifters were real. "And people will pay a lot of money for that kind of control. Particularly people in the public eye. Entrepreneurs. Actors. Politicians. Imagine how the public would react if the president turned into a poison-spitting were-newt in the middle of a White House press conference?" Lucien glanced up with a smirk. "Bad example. He's clearly not bothering to use our tech."

Theia laughed again, her nose wrinkling. He definitely liked making her do that.

The main course arrived, and they were distracted for

a bit by both the presentation and the flavor, truffle and fungus in wine sauce drizzled over the top of the perfectly grilled steak and an artful swirl of béarnaise surrounding mashed root vegetables with edible flowers on top. Lucien found he liked watching Theia eat food that delighted her almost as much as he liked making her laugh. But not quite as much as he was sure he'd like tasting her mouth the way she was tasting that filet mignon.

Lucien focused on his own food for a moment, trying to think more appropriate thoughts.

"So what is it you'd want me to do?"

He glanced up sharply, nearly choking on a mouthful of mashed turnip as he inhaled at the wrong moment. It would really be something if she had to return the favor from the wedding reception by performing the Heimlich maneuver on him.

"At the lab," Theia clarified, eyeing him suspiciously. "Why do you need me?"

Managing not to choke, Lucien set down his fork to take a drink of mineral water. "We have an excellent staff of researchers but only a handful of lab techs who know the full extent of what we do. I thought it would be good to have someone on staff that I don't have to hide things from." Not those things, anyway. He'd gotten used to hiding everything else. "And you'd be well compensated," he added. "In case that wasn't clear."

"You want me to be a lab technician?"

"More than just a lab technician. I mean, that, too. But…" He hadn't really thought about how he was going to broach the subject of her gift. They'd talked around the reputation of the Carlisle sisters, but he hadn't actually mentioned clairvoyance outright. "Someone with both technical and esoteric knowledge would be invaluable. Someone who could make…educated predictions of the likely outcomes."

Theia's body language had loosened up significantly

over the course of the meal, but in an instant she was back to being stiff and tight and on guard.

"Sorry, did I say something wrong?"

"What exactly is it that you think I can do, Mr. Smok?"

Oh, crap. He was Mr. Smok again.

"I…understood you had oracular powers."

"Oracular." Her forehead creased with irritation. "You think I can see the future. That I can just look into my little crystal ball and tell you how Smok stock is going to do tomorrow."

"Well, not exactly—"

"Who told you I had these oracular powers?"

Lucien was beginning to feel uncomfortable under her gaze. She might not have oracular powers, but he was starting to think she could burn a hole in his family jewels with those eyes.

"It's common knowledge in the community. The magical community."

"And the magical adjacent, of course."

Lucien shrugged helplessly. "Sorry. I've obviously stepped in it here, and I'm not really sure how."

"Let me ask you something, Mr. Smok."

"Fire away."

"Do you and your kind think my sisters and I are some kind of magical Pez dispensers? Is there a creep board out there on the internet somewhere, some ugly little masculinist corner of the deep web where you guys swap stories about how to hit on magically gifted women?"

Lucien nearly choked again at the word *masculinist*.

"I'm not sure what you think my kind is, but I think you're taking my interest the wrong way."

"So you don't want to sleep with me to get your magical rocks off."

Something in her words made him snap, like a percussion grenade had gone off inside him. "Listen, sweetheart, if all I wanted to do was sleep with you, I wouldn't have wasted the company money on a fancy dinner. I would have just done it, and right about now is when you'd be gathering your clothes and making your exit so I could roll over and go to sleep."

Theia pushed back her chair and stood, her napkin falling to the floor. "Thank you for the dinner, Mr. Smok. Enjoy rolling over and sleeping next to your hand."

Still suffering the effects of the mental percussion grenade, he wasn't entirely sure what had just happened, but it was both delightful and painful to watch her walk away in those heels and that skirt.

Chapter 5

Theia ordered a car on her way outside, and in fifteen minutes she was back at Phoebe's ranch house yanking off the skirt and kicking off her shoes and grabbing a startled Puddleglum for a forcible cuddle in the papasan chair by the picture window.

Who the hell did that asshole Lucien Smok think he was, anyway? God's gift to women, obviously. Showing up at Phoebe's wedding trolling for Lilith blood was bad enough, but making up a job offer to get into her pants was pathetic.

Her phone rang underneath Puddleglum, and she ended up accidentally answering as she wrested it from under him before she saw who was calling.

Lucien's voice carried from the speaker as she stared at it. "I didn't think you'd answer."

"I didn't. It was my sister's cat."

"Her…cat?"

"His butt. Some people butt dial. He butt answers. Goodbye." Her finger was poised over the button.

"Wait. Please hear me out."

For some reason, she did.

"I'm calling to apologize. I screwed up."

"Ya think?"

"I really did ask you to dinner to talk about the job. There was no ulterior motive. I'm sorry I handled the topic of your gift badly. I didn't realize it was a touchy subject and maybe not for public consumption. And I'm sorry I snapped at you. I'm not sure why I overreacted. But what I said was inexcusable."

Well, damn. That was an unexpectedly sincere apology.

But maybe this was part of his game. She wasn't going to be stupid enough to fall for it twice.

"Okay, well, thanks for calling. Have a nice evening."

"Theia?"

Something about the way he said her name, almost a plea, made her hesitate.

"Are you still there?"

Theia's thumb hovered over the button. "Sort of."

He laughed softly. "Sort of? Listen, the job offer was genuine. I realize I made assumptions, but I think you'd be an asset to the enterprise, gift or no gift. Is there any way we can start over and discuss it?"

She did need to learn more about the Smoks, and the whole trigger-suppression concept was intriguing.

Theia sighed. "I'm not a psychic, I don't read people's fortunes and I don't perform on command."

"Of course. That's perfectly understandable. Can I ask…" There was a rustling sound as he changed position. "Can you tell me how it does work? If it's none of my business, that's perfectly cool."

Theia hesitated, and Puddleglum jumped down to wander to the kitchen, offended at no longer being the center of attention. "I've been known to have dreams. Visions. But honestly? I don't even know if they're anything."

"I think you underestimate yourself."

"How would you know?"

"Just a feeling."

Theia smiled despite herself. "That's usually my line."

"Why don't we put the feelings and intuitions aside then? I'll be at the lab tomorrow around two o'clock. Just come by and take a look around, see what we do. If it doesn't interest you, no harm done. You can walk away. And if you do get any impressions of a possible prophetic nature, I'd be happy to hear those, too. But no pressure."

"No pressure."

"Cross my heart and hope to die."

"Let's not go that far."

Lucien gave her that soft laugh again. "I get the feeling you doubt my sincerity. Suppose I can't blame you. So will I see you tomorrow?"

The word *tomorrow* seemed to float before her in brilliant blue letters. Synesthesia wasn't unusual for her, but it was often a precursor to a waking vision. Either way, it seemed to indicate that tomorrow was significant. A sign she should heed. Interpretation, of course, was always the tough part. Was her gift telling her she should go tomorrow? Or stay away?

"Theia? You still there?"

"Yeah, sorry. Tomorrow it is."

The same brilliant blue haunted her sleep. Not letters or words this time, but blue in the form of a small dragon. Like the cockatrice she'd dreamed of before, it had webbed, bat-like wings, the joints ending in sharp claws, and stood on two legs, the head and barbed tail the classic shape of a dragon from fantasy—the sort Rhea had collected as figurines when they were kids. But there was something wrong with this dragon. It dragged itself along the desert floor the way a wounded bat might, using its winged forelimbs to "walk." And above it, the shadow of the carrion-eating cockatrice circled as before. And it was growing closer.

She forgot about the dream images by the time she'd finished grading papers from her Friday morning class and headed over to the lab.

Smok was using the university biotech labs while a larger, permanent facility was being built off campus. Theia already had an access card for her own research, though she'd never been in the biotech section.

Lucien greeted her in the atrium, looking almost surprised that she'd actually shown up. "Theia. Welcome." He squeezed her hand like they were old friends. "It's nice to see you in something more comfortable."

She'd worn ruby plaid skinny jeans and a black fitted T-shirt—not exactly something she'd just thrown on, but she wasn't trying to look good for him. The words of Violet Bick from *It's a Wonderful Life* popped into her head: "*This old thing? Why, I only wear it when I don't care how I look.*" Theia, of course, couldn't pull off the sassy hair flip.

She just wanted to feel confident, and looking exceptionally cute made her feel confident. So did the approving look he gave her as his eyes lingered over her curves for just the briefest moment. Not so long that it was obtrusive and objectifying, but long enough that she knew she'd chosen well. And as much as she hated to admit it, that little feeling of breathlessness was back.

She'd tried to ignore it at dinner the night before, tried not to think about how his arms had felt around her, like he was protecting her from the world—or like there was no one else in it but her. But every time she'd looked up from her food into those depthless ice-blue eyes, her lungs had tightened like when she was a kid and had felt an asthma attack coming on. She'd had to chew very carefully to make sure not to end up in a repeat performance of the moment they met.

Today, of course, she'd gone with comfortable black cotton Mary Janes instead of the velvet heels, which made Lucien seem exceptionally tall, though he was probably just under six feet. She'd been wearing heels both times they'd met before, but now she was at her full height of a whopping five foot two.

Beside Lucien, an older woman in a lab coat held out a clipboard. "Before you go in, we'll need you to sign a standard confidentiality agreement."

Lucien gave her an apologetic smile and a little shrug. Once Theia had signed it and returned the clipboard,

Lucien led her into the Smok wing of the lab, which required a special passkey. "I can have them add the access code to your existing card right now if you like." He held out his hand as if expecting her to put her card in it.

Theia kept her arms crossed. "I haven't agreed to your offer yet."

Lucien smiled. "You will."

Researchers were hard at work despite the lab only having been in operation for a few days. The equipment—and presumably the technology behind it—was cutting-edge. Theia had microscope envy.

Lucien seemed pleased by her reaction. "This is our pharmacogenomics division."

"Pharmacogenomics?" Theia wondered if she'd heard wrong. "Not pharmacogenetics?"

"Nope. Genomics. That special project I told you about is particularly dependent on genome-wide study. Smok is currently trying to pinpoint variations in a single nucleotide within the genome to understand the pharmacokinetic and pharmacodynamic effects for our newest drugs in development."

Theia's heart skipped a beat at the way the words rolled off his tongue. Most people's eyes glazed over when she talked genetics. She was starting to see Lucien in a new light.

Encouraged by her interest, he gave her a little smile and went on. "The market for this drug is unique, as you know, and every patient responds differently. Understanding the epigenetics involved is crucial."

Epigenetics. Now *there* was a term that was near and dear to Theia's heart. The Lilith blood phenotype she'd postulated was epigenetic in nature, not caused by changes in the DNA itself, but by changes in gene expression.

"Have you been able to isolate the autosomal mutations responsible for the…condition?"

"We have, indeed. We're well past that stage." Lucien looked thoughtful before moving toward an isolated room at the rear of the lab. "Let me show you something." He used his key card once more on the door. "Another access code I'll provide you with. This one's highly classified, since it has to do with our special research."

He held the door for Theia and she stepped in, not realizing at first the significance of what she was looking at. Cages lined the walls of the small room, containing what seemed to be perfectly ordinary specimens—mice, rats, a snake.

Lucien closed the door behind him. "These are all animals in which we've been able to induce lycanthropy through gene manipulation."

"Lycanthropy?"

"As a generic term, it doesn't refer strictly to wolf-human forms but to any kind of trans-species shift."

Theia moved closer to the snake—a juvenile albino ball python—to get a better look. "You mean…they all shift?"

"It makes it easier to study the triggers and suppression mechanisms when we know exactly what genes we're dealing with." Lucien pushed a button next to the glass of the python's cage.

"What does that do?"

"Triggers the shift by introducing a mild toxin into the sealed environment."

Theia bristled. "A toxin?"

"It won't harm it. It's more of an irritant. We'll remove it and rebalance the environment in a moment."

Theia was about to give him a piece of her mind about humane lab practices, but the snake had begun to uncoil, raising its head as if sensing them or perhaps just sensing the change in its air. And as it lifted its snout, the yellow and white pattern of the scales began to ripple and grow, becoming feathery, while the snout elongated into a beak.

The reptile shuddered as it morphed, although she'd seen much more violent transformations. This, at least, didn't appear to be painful.

The body shortened. Limbs grew—a pair of legs with talons. Soon it was covered in feathers, wings bursting from the flesh at its sides and a comb and wattles elongating out of the remaining scales on the head. A rooster...a cock. Theia shivered.

"Amazing, isn't it? And just as we've triggered the metamorphosis, we can trigger the reverse." Lucien pressed the button again, and in moments the creature was shuddering back into its original python form and curling up into its previous coil. "The gene manipulation is a shortcut, of course. We can't exactly experiment with genetic modification on human subjects. Although human trials for the serum are the next phase. We're not quite there yet, but we're actively recruiting volunteers who already have the shifter gene."

Theia turned to stare at him, thinking he might be pulling her leg, but his expression was serious.

"You see why we have a need for ethical oversight from someone familiar with the sensitive nature of the work."

"You expect me to help you experiment on human volunteers?"

"Like I said, the actual clinical trial comes later. Probably at least a year away. What you would be doing is helping us map triggers based on genome. And making sure confidentiality is maintained as well as helping to establish a sensitivity protocol for screening volunteers. Which is where your special skills would come in."

There was something unsettling about the idea of people volunteering such information to a large, profit-driven corporation, but she supposed someone with lycanthropy who was desperate to control it might be willing to sacrifice some privacy for the promise of a cure. Or at least the promise of a regimen for managing it.

The idea of mapping triggers, however—mapping them to *genes*—it almost made her toes tingle with giddy excitement.

Lucien smiled knowingly. "It's a lot to take in all at once. I don't expect you to answer right away. Take your time and think about it."

Once he'd started talking pharmacogenomics, there wasn't really any question of what her answer was going to be, and she suspected he knew that. But it wouldn't hurt to sleep on it and think it over rationally. Or pretend to.

Theia held out her hand and gave him what she hoped was a businesslike handshake. Her palm felt small in his. Despite his claim that he didn't do physical labor, his hands were surprisingly muscular. Not in an unpleasant way, but like he was used to using them for more than just writing checks from his trust. Maybe he worked out a lot and it was from gripping weights or something. As with his earlier greeting, his grasp was warm and familiar. Not businesslike at all.

Theia tried to keep from blushing at the contact. "I'll definitely think it over. Thanks for taking the time to show me around."

After holding her hand a moment longer, Lucien winked as he let it go. "Anytime, darling." There was something in the way he said *darling* combined with the wink that seemed deliberately alienating, as though he'd realized he'd been behaving much too civilly. Like he was reminding her that he was a jackass. *Well, it worked, buddy.* She didn't feel flushed or breathless anymore, just annoyed.

Chapter 6

For some reason, the meeting with Theia had agitated him. Lucien took the company Maserati and drove south from Flagstaff with the top down, deliberately speeding, taking the switchbacks and hairpin turns down Highway 89A without slowing, just to hear his tires squeal.

He liked her more than he wanted to. He didn't really want to like anyone. Wanting something—wanting *someone*—made you vulnerable, and that was something Lucien didn't intend to be. He needed to be vigilant. The family curse might be nothing more than a legend, but he wasn't about to be caught with his metaphysical pants down. The last time a firstborn son of the Smok family had been required to pay the price demanded by the witch in Briançon before she burned, the Smoks had only just immigrated to the New World. Every seven generations, so the legend went. The last Smok to pay it had fought against the British in the American Revolution.

Lucien wasn't going to be the next.

At the same time, he kind of hated himself for turning on his manufactured "Lucien Smok, spoiled brat" persona just as he'd parted ways with Theia. He could see the disappointment in her face. She'd been warming up to him, and he'd yanked the rug out from under her on purpose.

When he got back to his rented suite, he found an envelope had been slipped under his door. It was a little unsettling not knowing who this "helpful citizen" was, but the source had been right on the money every time. It was better intel than he could get at Polly's—at least not without her expecting something in return. Then again, everything had a price. He just didn't know what it was yet. It ought to worry him more, but right now he needed to send something to hell.

He opened the manila envelope, expecting another name, maybe an active vamp who preyed on the living—unlike the pasty poseurs at Polly's—or an animated corpse. Instead, it was a URL. Lucien was surprised to find it took him to a genealogy website. The page was for the Carlisle family. What was the point of this? He already knew their history. They were descendants of the witch, and they'd inherited her gifts. Witches might have the potential to create supernatural havoc, but they weren't supernatural themselves. It wasn't like *they* were demons.

Lucien closed the browser just as a message appeared on his phone from Polly.

Got something juicy for you, hon. Come by tonight.

He headed to Polly's after dark, trying for low-key in a tan Versace suit.

Polly laughed when she saw him. "What is this, the Obama surprise?"

"Hey, that was a damn fine suit. So's this. Just because some people have no appreciation for style…"

"Whatever you say." She was at her usual booth, surrounded by pretty-boy vegan bloodsuckers and assorted half-shifted weres, and she gave no indication that she intended to dismiss them.

"So what is it you wanted to tell me that you couldn't just text me?"

Polly pretended to pout. "Now you're just being mean. Is it so terrible to have to see me in person?"

Lucien sighed. "That's not what I meant, and you know it. It's just that you look awfully busy, and I wasn't really planning on hanging out and drinking tonight. I felt like shit the next morning after the last time we chatted."

"It's not my fault you can't handle your liquor. Anyway, I thought you might want to be here tonight, because there's someone special visiting."

"Who?"

She nodded toward a table near the stage, partially lit by the spillover of the spotlight on the singer. "Check out the Amazon with the short bald guy."

Lucien noted the tall, leggy blonde and her considerably less impressive companion. "So? Who are they?"

"Who cares who he is? Probably a snack. *She's* Brünnhilde."

Lucien's brows drew together. "Who the hell is Brünnhilde?"

Polly gave him a smug grin. "She's a Valkyrie, baby. I found you a Valkyrie."

The bloodsucker beside her frowned. "Who's this asshole? Why does he get a Valkyrie?"

Polly slapped his hand. "I'm not giving her to him, you idiot. She's a freaking *Valkyrie*. And have some respect. This is Lucien. He's the—"

"Thanks, Polly. You can quit there. A little discretion?" He turned toward the table where the Valkyrie sat, but Polly put her foot in his path.

"Hey. No thank-you? Not even a little kiss?" She tilted her head and pointed to her cheek.

Lucien smiled, remembering his manners. He'd be wise to keep Polly on his good side. And she *had* done him a favor. He leaned in, but instead of kissing her cheek, he lifted her hand from around the vamp's shoulder and kissed the back of it, to the annoyance of both parties.

Polly flipped her hair, black this evening, over her shoulder. "Come by tomorrow at two. You can thank me properly."

Lucien approached the Valkyrie's table, realizing half-way there that he didn't know what to offer for information from a Valkyrie. What did Valkyries want? Souls? They didn't need him for that. And he wasn't likely to be able to give them any valiant, heroic ones. He lucked out, though, as she seemed thoroughly bored with her companion.

He smiled winningly at her as she glanced up. "Pardon the intrusion, but would you care to dance?" No one else was dancing, but Brünnhilde rose and accepted as if eager to escape.

The song that had been playing was more on the swing spectrum, but the band switched to something slow and melodic. Lucien put his arm around her waist and took her hand, feeling like an adolescent next to her. It was like dancing with a tree.

"I'm Lucien," he offered.

"Brünnhilde."

"That's a lovely name."

Brünnhilde's brow arched. "Is it? In 2017 in the Southwestern United States?"

Lucien laughed. "Well, Lucien isn't exactly in fashion, either. Your name stands out. And it suits you."

"I get the impression you want something from me, Lucien."

"Can't a guy ask a beautiful woman to dance?"

She gave him another brow arch, this time without amusement, and he laughed.

"All right. I'll cut to the chase, since you've been gracious enough to indulge me. I understand you're a Valkyrie. I hope that's not out of line to say."

Brünnhilde shrugged noncommittally. "Perhaps."

He wasn't sure if she was half-heartedly confirming her identity or agreeing that he was out of line, but he forged ahead. "I wondered if you might have heard anything about the Wild Hunt."

"You speak of Odin's Hunt."

"I believe so, yes. But one that's out of season."

Brünnhilde's green eyes flickered with annoyance. "Indeed it is. The Chieftain of the Hunt defies propriety. No surprise, given his protector."

"His protector?"

"A mortal who wields peculiar magic. She somehow bested one of my sisters to win him."

"That's surprising. Why does he need protection? And from a mortal, no less?"

"Because his body is meant to sleep while he rides. But when Kára removed her own protection from him, she also gave him the power to ride while in his skin. It's a disgrace. Of course, Kára was a disgrace long before this latest stunt."

"Kára? She's your sister?"

Brünnhilde nodded tersely. "She calls herself Faye these days. She was once a great warrior, but she defied the Norns to coddle this man, fallen in battle. Instead of taking him to his reward in Valhalla, she kept him as a pet. In exchange, he was cursed to lead Odin's Hunt."

"This man, the chieftain—you say he was fallen. You mean he died?"

"Precisely. Died in battle, but Kára broke the laws of the Valkyries, the laws of Odin himself."

"So he shouldn't be here. His life is unnatural."

Brünnhilde shrugged. "Well. None of the wraiths of the Hunt *should* be here. And yet they are. They are all unnatural. That's what makes them wraiths, does it not? How else would we have the Hunt?"

The music ended, and Lucien thanked her for the dance.

Brünnhilde glanced back at the table where her inexplicably dull companion was waiting for her. "I suppose I'll have to take him now. Warriors aren't what they used to be. She sighed and headed back to her table.

Lucien had the answer he needed. Leo Ström was as unnatural as a man could get. His soul might once have been
destined for Valhalla, but now it belonged in hell.

He donned his hunting attire and made sure the arrows
in his quiver were all equipped with his specially designed
arrowheads. Having Smok labs at his disposal had come
in handy in his quest to rid the world of revenants and demons. The exploding tips were filled with a serum known
at the lab as the Soul Reaper. Developed for those dangerous and recalcitrant creatures they occasionally came across
on their consults, it was deadly to the inhuman. And if the
inhuman creature it struck happened to have a human soul
remaining in it, the remnant was dissolved and relegated,
presumably, to hell.

In all honesty, Lucien wasn't sure he believed in an afterlife of reward or punishment, but he'd seen plenty of
evidence of an underworld—or perhaps underworlds—
a plane where the supernatural elements of living things,
whether spirit or soul or something else, could travel. Virtually every religious tradition had its own version of this
soul realm—and a ruler of it.

He took a more discreet car this time and drove to the
home where Rhea Carlisle and Leo Ström were staying.
No point waiting to see if the Hunt would ride tonight. He
knew what Leo was. And if the revenant was already out
for the evening, Lucien would wait. He'd brought a ski mask
to avoid revealing his identity to Theia's twin.

A little twinge of conscience tugged at him, reminding
him that an insult or injury to one twin was likely to be
felt by the other. Not physically, necessarily, but in terms
of emotional harm, regardless of how close they were. And
these two had seemed particularly close when he'd seen
them together. He and his sister Lucy didn't see eye to
eye—after years of sibling rivalry fueled by their father's

vagaries, sometimes they downright hated each other—
but he knew that if anything happened to Lucy, if anyone
dared to hurt her, he'd be furious. He'd want retribution.

But he couldn't allow his feelings to get in the way of
his mission. This wasn't about him, in any event. It was
about the kind of people the Smoks had cozied up to for
hundreds of years. No, not people, but *things*. Lucien felt
it was his duty to make up for the evil his family enabled.

Helping a foolish family that had invited a demon into
their home was one thing, and the routine cleansing of
unwanted spiritual activity was a necessary service, but
Smok Consulting had covered up depravities—cleaning
up blood-spattered rooms after a nest of bloodsuckers had
engaged in a Caligula-style orgy and fed on their half-dead
victims for days; disposing of bodies when a shape-shifter
lost control and slaughtered its own family, and then allowing that shape-shifting abomination to start a new life
somewhere else with no consequences. The thought of how
many lives his own family had allowed to be destroyed,
looking the other way in the name of professional reputation and profit, sickened him.

One of the key sources of tension between Lucy and him
was her blasé attitude toward all of it, her seeming accep-
tance of the status quo. She was ambitious and had made
it her life's goal to show Lucien up and prove to their father that he'd made a mistake in choosing his heir. It was
never going to do any good. Edgar was immovable, but
Lucien was happy to let Lucy take the lead and the credit,
to let himself seem lazy and spoiled. The longer his father
was motivated to keep putting off retirement, the better.
And Lucy was just better at business, which didn't interest Lucien in the least.

Rhea and Leo were staying at one of Rafe Diamante's
properties in his absence—Lucien had been tracking them
since the reception—a gated community in northeast Se-

dona. Luckily, the Smok family connections gave him access to any of a number of exclusive communities here and around he world. He had no problem getting in. Rhea's car, a red Mini, wasn't parked in the drive at Diamante's house, which could mean they were both out. But the lights were on inside.

He pulled his ski mask over his face as he got out of the car, loaded an arrow in the crossbow and lined up the sight on the scope.

Luck was on his side tonight. The revenant walked in front of the large picture window, looking down at something on the coffee table in the great room. Sheer curtains were drawn across the window, giving Lucien the advantage. He could see Leo perfectly through them but wouldn't be visible from within.

The image of Theia's face popped into his head, making him hesitate just for a moment. But Lucien wasn't responsible for the fact that the Valkyrie had created an abomination Theia's sister happened to be dating. This creature had stalked the earth long enough. It needed to be put down. *Forget about Theia.* Easier said than done, but anger at himself propelled Lucien forward, and he took his shot straight through the glass, not wanting to waste the opportunity.

The split second between the penetration of the glass and the arrow's impact in his target wasn't long enough for a normal person to react, but the revenant turned, causing the arrow to hit him in the shoulder. It had missed bone and gone straight through. Lucien grabbed another arrow, but Leo moved faster, charging through the broken window, and the arrow wasn't fully loaded as he came at Lucien.

Lucien dropped the bow, ready to defend himself in hand-to-hand combat. He only had to hold the revenant off for a little while. Despite the miss, the arrow tip would have delivered its poison, and it should be taking effect any minute.

But Leo didn't even seem impaired. Lucien bobbed and wove as Leo grabbed for him, throwing a right hook. Leo was faster, his fist catching Lucien on the jaw. The revenant barreled into him as he tried to take another swing, flattening him on the ground. Gravel and cactus tines from a decorative cholla ground into Lucien's shoulder as the revenant pummeled him. The Soul Reaper wasn't slowing this guy down a bit.

A knee to Lucien's groin ended any chance of regaining the upper hand.

Leo climbed on top of him, hands around Lucien's throat, the shaft of the damn arrow still skewering his left shoulder. "Who are you? Who sent you? Was it that necrophiliac?"

The lack of oxygen to his brain as the large hands constricted his airway must be impairing his understanding. That couldn't have been what the revenant said.

Lucien's vision was going gray.

"Leo! What the hell are you doing?" Theia's voice rang out as a car door slammed, and she was running toward them. "What's going on?"

But it was Theia's twin, not Theia herself—which made a lot more sense, Lucien realized before he lost consciousness.

Chapter 7

Rhea's message was baffling.

That guy you pretend you don't want just went rogue. Get over here. NOW.

Theia tried calling, but it went straight to voice mail, and her texts weren't being read. That was unnerving. What was going on? She hopped into her car and drove straight to Rafe's place, rattled enough to speed. Normally, according to Rhea, she drove like a granny.

A car Theia didn't recognize was parked out front, so she had to park farther down the drive. As she approached the house, she tripped over what looked like a quiver of high-tech arrows among scattered gravel and broken cactus littering the normally immaculate walkway. Theia dashed to the door and burst in without knocking after seeing shattered glass around the front windowpane.

"Rhea? Are you okay? Are you here?" She hadn't had any visions about Rhea being in danger, but her Spidey-sense was triggered like crazy.

"In here."

Theia breathed a bit easier at the sound of Rhea's voice. She hurried toward it and found her sister and Leo in the kitchen—with Lucien Smok tied to a chair. He looked like an angry bull had trampled him. Lucien glanced up at Theia out of one eye, the other swollen shut, and quickly looked down.

Leaning against the counter with his arms folded, Leo

had a bandage around his shoulder and blood soaking his white T-shirt. And there were bruises on his knuckles.

Theia found her voice after a moment of what was becoming a familiar sense of breathlessness, except this was breathlessness of disbelief. "Lucien? What in the world is going on? What happened to you? What are you doing here?"

"That's what we've been asking him, but he won't talk." Rhea kicked at the leg of Lucien's chair. "He shot Leo with a goddamn arrow." She indicated Rafe's large oak table with her gaze. A crossbow with a high-powered scope attachment lay on it.

Theia rubbed her forehead. "Lucien?"

He didn't glance up, but he finally spoke. "I'll talk to Theia. But not with *him* in the room."

Leo made an angry noise that sounded like a wolf growling, but Rhea took his hand. "Come on. Maybe she can get something out of him." Reluctantly, he went with her, and Theia closed the kitchen door.

She took a breath and turned around to find Lucien staring at her, his one open eye bloodshot and defiant. "Are you going to tell me what's going on? Did you really attack Leo with a…" She glanced at the table. "A *crossbow*?"

Lucien's voice was calm and measured. "Your sister is living with a man who ought to have died a millennium ago."

Theia crossed her arms. "I'm aware of that."

"You're aware."

"How is this any of your business?"

"Because *that's* my business. My real work. Putting unnatural creatures down. Demons. Revenants."

"Revenants?"

"That's what the reanimated dead are called."

Theia laughed, but Lucien wasn't kidding. "Leo is *not* a

revenant. You can see that, can't you? I mean, I know your vision is a little limited right now, but, seriously, Lucien."

"He died over a thousand years ago."

"He was *supposed* to die over a thousand years ago. I take it you're aware of the Valkyrie's bargain?"

"Dead is dead. The Valkyrie created a revenant in defiance of the Fates."

"Even if she did, what does that have to do with you? Why do you care?"

"I told you—"

"Yeah, yeah. You said. It's your job. Is this why you showed up at Phoebe's wedding?"

Lucien inclined his head. "One of the reasons. The other reasons were a demon and a necromancer."

Theia's temper flared in the face of his calm composure. "So your bullshit job offer was just that. Something you made up on the spot as an excuse to get close to my family so you could go on some purity crusade against them. Are you working with Carter Hamilton?"

Lucien opened his mouth but paused as her words registered before he spoke. "Hamilton?"

"The *actual* necromancer who crashed the reception. The man who murdered Rafe's father and apprentice along with at least two innocent women."

"I'm aware of who he is. Why would I be working with him?"

"Because he's made it his life's work to destroy my family, and you seem to be very conveniently helping his cause."

"I'm not trying to destroy your family. This isn't about your family at all."

"Could have fooled me."

Lucien sighed, glancing down at the floor, where droplets of blood had dried around him. "First of all, my interest in having you join the genome project at Smok Biotech was genuine. *Is* genuine. That has nothing to do with any of this."

"Any of this? You mean the trying-to-kill-members-of-my-family this? Did you think I'd just be like, 'Oh, that's okay, Mr. Smok, let me map these triggers for you. I don't need time off for the funerals. Can I get you a coffee?'"

"I didn't think you'd find out," Lucien burst out.

Theia unfolded her arms and clenched her fists, tempted to add to his bruises.

He had the sense to look embarrassed. "I mean, this is what I *do*. It has nothing to do with anything else. I compartmentalize the Lucien I have to be for the company so I can do this. You have no idea how dangerous these inhuman abominations are. Revenants rip people limb from limb. They're unstoppable. They're not human, and they do not experience empathy or remorse. My work with Smok Consulting means letting creatures like these walk free, and I was tired of being the cause of it, so I decided to take matters into my own hands—unofficially. I'm sorry it happens to affect you personally, but I can't let my feelings for you get in the way of what has to be done."

Through the haze of anger, Theia's airway did that funny tightening thing again. "Feelings for me?"

"I didn't mean *feelings*, I just meant—I mean, of course I'm attracted to you, that's not… Fuck." Lucien threw back his head in frustration but clearly regretted the movement as soon as he'd made it, judging by the sharp cry.

"What was that? What's wrong?"

Lucien looked a little green. "Nothing. I think I might have… I just have a little…" His eyes fluttered shut, and his head slumped forward.

"Lucien?" Theia tried to rouse him with a gentle shake, to no effect. She raised her voice as she turned her head toward the door. "You guys? I think I need some help in here."

The door opened abruptly, Rhea's palm flat against it

as though she'd been standing just on the other side with her ear pressed against the wood. "What did he do now?"

"I think he passed out. He moved his head sharply and it jarred some injury."

Leo grunted from the doorway. "Probably his broken arm."

Theia whirled on him. "You broke his arm?"

"*Arrow*," Rhea reminded her. She pointed at the table with a glare. "Crossbow."

"I'm not saying it wasn't warranted, but you don't tie up a guy with a broken arm and torture him for information."

Rhea snorted. "Nobody tortured him. He's a big goddamn baby."

"You have to take him to the hospital."

Lucien stirred and groaned. "'M fine. No hospital."

Theia rolled her eyes. "You're not fine. You got the shit beaten out of you by a Viking. Deservedly, it sounds like."

Lucien gritted his teeth like he was struggling to stay conscious. "Call Lucy."

Theia looked at Rhea, who shook her head and shrugged, then glanced back at Lucien. "Khaleesi?"

Lucien groaned, this time a sound of frustration rather than pain. "Call. *Lucy*. My sister. Number's in my phone." He paused for a breath. "Under 'Bitch.'"

"Um…" Theia raised an eyebrow.

Rhea picked up the cell phone lying next to the crossbow. It was a bit dented, and the glass cracked, but apparently it still functioned.

"Password?" Lucien gave it to her and Rhea typed it in. "Yep. Here it is—Bitch."

"She's my twin," said Lucien.

Rhea shared a look with Theia. "Seems about right," they said together.

Lucy Smok was at the door twenty minutes later. She had the same ice-blue eyes and long lashes as her brother.

The same dark brows and darker hair—though Lucy's was considerably longer and hung in a loose braid—contrasted starkly with the porcelain-fair skin in a slightly more feminine frame.

Lucien's twin leaned casually against the entryway, a black leather attaché case in her hand, glancing from Rhea to Theia as they opened the door. "Which one of you is the biologist?"

"I'm Theia." She stepped forward and shook Lucy's hand as though they were meeting in a normal social situation. "This is Rhea. Please come in. He's in the kitchen, through here."

Rhea had agreed to let Theia untie Lucien, but he still sat in the chair, guarded by a scowling Leo.

Lucy took in Leo's size with a glance and burst out laughing at her brother. "God, you're an idiot."

Lucien glared, holding his right arm awkwardly in his lap. "Thanks." His voice was tight and clipped. "Knew I could count on you."

"You'll have to forgive my brother." Lucy smirked at him from the doorway. "He thinks he's some kind of vigilante superhero." She stepped into the kitchen and set down the bag to look him over, clucking her tongue at his bruises.

He swore loudly when she touched his arm. "I think it's broken," he said through gritted teeth.

"That's what they told me."

"Did you bring it?"

"I did. You sure you want it?"

Lucien nodded curtly.

Lucy straightened. "We're going to need to get that shirt off." She looked around. "Got any scissors?"

Rhea rummaged through the kitchen drawers and dug up a pair. "Looks like you've got this covered." She handed them to Lucy. "I think Leo and I should leave you to it." She nodded at Leo, who pushed away from the counter with a sigh and followed her to the door. Before she left, Rhea turned back to Lucien. "And by the way? He's not a revenant, you jackass. He's mortal."

Lucien hissed in pain as Lucy cut the black sweater up the side, muttering something under his breath.

Lucy shook her head, continuing to cut without pausing. "You shot a mortal with that thing, idiot. You're lucky he didn't kill you."

The sleeve came away, revealing an odd twist to Lucien's elbow that made Theia's stomach churn.

From the black case, Lucy retrieved a small glass vial and a disposable syringe and ripped open a sterile wipe, which she used on his elbow. "This is going to hurt."

Theia peered over Lucy's shoulder as she opened the vial and filled the syringe. "What is that?"

"It's like Fix-a-Flat for bones." Without a warning, Lucy jabbed the needle directly into the joint, and Lucien let out a barrage of obscenities.

Theia had to turn away to keep the sudden lurch of her stomach from becoming something more. When she turned back, the twist in Lucien's arm seemed to have magically straightened.

"It's a little something we make at Smok Biotech." Lucy nodded to her brother as he cautiously flexed the joint. "You'll need to have it set properly before it starts to mend wrong. But for now, you should be able to use it."

As Lucien pulled off what remained of the sweater, Theia caught a flash of blue ink on his back just below the right shoulder. Brilliant blue, like the color she kept seeing everywhere—in her dreams, evoked in sounds and words.

Lucien glanced at Lucy. "Did you bring me—"

"Of course." She handed him the sweater she'd taken from the case, the same as the one he'd been wearing.

He turned as he stood to pull it on, giving Theia a good look at his ink.

It was a tattoo of a small web-winged dragon in flight.

Chapter 8

As Lucien struggled to pull on the sweater without showing that it was a struggle, Lucy stopped him.

"You've got something sticking out of your back."

"Cactus." He'd rolled in plenty of it. The minor irritant had paled against the other aches and pains he was beginning to feel now that his arm wasn't killing him. He couldn't remember ever taking such a beating, even from a raging wendigo. He'd been overconfident and unprepared.

Lucy sighed and got a pair of tweezers from her case. "Sit down. Let me get them." She went to work pulling out the tiny spines as he eased back into the chair. "So I understand you're going to be working at Smok's new lab," she said to Theia.

Lucien snorted. Like that was happening now.

Theia stayed behind him, watching Lucy from a few feet away. "I hadn't made up my mind."

"Well, if you don't mind a little unsolicited advice, I suggest you don't."

Lucien tried to turn, but Lucy held his shoulder—the one that was still sending out flares of pain.

"Oh?" Theia's voice was cool. "And why not?"

"I think it's a little beyond your abilities."

Lucien wanted to slug her, but her grip on his shoulder was firm.

"I mean, I'm sure you'll be a fine scientist someday, but this is serious work. It's not a graduate project."

"Give it a rest," Lucien growled under his breath.

"On the other hand, I hear you've already been in the White Room."

"The White Room?"

"Our special project. *Lucien*'s special project, really."
She was yanking out cactus spines roughly to let him know
she thought he'd overstepped his authority. "It's highly classified. Even the government doesn't know about it. But
you...you know about it."

Theia stepped closer. "Is that some kind of threat?"

"Threat?" Lucy stopped plucking and turned to look up
at Theia. "No, of course not. That's a little paranoid." She
went back to her work. "It *is* a warning, however. I know
you've signed our nondisclosure agreement. Not sure if
you read the fine print."

Theia's voice hardened. "What fine print?"

"*Lucy,*" Lucien warned, but she ignored him.

"The fine print that says you've agreed to return any intellectual property you may have removed from the lab."

"I didn't take anything. What are you talking about?"

"Your memories." Lucy stood and dropped the tweezers
into the case, turning to face Theia as Lucien rose, wanting to shut her up but not knowing how—and realizing as
he stood that the room was spinning.

"And how exactly am I supposed to give back my memory of the visit?" Theia scoffed.

"We've developed a special technique."

Lucy had a syringe in her hand, and Lucien grabbed for
it, but the floor seemed to tilt under him, and he grabbed
her arm instead as he pitched toward the table.

Theia stepped in to steady him while Lucy regarded
him with cold eyes, as if she would have let him fall. He'd
fucked up, and he was on his own.

She stood back while Theia helped him into the chair.
"I suppose you got your head knocked around by that delicious Viking."

"I may have hit my head on the concrete once or twice,"
he acknowledged.

"Are you having trouble seeing?"

"Not much." Things *had* been a little blurry.

"Not *much*?" Lucy shook her head. "Looks like you've earned yourself a pretty good concussion there, little brother. Someone's going to have to keep an eye on you overnight. And it's not going to be me. I have a date."

"Well, he's not staying *here*," Theia's sister objected from the doorway.

"I'm fine," Lucien insisted. "It's just a little vertigo and blurred vision." He stood again but couldn't seem to find the room's level.

Theia grabbed his arm once more. "I'll give you a ride home. I'd like to discuss this intellectual property issue a bit more, if you don't mind."

With both Rhea and the Viking now standing in the doorway, Lucy was reluctant to make a scene. Lips pressed together, she discreetly dropped the syringe back into her attaché case as she picked it up. "Suit yourself. But I warn you, he's a pain in the ass when he's convalescing."

"Thanks for all your help," Lucien said to her sweetly. "I think we can take it from here."

Lucy shrugged. "Get that bone checked tomorrow. And don't come crying to me if you slip into a coma."

"If I slip into a coma," said Lucien, "I promise you will be the last person to whom I come crying."

Lucy gave him a saccharine smile and headed for the door.

Theia's sister frowned at the two of them. "You sure about this, Thei?"

"No. But I'm doing it anyway." Theia picked up the crossbow and gave Lucien a stern look. "I'm going to hold on to this for you. If you can convince me you're not a danger to my family, maybe I'll give it back."

Leo stepped in the way as Theia led Lucien toward the

door. "Don't come at me or mine again. Next time you won't be walking away, with or without assistance."

Lucien was too tired to argue with any of them. All he wanted to do was lie down and go to sleep. He let Theia walk him to her car without comment or protest, leaning back in the seat and closing his eyes once he was inside.

"I'm going to talk to Rhe for a minute," Theia said. "Don't fall asleep."

"That's not actually a thing," he murmured. "It's a myth that you shouldn't fall asleep after a concussion."

"I meant because we're going to have words. A lot of them." She slammed the car door, and Lucien wanted to grab his head to stop it from ringing, but his arms were too tired.

Theia glanced back at the car as she gathered the scattered arrows. Lucien might be dangerous, but his sister was definitely more so. She hadn't exactly been subtle in her threats. Smok Biotech might not literally have a way to wipe Theia's memory, but she wasn't about to give Lucy the chance.

The rhythmic snap of a pair of flip-flops announced Rhea's approach on the stone path. "You're not really going to give those weapons back to him?"

Theia straightened and put the last one in its quiver. "Not if he doesn't give me some satisfactory answers. But I'm sure he's got plenty more where these came from."

"He just tried to *kill* Leo."

"I know. I'm going to try to talk some sense into him about this obsession he has with Leo being a revenant."

"You realize there's a good chance that he's actually unhinged."

"Yeah."

"Want me to read that tattoo of his? I caught a peek from the doorway. Maybe we can verify his motives, see if any of this stuff about hunting down 'unnatural creatures' is true. And maybe find out a little more about him, if you know what I mean." Rhea raised an eyebrow suggestively.

Theia was 99 percent certain that whatever Rhea might read in Lucien's ink was the last thing she wanted her to see.

"Maybe some other time. I'm not sure how his mental state right now would affect it. And I'd prefer if we had his consent." Which Theia was going to make damn sure they never got.

Rhea studied her for a moment, her expression suspicious. "You call me when you get home. I want to know you're all right before I go to bed."

Theia booped Rhea's nose, guaranteed to distract her with aggravation. "You got it, Moonpie."

Rhea rubbed her nose with the back of her hand. "Gross. Weirdo. And stop calling me Moonpie."

Theia headed for her car. "But you look like a Moonpie."

"What does that even mean? I look like *you*."

"Go play with your Viking."

Theia tossed the quiver onto the back seat and climbed in. Lucien's eyes were closed, his head lolling against the headrest. Theia reached over to draw the shoulder belt across him and fasten it before starting the car. With a wave at Rhea, she headed out, only to realize once she'd exited the gates that she had no idea where Lucien lived.

"Lucien?" She nudged him gently. Nothing. God, he wasn't slipping into a coma already, was he?

His phone was propped in the cup holder under the dash. Maybe his address was in it. Theia pulled over and entered the password on the cracked screen and found the address in his contacts, committing it to memory. Before she set the phone down, a message notification appeared from Lucy. Theia couldn't resist taking a peek.

This one's for the little pixie girl.

Pixie girl? Theia glared at the screen and continued to read.

No doubt he's sitting next to you in the car snoring right now.

He was, a little bit, now that she listened for it.

Make sure you wake him up every two hours to check his responses. I don't like the blurred vision. If you can't wake him, call me. I'll send one of our doctors. Lovely to meet you. Finish our talk later.

Every two hours? She tried to respond, but the keyboard wasn't letting her press most of the keys. Theia sighed. She was going to have to take him to Phoebe's place. She'd left the house without feeding Puddleglum.

Someone was shaking him.

"We're here. Come on."

After a more vigorous shake, Lucien opened his eyes and focused on Theia's face. Still a little blurry. But eminently kissable. Shit. He was really out of it.

"Hey." She peered at him. "You awake? It's Theia Dawn. We're here. Time to get out."

Lucien looked around at the shrubbery laced with fairy lights in front of the cozy ranch-style bungalow. The night was silent except for the pleasant rhythm of chirping crickets, and the air was heavy with the perfume of jasmine blossoms. He was completely lost.

"Where's here?"

"My sister Phoebe's place. I'm cat sitting. And now apparently I'm babysitting. You," she clarified when he squinted at her in confusion. "Lucy told me to wake you up every two hours and check on you, so you're staying with me tonight."

"I thought Lucy left before we did. How long was I asleep?"

"About an hour. I let you sleep a little longer while I was feeding the cat. And she did leave before us."

"The cat?"

"*Lucy.*" Theia narrowed her eyes at him. "Are you sure I shouldn't take you to a hospital?"

Lucien rubbed his eyes. "No, I'm fine. I'm awake now." He tried to get out of the car, impeded by the seat belt, and finally managed to fumble in the dark and find the release. As he got to his feet, he groaned and clutched the door.

"Lucien?"

He stared at the ground for a moment, suddenly flushed, his forehead breaking out in a sweat. "I'm possibly going to throw up in your sister's front yard."

"Oh God. Please don't."

"I'd prefer not to." He stood still for several seconds, willing it down, and finally straightened. "Lead the way."

"To the bathroom?" she suggested as she took his arm.

"Sounds wise."

The ground tilted and swayed beneath him, echoing the motion of his stomach, as if he were navigating the deck of a ship on a choppy sea. He managed to make it to the little powder-blue room and close the door before pitching toward the floor once more. Lucien sank to his knees and grabbed the edge of the toilet, literally hugging the bowl as he dredged up what he was certain was every last thing he'd ever eaten.

By the time he was able to get to his feet and clean himself up, his head felt like someone had shaken his brain and bashed it against the inside of his skull—which he supposed was pretty accurate—but at least the dizziness and nausea had subsided.

Theia sat waiting for him in the living room when he made his way gingerly down the hallway. "So where do you want to start?"

"Start?"

"Explaining yourself."

Lucien stepped down into the living room with a sigh and grabbed for the couch. "I already told you that Leo Ström is a revenant, and—"

"Except he's not. He was immortal. He was never a revenant. In Leo's tradition, I believe, revenants are known as *draugr*. Rhea dealt with one once when she was fighting to save his life. It was what you said—an abomination. A shuffling, inhuman monster that tried to suck out her soul before Leo's warden spirit destroyed it. Leo isn't a monster. He's a good man."

Lucien studied her for a moment. He'd put down a *draugr* or two. They were just about the most unpleasant creatures he'd ever encountered. But that didn't mean that every revenant raised from the corpse of a Norseman had to be a *draugr*. Valkyries had great power over the dead.

"Your sister said he was mortal."

Theia nodded. "He is. It was part of the Valkyrie's bargain with the Norns when she released him."

"But he leads a hunting party of wraiths."

"Yeah, you'll have to ask Rhea how that one works, because I haven't quite wrapped my head around it. But it doesn't make him a revenant. I'm sure Leo would be happy to explain it to you himself after you've apologized for trying to kill him."

Lucien leaned forward and rested his arms on his knees, looking down at the wood floor as he contemplated the facts. He couldn't let guilt or desire sway him. Cold, hard, rational facts were the enemy of the esoteric. The stupid. Of supernatural shit. And feelings.

He lifted his head sharply and regretted it. "Where's my gear? My crossbow?"

"I've put it away for safekeeping."

The tip of the arrow that had hit Leo Ström should have exploded on impact with flesh, leaving behind its poison. A revenant would have gone down within seconds, the unnatural blood in its veins turning to acid and eating it from the inside until there was nothing left of it. But Leo hadn't. The serum hadn't affected him at all. The arrow had only wounded him. Those were the cold, hard facts.

"I may have made an error."

Theia laughed, and he smiled without meaning to.

She shook her head, the red tips of her hair swinging. "Jesus, you're a stubborn son of a bitch." She leaned back against the cushion of the round rattan chair, looking like Venus in her scallop shell. Perhaps he'd hit his head harder than he thought. Theia's velvety gray eyes fixed on his, her gaze piercing. "So about that nondisclosure agreement."

Lucien rubbed his eyes. "Lucy didn't have any business bringing that up. She tends to get a bit aggressive when it comes to the company."

"Is that really what I signed? An agreement to have my memory wiped? Can she do that?"

"Yes." He shrugged. "No. And yes. The NDA does include a clause about not removing any intellectual property, but, legally, I think we'd be hard-pressed to make the case that you were agreeing not to leave with your memories intact if you chose to reject the offer. As for Lucy, well… I wouldn't turn my back on her if I were you."

"So there *is* a drug that can erase my memories of what I saw."

"And any memory that we've had this conversation about it, yes. But it's not my intention to implement that protocol."

Theia lifted an eyebrow. "You say the darnedest things."

"None of that's relevant, though, if you choose to accept the offer."

"Oh, I see. So *if* I agree to keep my mouth shut and help you with your little genome-mapping database, you won't physically assault me and tamper with my mind."

Lucien closed his eyes against the increasing intensity of his headache. "Can we… Do you mind if we continue this in the morning?" He could feel her gaze intent on him, studying him, perhaps to see if he was bullshitting her.

"Of course." Theia slipped from the shell-like chair and held out her hand to help him up as he opened his eyes. "Or in two hours. Whichever comes first."

"You're really going to wake me up every two hours?"

"Still have the blurred vision and vertigo?"

"No." Lucien reached for her hand and missed. "Yes."

"Then, yes, I am." Her hand closed around his. "I've made up the guest bed for you. Actually, I was sleeping in the guest bed, so I didn't really do anything but straighten it— Are you allergic to cats?"

He tried to follow her train of thought as he rose and went with her. "Allergic? No."

"Good, because Puddleglum pretty much thinks that room is his, and there's no way to get all the fur off the bedspread."

"I don't want to displace… Puddleglum? Or you, for that matter. I could sleep on the couch."

"That would be stupid. It's a two-bedroom house." She opened the guest room door. A well-fed tiger-stripe Siamese regarded him from the center of the largest pillow with unblinking aquamarine eyes.

"That's his pillow," she said unnecessarily. "If you need anything, just let me know."

"Theia?"

She paused as she turned to go. "Hmm?"

"I'm not sure why you're being so nice to me after I... well, anyway. You don't have to be, and I appreciate that you are."

Theia wondered the same thing as she set the alarm in Phoebe's room. She could have ignored Lucy's instructions and driven him home. Yet here she was, preparing to interrupt her sleep every two hours to make sure Lucien's own arrogance didn't kill him.

But despite his misguided attack on Leo, she couldn't help being secretly pleased to learn there was more to Lucien than just a privileged rich boy for whom everything was a game—including seduction. If what he'd said was true, he'd taken a principled stand against his own family legacy. If Smok Consulting was in the business of covering up paranormal crimes for the wealthy, Lucien's clandestine efforts minimized the harm they caused in doing it. And Theia wanted to find out more about both.

Chapter 9

The alarm went off what seemed like minutes later. Theia rose bleary-eyed and shuffled down the hall to the guest room, where Puddleglum opened one suspicious eye from his perch on the pillow.

Lucien was hard to rouse, but he jolted awake when she put her hands on both shoulders to shake him. His hands closed around her upper arms, and he flipped her across his body onto her back on the bed and leaped over her on all fours, eyes looking slightly wild. Puddleglum disappeared under the bed.

It took Theia a moment to catch her breath and speak. "Lucien, it's me."

He blinked down at her, his feral stance slowly relaxing. "Sorry. I was deep in a dream. I was fighting off—"

"A thousand-year-old Viking who was kicking your ass?"

Lucien grinned sheepishly. "Something like that." He sat back on his heels, and she was intensely aware of his thighs—muscular and firm—on either side of hers. He might not be able to compete with Leo in size, but he was obviously extremely athletic. "So this is my two-hour wake-up, I take it."

"And I take it you're not in a coma."

"Not at the moment."

"And you know your own name."

"Of course. Anakin Skywalker."

"Interesting choice. Who's the president of the United States?"

Lucien scowled for a moment, pondering the answer. "Alec Baldwin?"

"Close enough. You're cleared for another two-hour nap." Theia waited for him to move, raising an eyebrow when he continued to stare down at her. "Are you going to get off me?"

Lucien seemed to color as he rolled onto his hip, but it was hard to be sure in the monochrome tones of the dark bedroom. Maybe it was just her imagination.

Theia turned to face him, head propped on her hand. "How long have you been…"

"Hunting unnatural creatures?" He considered for a moment. "It started by accident, I guess. High school. Junior year, on a job cleaning up a vamp den."

"As in *vampires*?"

"Yeah."

"They're real?"

"Everything's real."

A little shiver ran up her spine, and he must have noticed it.

"There's nothing sexy about them, I can assure you. Every one I've ever met was as dumb as a post. They exist on instinct, feeding their hunger. If they're part of an organized brood, they're fairly harmless, only clever enough to follow orders. The master negotiates with sources and puts them to work delivering shipments, doing busywork, so they don't wander off and try to hunt on their own."

"Sources?"

"Blood sources. There are black-market blood banks… and voluntary donors."

Theia shuddered, this time with revulsion. She could just imagine how the "voluntary" donor system worked. Probably a lot like Carter Hamilton's afterlife sex ring, where the shades of dead sex workers were coerced into servicing clients who paid to have sex with someone being controlled by a "step-in."

"The business runs pretty smoothly," Lucien confirmed. "The syndicates keep everything relatively clean. But every so often, a bloodsucker goes rogue. Sometimes a handful of them will splinter off the brood and try to go it alone. That's when it gets messy. Which is when they call in Smok Consulting."

"Your father's company."

Lucien nodded. "Edgar didn't trust me to handle the consulting work. Probably rightly so."

"Edgar?"

"My father." He shrugged. "It turned out a rogue brood had been keeping a…" Lucien swallowed, his expression no longer neutral. "An illegal blood farm. Kids they'd taken off the street—junkies, runaways. There's a strict set of rules for voluntary donors—consent forms, maximum donations, minimum nondonation periods to make sure the donors remain healthy, a mental-health screening process— these kids bypassed all that. Probably traded sex—or even a willing donation if they were savvy enough about who they were dealing with—for a place to sleep for a night. And then found themselves being harvested…indefinitely."

Theia's gut twisted. "Jesus."

"Yeah. Some of them lasted…" Lucien's voice trailed off, and he swallowed again before going on. "A long time. I was supposed to be cleaning up corpses, and there was this kid, this little girl, maybe twelve years old, chained to a radiator. Vamp tracks up and down her arms…everywhere. She was supposed to be dead, but she moved."

Lucien's face had gone white. "God, she *moved*." He sat up and drew his knees to his chest, and Theia stared, transfixed, not wanting to hear any more but unable to stop him. "I called in the crew foreman to get her help. I stayed with her, told her it was going to be okay, she was safe now. And when the foreman showed up, he…put a bullet in her head."

"Oh my God. Lucien…"

He dropped his forehead to his knees and shuddered, and Theia sat up and put her arm around him, rubbing his shoulder, not sure what to do.

"I don't know why I told you that. I've never told anyone that. Not even Lucy."

"It wasn't your fault."

Lucien straightened and jerked away from her. "Of course it was my fault. I'm a Smok. That's what we do."

"You tried to help her."

Lucien laughed bitterly. "Yeah, and you see how that turned out."

"You were a kid yourself." Theia was pissed on his behalf. "It's outrageous that your father would have put you in that situation. You were what, seventeen?"

"Sixteen. It doesn't matter."

"Of course it matters." She wasn't sure how to get him out of the dark place he'd descended to, and it seemed suddenly urgent and imperative that she did. "And that was when you got started with your own hunting? At sixteen?" The calm questioning seemed to work. The shadow in Lucien's eyes faded.

"Not right away. It was just the catalyst. I asked what was going to happen to the bloodsuckers who were responsible, and my father said their sire would deal with them. It's not good for business to have rogues on the loose, so they'd likely be put down." His affect had changed, his words now emotionless, as though he'd dissociated. "I couldn't stop thinking about it, so I decided to look for them and find out for sure. I used a fake ID and signed up as a donor."

Theia gaped at him. "But you didn't actually…"

"Of course I did. The ID said I was eighteen, the minimum age allowed. They paid by the hour. You could do a private donation with a single patron for fifty dollars an hour, or you could go to a party and be available on tap. Five hundred a night."

"On tap? Not a literal…"

"No, though that's not unheard of. Mostly with fetishists. Groupies. But this was purely a financial transaction. I signed up for a party. There were two other donors, both girls who looked like minors. I thought it would be like the movies, with everybody at a cocktail party, lots of velvet, vamps biting us on the neck." A slight, embarrassed smile animated his face for an instant and was gone. "But it was way less glamorous. Apparently the telltale wound draws too much attention for donors, and it's dangerous anyway. Too easy—and too tempting—to drain the donor dry. They needed access to less visible veins. We stripped down to our underwear. The girls were topless."

Lucien's expression had gone flat. "The party was in a hotel suite. We were told to circulate—that got some big laughs—and the vamps started feeding on us as we moved around the sitting room. We all tried to make small talk at first, but they weren't interested in us as people. We were food. The girls were more popular, and one of them ended up passing out because they drained her too quickly. They carried the other one off to the bedroom, and three of the vamps stayed in the outer room with me and pulled out the sofa bed. Apparently, they prefer to feed lying down."

Theia rested her hand on his wrist, wanting to stop him, but he seemed determined now to get it out.

"When they'd had their fill, they got a little more talkative, and I managed to turn the conversation to the rogues, pretending I was a groupie and I wanted to be owned. I said it was a shame they were gone, but one of the bloodsuckers told me they'd just relocated. He gave me an address, a ranch. I was taking archery at school, and I showed up at the ranch the next morning with my bow loaded with Soul

Reaper arrows—the kind I had tonight, to split the demon from the undead frame and send the soul to hell. And I staked every last one of them while they were sleeping." Lucien shrugged, as if the last part had been incidental. "Didn't do anything like that again until I was in college."

Theia was at a total loss for words.

"I've talked your ear off." Lucien had been staring at the wall, and he turned his head to look at her with an apologetic smile, but the smile faltered. "You're crying."

Theia put her fingers to her cheek. "I am?" She was. She hadn't even noticed. "I'm sorry." She wasn't sure exactly what she was apologizing for. The tears were coming faster.

"Theia. Don't." He reached out to her, taking the hand she was still holding in front of her, tears on her fingertips. "I didn't tell you that to play on your emotions."

"I know you didn't. It's just…my gift."

"Your gift?"

"It comes with the visions. Sometimes instead of images, I pick up on other people's emotions." She shrugged, again apologetic. It always seemed like a bit of an intrusion, and one she usually kept to herself. "These aren't my tears."

She could feel it now, like a physical blow to her soul. Lucien was in pain. Torn up inside as much as he was bruised and battered outside from his fight with Leo. More so, probably.

He squeezed her hand, wordless, shocked, and didn't deny it.

Theia started crying in earnest. "Okay, maybe they're a little bit mine, too." She grabbed for the tissues on the nightstand, but Lucien reached for her, stopping her. His hands went to either side of her face, thumbs brushing away the tears, and he lowered his mouth to hers and kissed her.

Every dark warning she'd ever dreamed was rising to the surface, threatening to engulf her. He was mystery. He was danger. There would be no turning back if she dived into these waters. There was no telling how deep they were or what was hiding in them. But she didn't care. She wanted to drown in him. His kiss was like air beneath the dark waves. As long as she breathed through him, she would survive. Theia threaded her arms through his, hooked them around his neck and let go, giving herself to the deep. The relief at no longer fighting was immediate and intense. She was immersed.

Lucien made a soft sound of pain, and it took her a moment to realize it was physical.

Theia drew back. "Your shoulder?"

"I think I may have sprained it a bit."

"Maybe next time be more aware of who you're going after."

Lucien nodded and lay back on the bed, pulling Theia with him. "I solemnly swear only to hunt actual revenants and demons from now on." He wrapped her in his arms and started to kiss her again, but Theia hesitated. Lucien frowned. "What's the matter?"

"About the demons…"

He stroked his hand down Theia's side. "What about demons?"

Theia grabbed his wrist and pulled his hand away with a scowl. "You've threatened certain members of my family. I need to know if you're still planning to harm them."

"You consider them your family."

"Absolutely. They're both my brothers-in-law, but they were family long before that."

Lucien cocked his head. "I thought Phoebe was the only one who was married."

"Apparently Dev and Ione eloped. No one is supposed to know. But that's beside the point."

She'd gestured with her hand, and Lucien took hold of it and kissed it. "Tell me about Dev, then. Is he possessed or isn't he?"

Theia sighed. "He's not. Technically. He was bound to a demon by a sorcerer he was apprenticed to. The demon was tortured and forced to occupy Dev's physical form as though it were a cage. Dev nearly died. He didn't even know what his mentor had done to him until after he woke up in the hospital and something triggered the demon's release for the first time. Dev has it under control now. They've come to an understanding, and the demon is contained by a magical sigil tattooed on his body."

"An understanding." Lucien scowled. "How do you come to an understanding with a demon? It's a monster. A killer."

"Kur is actually very sweet once you get to know him."

"*Kur?* The demon has a name? And you've met this abomination?"

"I have. And please stop using the word *abomination*. It makes you sound like a hellfire-and-brimstone preacher."

Lucien laughed. "My great-grandfather was a hellfire-and-brimstone preacher, as a matter of fact."

"Well, that's delightful." The touch of his skin, his hand holding hers, was distracting, but she didn't want to let go. "Listen, why don't you just meet with Dev? Let him tell you about Kur. Maybe he'll even let you meet Kur so you can see for yourself. He's not an abomination, I promise you."

Lucien seemed to consider it seriously. "If you want to arrange a meeting," he said at last, "I promise to hear Dev out—but I'll make up my own mind about the demon."

It was a start. "Now, about Rafe."

Lucien groaned and rested his forehead against hers. "Can we talk about him in the morning? I've only had two hours' sleep, and there's a beautiful woman in my bed, and everything hurts."

She smiled reluctantly, her cheeks warm. "I would, except…" She glanced at the window behind him. Pale streaks of gold and pink were visible on the horizon, peeking between the tips of the spires of Cathedral Rock in the distance.

"Except what?"

"It's already morning."

Lucien turned and followed her gaze. "Well, damn." He rolled onto his back with a slight wince. "Can I have my two hours anyway? Or do I get kicked out at dawn?"

Theia curled against his side with her head on his chest. "I'll tell you when I wake up."

Lucien tightened his arm around her and closed his eyes. "Tell me I'm not still lying in the gravel getting my head kicked in and you're not some fevered hallucination that will disappear when I open my eyes."

Theia yawned. "I'm pretty sure I'm not a hallucination. But you did hit your head pretty hard."

Chapter 10

When Lucien woke again, a cat was in Theia's place. It figured. Even though he knew this was the infamous Puddleglum, it would be just his luck if Theia were a shapeshifter. Puddleglum sat staring at him like some infernal imp, blinking knowingly as if to say, "Takes one to know one, buddy."

Theia saved Lucien from imminent hypnotism and enslavement by returning with coffee and a box of doughnuts.

"Thank God." Lucien sat up and took the cup she handed him. "I think your cat was plotting the trajectory to my jugular. I was playing dead, but I think he was onto me."

Theia grinned. "He's way too lazy to bother with live prey. He'd just sit there and wait you out until you died of starvation and then eat your corpse. And probably stalk off in a huff because you weren't the right texture."

Lucien took a powdered doughnut from the box with a little offended sniff as Theia climbed into bed and displaced the cat. "I assure you, my texture is everything it ought to be."

"I take it you're feeling better." She examined the eye that had been nearly swollen shut the night before. "I thought I'd let you sleep. I figured it would do you some good."

"Let me sleep?" Lucien took a bite of his doughnut. "What time is it?"

"One o'clock."

Lucien inhaled powdered sugar and nearly choked. "In the afternoon? Damn. I have to go." He kissed her and stuffed the rest of the doughnut in his mouth as he rolled out of bed as gingerly as possible while still maintaining a modicum of masculine dignity. The sharp sting from the cuts and scrapes and cactus spines had given way to an all-over throbbing ache and muscle stiffness.

"Go where? It's Saturday."

He couldn't exactly tell her he had a date with his ex-girlfriend to express his "gratitude" for the information she'd given him about Leo. "I have to meet with a client at two." He kept his head down over his coffee cup, hating that he was already lying to her. This was the other problem with having feelings for someone.

Theia set down her cup and got up. "Your car's at Rafe's. I'll have to drive you. I don't think you should be driving with your vision messed up, anyway."

He'd forgotten he'd left his car. There was no time to go across town to get it and still meet Polly by two. And she was very unforgiving of people who made her wait.

"I can have a car pick me up."

"Lucien, I'm right here with a car right now. What's the big deal? I can wait in the parking lot while you meet your client."

If he made this an even bigger deal, she was going to get suspicious. "You promise you'll stay in the car? It shouldn't take long." He crossed his fingers behind his back, praying to whatever forces controlled the universe that Polly wasn't going to want something he couldn't give her with Theia waiting outside.

Lucien was moving like an old man, and the broken bone in his arm was starting to feel stiff and cold as the ecto-plasmic gel Lucy had injected began to solidify. It wasn't intended as a long-term fix.

Theia pulled into the parking lot at Polly's, obviously curious but not asking any questions, and Lucien drew himself up straight to walk in with his usual casual aplomb. It took every ounce of control he had.

Polly's hair was blue today, clipped up in a loose fall of sapphire curls. Seated at the bar reviewing the books, she glanced up at his entrance and let her gaze wander over him with amusement.

"Just coming from goth yoga, are we? Where's your mat?"

"Very funny."

"Oh, wait, I know…you left her in the car." She glanced up at the television over the bar, tuned to a closed-circuit security camera on the parking lot.

Lucien slid onto the stool beside her with manufactured grace. "Jealousy, Pols? Aren't you above that?"

"I wouldn't call it jealousy. I'm just looking out for you, sweetie. I warn you about her, and the next thing I know, she's chauffeuring you around town. In the clothes you obviously slept in. And apparently were mauled by a bear in." Polly scrutinized him more closely, touching his puffy eye with a metallic-teal fingertip. "Took him a while to go down, did it?"

Lucien picked up the highball she was drinking and tossed it back. "He didn't go down."

"You're kidding. Your fancy arrows didn't work?"

"He was human, as it turns out."

Polly covered her mouth, trying not to giggle—and not trying very hard. "Oh, no. Oh, Lucien."

"Did you know?"

Polly didn't answer right away, reaching over the bar with her ass in the air to get the bottle of bourbon and re-fill the glass. "How would I know? He hasn't been in here in years. He certainly wasn't a human then. At least not a mortal one. I guess he broke the curse." She took a sip and smiled, savoring it in her mouth. "You asked for information on the Valkyrie. I got you a Valkyrie so you could get it straight from the horse's mouth. I can't help it if you didn't ask her the right questions."

"I'm so glad this is amusing for you."

"Oh, come on, sweetie. I'm sorry." Polly kissed his cheek, her lips damp with bourbon. "You really took a beating, didn't you? And the girl? The psychic sidekick? Does she know how you got hurt?"

Lucien turned the bottle on the bar, feigning interest in the label. "Theia isn't psychic, as it turns out. She's an empath."

"Lucien." Polly moved the bottle out of his grasp, all teasing gone. "You're playing with fire. I'm the one who picked you up out of your own vomit when you couldn't stand to stay sober long enough to have an emotion. She'll end up knowing everything about you. Things you don't even know. That self-loathing that eats away at you that you manage to project as cockiness and arrogance, the fear that made you run away from Edgar and his ice-in-his-veins ideas about family and duty straight into my bed." Polly smiled sadly and lifted his chin. "Your Maggie May. All of that is going to be laid bare to her. You might as well be walking around without skin, waiting for her throw salt on your raw flesh."

"I don't need you to tell me that."

"Don't you?" Polly turned his chin toward her and shook her head. "Poor baby. I wish I could give you immortality, make you immune to human weaknesses like love."

"You know I don't want to be inhuman."

"Oh, I know that, sweetie. Which is what makes your path so much harder. Be careful, sweet boy. She'll break your heart."

"I didn't come here for a lecture. I came to thank you for the information you facilitated—as unfortunately inaccurate as it turned out to be. You wanted me to meet you here, and I'm here. So what do you want?"

Polly turned her wrist, the jewels in her charm bracelet catching the light. "I was going to ask for a drop of blood." She fingered a garnet teardrop. "But just look at you." She shook her head and sighed. "Considering what's waiting for you outside, I suppose I'd better have what you gave her."

Lucien's brows drew together. "What I gave her?"

"A tear, sweetie. Before she drains you of all of them." Polly held her finger to the corner of his eye and a tear fell onto her fingertip as if commanded, solidifying into something that strongly resembled a diamond. "Lovely, isn't it? The devil's tears. It'll be worth a pretty penny one day."

Chapter 11

Lucien was quiet. Theia didn't ask what the meeting was about. After what he'd told her last night, she wasn't sure she wanted to know. She drove him to his car, which he insisted he was okay to drive home. He needed a shower, he said, and some more rest, but he'd see her later.

Theia wasn't sure what later meant, precisely, but he kissed her goodbye, and the kiss was promising. In the meantime, she was going to burst if she didn't talk to someone about what had happened between her and Lucien. She needed sisterly advice, but there was no way she could talk to Rhea about him after what he'd done. Ione had raised them after their parents were killed in a car accident, and Theia wasn't in the mood for her disapproval. Phoebe would have been perfect—she was always easiest to talk to—but Phoebe was somewhere in the Yucatán climbing pyramids and getting laid by a demigod.

But Theia hadn't talked to Laurel in a while.

Laurel Carpenter was their half sister, one of three born to their father's secret second wife.

Rhea wouldn't be happy about it, but despite Laurel's past sins against them as Carter Hamilton's apprentice, Theia considered her a friend. Laurel had grown up in foster care, unaware of her own magic and resenting the half sisters who'd gotten all her father's attention. She'd been ripe for Carter's head games. Theia couldn't hold that against her.

She needed to pop into her apartment in Flagstaff anyway to get some materials for the final exams for a class she was teaching, and Laurel, it turned out, was more than ready to take a break from studying for her own.

As they set out the tea things on Theia's balcony, Laurel watched her, cautious as always. "I guess you've heard about Carter's conviction being overturned. In case you're wondering, no, he hasn't contacted me, and no, I have no interest in ever speaking to him again."

"I did hear, actually." Theia grimaced. "When he magically crashed Phoebe's wedding reception."

"Oh, shit. He didn't."

"Sadly, he did. But don't worry. That's not why I called you. Although I do have a bit of an ulterior motive." Theia grinned as she poured the tea. "To be honest, there are some things I can't talk to anybody else about, and I really need some advice."

"From me?" Laurel set out the plate of homemade lemon bars she'd brought. "I'm not sure what advice I could possibly give you."

"I've had these visions lately—one in particular that I've had since I was little." Theia sat and took a lemon bar. "I think it started when I heard a story in church about being the bride of Christ. The priest said if we weren't Christ's, we would be the devil's. I dreamed I was wearing a red wedding gown and veil and running from someone hiding in the shadows. The faster I ran, the closer the figure got, until I realized I was running straight to hell. At the end of the path was a throne. And the dark figure that had been chasing me was sitting on it and holding out his hand."

"And now you think you've met the dark figure."

Theia shivered despite the balmy weather. "Bingo. You're good."

Laurel smiled as she stirred sugar into her cup. "You know I see things, too." Laurel's gift was a true ability to see the future without all the interpretation Theia's visions required.

"So...what exactly have you seen?"

"It's not always perfectly clear, you understand. I see future events like they're on a layer of film laid over the top of what's in front of me, and right now... I see some kind of contract in your hand."

"And?"

Laurel set down the spoon and smoothed her fingers over her closely cropped hair. "And I think it says you've promised the devil your soul."

"Ah."

"I take it you were hoping for something a little less literal."

"Well, it is very specific. The thing is, this man I met... there's more to him than this 'dark prince' persona he shows the world. I guess I was hoping I was imagining things. It wouldn't be the first time I've avoided getting close to someone because of my dreams. But I..." The look on Laurel's face when she glanced up made her pause. "What?"

Laurel colored. "It's not important. Sometimes I get flashes of events that aren't any of my business."

It was Theia's turn to blush. "I'm going to sleep with him, aren't I?" She groaned into her hands for a moment before looking up again. "See, this is another thing I can't talk to Rhea about. As close as we are, I've never told her that... I've never actually...done it."

Laurel's eyes widened over her cup.

"Yeah." Theia lifted her shoulders helplessly. "I've been having visions all my life, and every time I got involved with a guy, I'd see something about him that just, I don't know, made me think the devil was around every corner. And I don't even believe in a literal devil. Of course, with the things we've seen lately, I don't even know what to believe. And Lucien—that's the guy—has been telling me about a whole underground society of 'unnatural creatures,' things I had no idea were real."

Chapter 12

Lucien stared at the laptop, trying to get a grip on the sudden rage filling him. He'd given her the benefit of the doubt despite her sisters' penchants for unnatural men—and now here it was, a confession in her own words that she herself was unnatural, that she was the worst kind of unnatural. Theia was what he'd been trying to escape his entire life. In fleeing Edgar and his stupid rules, Lucien had been fleeing the stain of the demonic—the Smok legacy: that he was doomed to serve in hell. Though the story had seemed allegorical when he was younger, it had become more theoretically probable once he'd been initiated into the family business.

The family made its money fulfilling the needs of demons and unnatural beings, hobnobbed with them, protected them. It had begun to seem unlikely that the legend was only that. By the time Lucien had started college, he'd been bitterly determined not to become what his father wanted him to be, what he was trying to make him into. He'd tried to drown his fears with drink—and then he'd met Polly. He'd followed the song of the siren, jumping headfirst into the world he'd been resisting.

It was a double standard, but becoming a slacker who hung out almost exclusively with inhuman and unnatural beings had been another kind of rebellion. Doing business with such creatures was one thing. One did not *party* with them, as Edgar had once told him in disgust. And they sure as hell didn't sleep with them.

Lucien had lost himself in that world for a time, not caring what fate meant him to be and not caring if he became

"I see it," said Laurel. "That underbelly. Things no one else sees. Until I met Carter, I thought I must be schizophrenic or something when I'd see shades and ghosts. I was afraid to tell anyone when I was in the foster system, so I just kept it to myself."

Theia glanced at her, impressed. "I didn't know you could see ghosts. It's good to know I have another sister I can turn to for supernatural help."

Laurel paused with her cup halfway to her mouth. "You think of me as a sister?"

Theia couldn't help but laugh. "Well, not to state the obvious, but we *are* sisters. Just because we didn't grow up together doesn't mean we aren't."

Laurel set down her cup, visibly moved. "I've never really had a sister before. I know that sounds funny, but Rowan and Rosemary always seemed so much older than me. When our mom died, we went to separate foster homes, and we lost touch." Laurel shrugged. "Nobody's ever needed my advice. About anything."

Theia smiled. "Well, I do. Do you have any?"

"I don't exactly have the greatest track record. I mean, the last guy I was into was, you know. Ugh."

Theia poked at the crumbs of her lemon bar. "That's kind of the advice I want. How do you know when you're into someone who's not good for you? Should I run away from this? Or toward it?"

"I guess you have to trust your instincts. I didn't trust mine. I was looking for external validation because I didn't believe in myself. And now—I mean, I'm still struggling with that, but I'd never fall for someone like Carter today. He only told me what I wanted to hear."

The question was, what was it Theia wanted to hear? That Lucien wasn't dangerous? That he wasn't the Prince of Darkness after all? Or was she looking for someone to tell her it was okay if she sold her soul to the devil?

* * *

Lucien stood in the shower with his head bowed under the water, letting it pour over him. Every muscle in his body ached, and the broken bone felt like it had been replaced with solidified latex polymer, like rubber cement that had been left out with the cap off. Using it was going to become more difficult if he didn't see the company doctor soon.

When he emerged at last, the corner of an envelope poked out from under his door. After towel-drying his hair and wrapping the towel around his waist, Lucien bent to pick up the envelope. His body protested. Inside was the same URL his source had sent before. Had he missed something last time? Lucien looked at the Carlisle family tree once more, still baffled by what this had to do with hunting rogues. He already had the information the source had provided on Rafael Diamante and Dharamdev Gideon.

But there was something here he hadn't seen before. A document had been added to the family records, some kind of research paper on recessive genes.

As he examined it, he realized it was Theia's research on her own family, documenting her discovery of her father's polygamy—a second wife he'd taken in secret without divorcing the first. Lucien started to feel uncomfortable. How was this a public document? Maybe he should just close it and forget about it.

But something farther down the page caught his eye. Theia had discovered a genetic mutation. *Lilith blood*, she called it.

Lucien's own blood ran cold. According to Madeleine Marchant's claim, she'd been descended from the first demoness. Lucien had never believed it. But Theia had written this history as though it was fact. If her research was accurate, the demon blood was real, and all the Carlisle sisters possessed it. Their magical abilities, their gifts of vision and prognostication and communicating with spirits—they were all aspects of the demoness. The Carlisle sisters weren't just the gifted descendants of a powerful witch, they were literally part demon. *Theia* was part demon.

it. If his father found it distasteful, then Lucien would wallow in it. And Polly had been more than happy to help him in that endeavor. Though she'd been less enthusiastic when he'd decided to hunt rogue unnaturals. Polly brooked no nonsense in her club. Any unnatural creature that tried to do business there involving humans without their consent was summarily tossed out on its ass. But hunting them down was something else altogether.

Avenging the little girl he'd found at the blood farm had been an act of grief and rage. But the first time he'd taken out a rogue in cold blood had been intensely clarifying. He'd found his calling. Eventually, it replaced his need to wallow in vice, and he'd moved on, parting ways with Polly amicably enough. He'd told himself then he was through being ruled by his fate, and he intended to dedicate his life to resisting it. And that meant staying clean in terms of unnatural contact—which included anyone not fully human. His vow had hurt Polly, though she would never admit it.

And until now, Theia hadn't threatened that. He'd resisted his feelings for her because of the inadvisability of entanglements, but this morning he'd allowed himself the luxury of ignoring his own rules. And despite his doubts about her family—and about himself—kissing Theia had felt very right. He'd never felt so instantly at home with anyone. From the moment his lips had met hers, he'd felt as though he'd been broken, missing something, and now he was whole. He hadn't wanted to talk; he'd wanted to touch her mouth, taste her skin, run his fingers over every inch of her and explore this wondrous thing that had happened.

But now…now she was the goddamn enemy. This was fate's cruel trick, getting him to let down his guard and share himself with someone—when fate had been steering him toward that someone all along. More than just Madeleine Marchant's descendant, she was the embodiment of Madeleine's curse. "Blood for blood," the witch's last words had been before the pyre was lit. She seemed to be mocking him from the grave. He couldn't escape.

Lucien slammed his fist into the laptop screen and shattered the LCD. Stupid, but momentarily satisfying. He'd once surrendered fully to the darkness and the deep to spite his father, willfully drowning himself in the seamy underbelly of the world Edgar inhabited only on the periphery. And now he was drowning again—only this time it was an unwitting submersion.

The question was: Who wanted him to know? Polly? Was this her way of trying to warn him away from Theia? But she'd done so directly earlier today. Why bother with cryptic game playing? And if she'd known this detail about Theia's blood, why not just mention it outright when they spoke? No, this wasn't Polly's style. Someone else was apparently as interested in his fate as he was.

His phone buzzed, and he remembered the screen was shattered on that as well. But at least it was still readable. It was Theia, wanting to know what his plans were for the rest of the day. Their conversation was still unfinished. She'd wanted a chance to persuade him of Rafe's "worthiness."

Lucien realized he couldn't respond. The screen was readable, and a few of the apps were responsive if he pressed hard enough, but he couldn't get the keyboard or the number pad to work. He supposed it was just as well. Let her think what she wanted about why he didn't text back. It was a coward's resolution to the situation, but Lucien was tired, in his head and in his bones, the aches and pains from last night's disaster demanding his attention. The decision was out of his hands. Fate had once again intervened.

Mindful of the bruises on his backside, Lucien flopped onto his stomach on the bed and fell asleep.

* * *

He wasn't expecting to find Theia standing on his doorstep when he awoke from his nap.

He'd answered the door half-asleep, the towel he'd wrapped around his waist barely tucked in, not quite registering that he was answering a door and not a telephone.

There was Theia. He'd been dreaming about her. What was the dream about?

Lucien rubbed his eyes. "Theia?"

"You weren't answering my texts, and then I remembered your phone was broken so I thought I'd stop by on my way back from Flagstaff."

"Flagstaff?" He was drawing a blank on what she was talking about. Or what day it was. "What time is it?" It was dark out but not fully.

Theia laughed, and the sound tugged at his heart even as something else about her was filling him with anxiety. "It's 7:30. I drove to my place in Flagstaff to get some things and I was heading back to feed Puddleglum. I told you in my text…which of course you didn't get."

"No, I got…something." He was starting to remember.

Theia gave him an amused smile. "Are you going to invite me in?"

An invitation. It was how one let in vampires. And the devil. Lucien shrugged and held the door wide. His towel slipped off, and he managed to catch it and tie it back on as she entered.

Theia's cheeks went charmingly pink, but she frowned at his reticence. "Did I do something wrong? You seem upset."

"I'm not upset." Of course he was upset. He wanted to scream at the universe and punch the Fates in the face. Theia had demon blood. And she smelled like sunshine and citrus, and he just wanted to kiss her and shut his brain up.

On the coffee table, the laptop displayed its spiderweb of bleeding crystal behind the cracked screen.

Theia glanced at it and back at him. "Lucien? Is everything okay?"

"Yeah. No." He closed the door and sighed. "You didn't tell me about your history."

"My history?" Theia stared at the broken screen once more. Enough was visible through the bleeding colors to know what he'd been looking at when he smashed it. She looked up, her smile gone. "Is that my research? How did you get that? That's private."

"It's not important how I got it."

"The hell it isn't. Have you been investigating me?"

Lucien folded his arms. "No. But I should have. You're not human."

Theia's face blazed with anger. "Of course I'm goddamn human. Who the hell do you think you are, anyway?"

"I don't know, Theia. I honestly don't. But I know I'm not a demon." No matter what the family legend said. "And after last night, I'm sure you know how I feel about demons."

"I'm not a demon, either. I'm the distant relative of Madeleine Marchant. Maybe you've heard of her. It seems your family and mine go back a long way."

"So *you've* been investigating *me*."

"Damn right I have been. When you showed up at Phoebe's wedding acting completely full of yourself and trying to tempt me with the position at Smok Biotech, you may recall you told me to ask Rafe about your family. What information did you expect him to give me?"

Lucien faltered. He'd forgotten he'd encouraged her to talk to Rafe. God, what had Rafe told her? What did Rafe even know?

"I expected him to tell you about what Smok Consulting does, how he and his family have contracted us a number of times. It was a reference."

"Well, he didn't have time to give me a reference. He

was leaving on his honeymoon. So he gave me his father's papers. And Rafael Sr. apparently collected old Covent records. *Very* old ones."

"So you know." The realization tied his stomach in knots. She had utterly turned the tables on him, and he had no defense. "You know what my family did."

"You mean that they essentially owned mine."

Lucien blinked at her in confusion. "Owned? They were Madeleine Marchant's patrons, if that's what you mean."

"So they received her *property* when she was burned at the stake. Including her daughters. They became the wards of the Vicomte de Briançon, who sold them off to his cronies."

This was something Lucien had never heard. There was only one daughter he knew about. The one who'd married the vicomte's youngest son.

"You didn't know about that." Theia studied him. "So what were *you* talking about? What did your family do?"

Lucien rubbed his hand over his mouth, smoothing his fingers over his stubble. Hell. Might as well just tell her. Everything was fucked anyway.

"The vicomte's family—his wife—denounced Madeleine Marchant."

After a stunned silence, Theia lowered herself to the couch. "Wow."

"It was apparently a not-uncommon practice. A way for noblemen to steal what little their vassals had. Unless their families could prove to have had no knowledge of the witchcraft, the belongings of the accused went to their patrons by default to pay for the execution." Lucien shrugged helplessly. "I'm sorry."

Unexpectedly, Theia began to laugh.

"What in the world is funny about that?"

"Everything. This entire fight. I'm supposed to be mad at you because of something some people who were distantly related to us did over five hundred years ago? I mean, it's ridiculous. You're apologizing for the Vicomte de Briançon."

Her laugh was infectious, and Lucien had to lower his eyes to keep from smiling. It *was* ridiculous, but she was still a demon. And she was still part of the curse Madeleine had put on his family.

Theia's laughter subsided. "But you're still mad at me."

Lucien looked up. "I'm not mad at you. I'm mad at the universe. I mean, yes, I'm angry that you kept the fact that you have demon blood from me—"

"I thought you knew. You're the one who brought up my tattoo at the wedding and kept talking about blackmail and witches."

"Your tattoo…"

Theia held out her arm. "You called it the mark of Lilith. You obviously knew about Madeleine's claim."

"Her claim, yes, but not what it meant for her descendants. Not about the Lilith blood and the generations of seven sisters."

"And now that you do, I suppose I'm on your list." Theia rose, her gray eyes darkening. "Should I watch my back, Lucien? What would one of those arrows do to me?"

"I would never come after you."

"Oh, well, that's a relief. You know what? You can take the job at Smok Biotech and shove it up your ass." She brushed past him, reaching for the door, but Lucien grabbed her arm, and tears spilled over her cheeks.

"Don't go."

Theia looked up at him, miserable. "Why?"

He was too close to her. His skin touching hers. It would enhance any empathic vibrations she was picking up. Polly had warned him to stay away. His own instincts had warned him. She could read him now. He was an open book.

"Because I need you," he said simply and drew her into his arms. "I don't want to, but I do."

Theia's tears were still falling. "Then I guess I'm insulted and flattered."

Lucien laughed, the release of tension he needed, and kissed her.

It was a mistake. All of it was a mistake. But right now it felt like the most delicious mistake he'd ever made. Screw the Fates and his own infernal blood.

Theia tasted like lemon drops, and her hair smelled like violets, and nothing mattered. Lucien had been with his share of women—he hadn't been kidding when he'd bragged to her at the reception about the effect the Smok name seemed to have on some—but he'd never felt anything like the jumbled-up confection of desire and nervous excitement and worry and affection and, yes, *need* that was threading through his veins as he drank her in. He gathered her to him like she was a figurine made of glass, delicate and hard at once. He couldn't stop touching her, stroking her arms and her hair, holding her face between his hands as he kissed her deeper and with greater desperation until he finally had to let her go to breathe.

Theia's skin was flushed and her pupils dilated, her eyes shining as liquid danced in them in the dim light of the one lamp he'd fumbled on as he'd made his way to the door.

Lucien stroked his thumb across her still-damp cheek. "These are yours, right?"

Theia laughed weakly. "I think so. Unless kissing me makes you sad."

Lucien smiled. "It does not." He kissed her again to prove it, this time less desperately, lingering over the texture and taste of her lips. "You taste like lemon candy," he murmured against them, and Theia laughed again.

"Laurel made lemon bars. I had them with tea."

"Laurel?"

"My sister. My *half* sister."

"You have a half sister?"

"Three of them."

"Three…"

Theia nodded. "And four makes seven."

That little feeling of alarm was back, rattling against the walls of his skull, but Lucien wasn't about to give it free rein. Not now.

"I guess you didn't read through all of my research." Her body had gone tense.

Lucien was determined to drive the tension out. He let his hand slip down her arm and wordlessly led her to the bedroom. Sitting on the edge of the bed, he drew her onto his lap and kissed the back of her neck beneath the little point of hair at the center of her bob.

"What are you doing?" she murmured, softer already.

"Tasting you."

Theia shivered delightfully.

Lucien was only wearing a towel, and there was no way of hiding what that shiver did to him. The little moan she followed it up with only made things worse.

He wrapped his arms around her, stroking hers once more. "I like touching you."

"I can see that." Theia's arms crossed over his.

Lucien chuckled. "Well, I don't think you can see it, exactly. Not yet." He pressed his lips to her nape once more and began working his way toward the front, lingering in that spot just beneath the hollow of her jaw.

"Lucien." Theia's voice was a soft gasp.

He tucked her hair behind her ear and licked her earlobe. "Hmm?"

"I should probably…tell you something."

Lucien shook his head, planting more kisses along her collarbone as he peeled back the edge of her shirt. "You don't have to tell me anything."

"I think you might want to know…this thing." Theia gasped again and grabbed his hand as it slid downward between her legs, not pulling it back but not letting him move it any farther. "I think you might *need* to know it."

"What is it? Is something wrong?"

"Not wrong, exactly. It's just that, well…" Theia cleared her throat. "I'm a virgin."

Chapter 13

She waited for Lucien to laugh or for things to get awkward. Guys generally had one of two reactions to this announcement: pulling away or pressuring her. But Lucien did neither.

He kissed her neck again. "So?"

"That's...not a problem for you?"

"I guess it depends on what you want to do about it."

"Well, I... I'm not sure." Theia turned to look at him, and he caught her mouth in a kiss that made her forget what they were talking about.

After a moment, Lucien moved his mouth to her neck once more, nuzzling beneath her ear. "You don't have to decide right now, if that's what you're worried about. I just want you near me. We can just cuddle. Or I could..."

"Could...what?"

Lucien smiled, a devious little upturn to one corner of his mouth. "I could keep tasting you."

"Oh." Theia felt her whole body blush, heat rising in her skin for a multitude of reasons. She could also feel his heat beneath the towel. It wasn't that she hadn't gone that far before—she had, once or twice—it was how much she suddenly wanted him to that was making her flushed.

Lucien slid her off his lap onto the bed and ran his fingers along the hem of her T-shirt. "Can I take this off?"

Theia nodded and let Lucien draw the fabric up, lifting her arms so he could pull it over her head. He tossed the shirt on the floor, tracing her curves through the thin barrier of her bra. Fortunately, she'd worn a nice one, black mesh lace with a halter closure. Theia closed her eyes, clutching the edge of the bed, as Lucien lowered his head and closed his mouth over the fabric, the heat and damp of his tongue making a mess of it.

She opened her eyes with a whimper of disappointment when he let go, but he'd dropped to his knees and was staring up at her with his hands at the button of her jeans. "These, too?"

Theia nodded again, not trusting her voice, raising herself off the bed as he unbuttoned them and worked them off and down, pausing to take off her canvas flats. He positioned himself between her legs with his hands against her thighs, looking like a Roman centurion in his towel, and without removing her panties he parted her with the flat of his tongue.

Theia bit her lip, fingers curled around the bedspread, as Lucien's tongue prodded and teased against the cotton. If the bra was a mess, the panties were going to be wrecked, wet from without and within. Lucien's teeth nipped at the fabric, tugging the damp cotton and shaking it with a little growl like a puppy playing tug-of-war as he grinned up at her. At the same time, he'd moved his hands along her thighs, his thumbs slipping inside the legs of the garment, and Theia gasped as he pulled the panties away with a swift motion of thumbs and teeth.

As they fell to the floor, Lucien gently loosened her grip on the bedspread. "Let go. Hold on to me instead." He threaded his fingers through hers and locked them tight, as though to keep her grounded in case she floated away.

Theia let out a moan as he buried his head in her lap, tongue persistently and enthusiastically opening her until she was writhing and rocking into him and forgot to care about how much sound she was making. And Lucien seemed to revel in it, rewarding her with faster, deeper strokes of his tongue and answering moans of his own the more noise she made, until she arched back, hips raised, and crooned as the waves of her climax rolled through her. Her vision had gone blue.

Completely spent and utterly relaxed, Theia flopped back onto the bed, and Lucien persisted until she had to stop him, overstimulated. He responded to the little twist of her hips without her having to say a word, raising his head and resting his cheek on her thigh.

Lucien softened his fingers in hers and stroked his thumb along the heel of her palm. "You okay, beautiful?"

Theia giggled, not sure if it was more at the question or the endearment. "I am very okay."

He lifted his head from her thigh and climbed onto the bed, the towel catching and sliding off, revealing his still very enthusiastic erection.

Theia rolled onto her stomach beside him. "Do you want me to…?"

Lucien leaned back against the pillows, stroking himself idly. "Take this off," he murmured, tugging on the band of her bra.

Theia sat up and loosened the halter at her nape to let the bra drop open, cheeks warming at the little sound he made as she unhooked the back.

He shook his head. "Damn, girl. Just stay there, just like that." His fist around his cock was sliding up and down in more deliberate strokes.

Theia sat back on her heels, watching with fascination. She'd never actually seen a guy jerk off before. Lucien's hand picked up pace, and his breathing matched it as he watched her back, the soft sighs and grunts of his exhalations punctuating the sounds of skin against skin. After a moment, he screwed his eyes shut and let out a whispered string of obscenities and went off like a geyser, pearly white drops spattering the tight washboard of his abs as he choked the blushing head.

With his eyes still closed, the long, dark lashes stood

out against the flush in his cheeks. "Come here," he whispered, holding out his hand.

She crawled toward him and curled beneath his arm, and Lucien kissed her, his lips still sticky with her and her taste still on his tongue, unexpectedly pleasant.

Theia cuddled against his side. "Why didn't you want me to…return the favor?"

"It wasn't a quid pro quo, darling."

She flinched at the sardonic tone in his voice. She hadn't heard it since he'd given her the tour of the lab.

Lucien opened his eyes. "Sorry. Reflex." He rolled toward her, tucking her hair behind her ear. "I'm not used to not behaving like a prick just because I can." He kissed her again, the honesty in his touch reassuring. "When someone asks, 'Do you want me to?' it's generally not because *they* want to but because they think they ought to."

"It's not that I didn't want to—"

"Theia, it's okay. I would never want you to do something you weren't ready to do just to appease my arousal. I'm not one of those men who thinks he's owed something just because he's given something. The pleasure was in the gift." Lucien grinned. "Believe me."

Theia smiled. "Well, I'll keep that in mind. In case it… comes up again."

Lucien laughed. "And I have no doubt that it will." He snuggled closer to her. "Possibly after a short nap."

Theia closed her eyes for a moment, but they opened in a flash. "Oh, shit."

"What's the matter?"

"I was supposed to feed Puddleglum."

"Can't he wait until morning?"

"Seriously?"

"I don't know. I've never had a cat."

"Well, you have a stomach, don't you?" Theia sat up,

scrambling for her clothes. Her panties lay in a soggy heap at the foot of the bed.

Lucien laughed as she held them up and scowled at them. "Just toss them in my hamper. The cleaning lady is coming in the morning."

"I can do laundry at Phoebe's."

Lucien took them out of her hand and tossed them into the hamper across the room. "I'm sure you can, but that's what I pay the cleaning lady for."

Theia wasn't a fan of going commando, but she'd have to grin and bear it. She pulled on her jeans, zipping them carefully, and wriggled into her top while stuffing her feet into her shoes. The bra she tucked into her back pocket.

Lucien's phone buzzed, and he picked it up from the nightstand, studying the message with a frown.

"Bad news?"

"No, just a client. I have to go to Tucson."

"Tonight?"

"Yeah, somebody's got a poltergeist problem at the university. Lucy's on her way over to pick me—"

The bell chimed on the door.

Lucien inclined his head toward the sound. "—Up."

But Lucy hadn't waited for an answer. The front door opened, and Theia stood frozen in her tracks as Lucien's sister came down the hall, while Lucien remained where he was—nudity, sticky abs and all.

Lucy paused in the doorway, staring at Theia a moment before glancing at Lucien and rolling her eyes. "I see you found your way home just fine, Lulu."

"Don't call me Lulu."

"I should go." Theia scooted past Lucy through the door.

"Hang on." Lucien followed her to the front door as if his nudity were incidental and gave her a kiss. "I'll call you tomorrow."

"With what?"

Lucien shrugged in acknowledgment. "I'll get another phone in the morning."

Theia lowered her voice. "Aren't you a little uncomfortable...like this...with Lucy being here?"

"Why?" Lucien shrugged. "She's seen me naked. Don't worry about it." He kissed her again and opened the door. As it closed behind her, Theia realized her bra was dangling out of her back pocket.

"Give me five minutes," Lucien called over his shoulder as he went into the bathroom.

Lucy appeared in the doorway as he stood over the toilet. "You really think this is smart?"

"What, taking a piss?"

"Fucking that witch."

"She's not a witch. She has visions. She's an empath."

"Oh, well, that's fine, then. Nothing could go wrong there."

"Why does it matter to you?"

"You just seem a little bent on giving away all your secrets to someone you barely know. And some of those secrets belong to me."

Lucien flushed the toilet. "It may surprise you to know, but we didn't actually spend any time talking about you and your secrets when we were in bed. We were occupied with more interesting things."

"Just clean yourself up and let's go. Our ride is waiting for us at the airport."

The ride turned out to be a helicopter. At least he could avoid small talk with Lucy on the flight.

Rhea called just after Theia got out of a long, luxurious soak in the tub and started getting ready for bed. She thought about not answering, but that would only make Rhea suspicious.

She hit the speaker and tossed the phone on the bed. "What's up, buttercup?"

"You sound cheery."

"No, I don't. I'm just getting ready for bed. I do have a big bowl of ice cream waiting for me, though. I'm pretty pleased about that."

"I told you to call me when you got home last night, and you didn't."

"Oh." *Shit.* "Sorry. You're right. I forgot."

"Did you have any trouble getting Oliver Queen home?"

Theia laughed at the Green Arrow reference—probably a little too enthusiastically. "No, he was pretty subdued. I straightened him out about Leo. He shouldn't give you guys any more trouble."

"Thei…is there anything you want to tell me?"

"Tell you? What would I want to tell you?"

"Is he there with you right now?"

Theia felt her face blaze scarlet. "What? Why would he be here?"

Rhea sighed into the phone. "You really think I'm dumb, don't you?"

"What in the world are you talking about?"

"I may not be the one getting a master's degree in molecular biology, missy, but I know when something's going on with you. We shared a womb. And Rafe's alarm has been set to record and report entries at the security gate ever since the paparazzi incident. I saw your key code on the security log from this morning when you came to get Lucien's car."

"Oh. Fudge."

"You slept with him."

"In the sense that we spent the night together in the same bed? Yes. His sister told me I had to wake him up every two hours to check his responses, so I brought him back to Phoebe's place, and we ended up talking after I woke him up. That's when I straightened him out about Leo. And Dev. We didn't quite get to Rafe because the sun came up, but I'm pretty sure he's not going after any of our family members again." Theia was talking fast, trying to avoid a lull in the conversation that would let Rhea pin her down on what had happened today. Which was of course a dead giveaway that something had.

"You talked."

"*Most*ly."

"*Theia.* I can't believe you're holding out on me. I could hear it in your voice the minute you answered the phone. You just got back from his place, didn't you? You've been there all day, and he screwed your brains out. The lunatic who tried to kill my boyfriend screwed your fancy little molecular-biologist brains out. And you *loved* it."

"I was not there all day."

"Ha!"

"And there was *no* screwing."

"Theia."

"I…there might have been…licking."

"Oh my God. Who licked whom? I want details. Juicy, disgusting details. It's my birthright."

"That is not even a thing."

"It is so a thing. Leo is out hunting, and you're hoarding ice cream, Puddleglum and juicy licking details. I'm coming over there."

"Don't you dare. There is *not* enough ice cream for you. It's Häagen-Dazs Deep Chocolate Peanut Butter, and it's all mine." Theia realized the phone had gone dead. "Goddammit, Rhe." There was no way her story would hold up under Rhea's in-person scrutiny.

Chapter 14

Luckily, Rhea brought her own ice cream—a pint of Ben & Jerry's Chocolate Fudge Brownie.

Theia opened the door in her PJs and looked down at a pair of fluffy slippers that matched her own. "I compliment you on your excellent taste in footwear."

Rhea pushed her way in. "They're yours. I stole them the last time I visited you in Flag."

"I thought I'd left them at the Laundromat."

"You did. That's where I stole them."

"Dammit, Rhe." Theia had spent hours online finding a replacement pair.

While Theia took her ice cream from the freezer and grabbed some spoons, Rhea commandeered the papasan chair.

"So spill," said Rhea after Theia tossed her a spoon. "How exactly did you get from wounded commando recovery to licking? And who licked whom?"

Theia sat at the breakfast bar separating the living room from the kitchen, swiveling on her stool so she could see Rhea without facing her. "He told me what Smok Consulting does—they clean up paranormal situations that get out of hand. It complements the biotech business, where they're working on developing pharmaceuticals to suppress the effects of certain switched-on genes—"

"Blah, blah, sciencey words, blah, blah, and?"

"And Lucien needed an outlet that would let him balance the harm he felt Smok was doing, so he started going after what he considered to be dangerous elements. The serum-tipped arrows are specially designed to destroy un-natural creatures."

"And he shot one into my very human boyfriend, got his ass handed to him and you nursed him back to health with erotic licking."

"That is *not* what happened."

"Was it like this?" Rhea licked a ribbon of fudge off the back of her spoon.

"Oh my God. I did *not* lick him."

"Aha. So he licked you. Did you pass out after? No? Didn't think so. My man can lick your man under the table any day." Rhea paused. "Which does not sound quite like I meant it to."

"He's not my man." Theia kept her head over her pint to keep the heat in her cheeks from showing, but Rhea never missed anything.

"You are such a terrible liar."

Considering everything she'd been keeping from Rhea for years, Theia might not be the greatest at verbal dissembling, but she seemed to be doing a bang-up job at sins of omission.

"So where is he now?"

"He got called away to a job with Lucy."

"Ah, Lucy. The bitchy twin."

"Yeah, you two have a lot in common."

"Yeah, we're both the hot one. Kind of gives you fuel for a twin fantasy, though."

Theia nearly choked on her ice cream. "I beg your pardon?"

"Not us, you dork. Ew. I meant him and her. You ever think about…?"

Theia gaped at her. "She's female, in case you didn't notice."

"What, you've never hung out at Muffy's Dive Bar? I thought that was what college was for."

Apparently Theia wasn't the only one who was good at keeping secrets. "You are totally blowing my mind right now."

Rhea winked, digging into her pint. "That's what she said."

"Speaking of dive bars…" Theia cleared her throat. "Do you know anything about a place called Polly's Grotto in West Sedona?"

"Polly's Grotto?" Rhea sucked on her spoon. "Sounds vaguely familiar, but I don't think I've ever been there. Why?"

"Not sure." Theia dug for a vein of peanut butter. "Lucien had to meet a client there earlier today, and it just seemed like an odd place for a meeting. Even for a paranormal cleaner." She pondered her scoop. "I don't think the place was even open yet, so whom was he meeting?"

"I can ask Leo about it. He knows a lot of sketchy characters from his years as an immortal." Rhea studied her for a moment. "So it sounds like you're kind of all in with this guy, huh?"

"I don't know about…" Theia felt her cheeks warming again. "Yeah. I guess maybe I am."

Rhea smiled. "It's about time. You've been weird about dating ever since that reading I gave you. I was beginning to think you were going to die an old maid." She ducked as Theia flicked peanut butter off her spoon. It landed on Puddleglum, who was hovering at the top of the papasan chair in hopes of sneaking a bite of Rhea's ice cream. The cat gave Theia an offended look but began studiously grooming the peanut butter glob from his fur.

"Just promise me you'll be careful," Rhea added after a moment. "This quest of his to hunt down 'dangerous elements' could be a hard habit to break." She smiled ruefully. "Take it from a hunting widow. And if he's still harboring doubts about any 'unnatural' members of our family, he could be trouble for all of us. I'd hate for him to end up being that dark prince you worry about."

Theia put the lid on her ice cream with a thoughtful nod and gave Rhea a sly look from under her lashes. "Guess you're not quite as dumb as you look."

"Yeah, well, joke's on you, genius, 'cause you look exactly like me."

Theia got up to put her pint in the freezer. "No, I don't. Moonpie."

Lucy eyed Lucien as their escort at University Medical Center led them off the helipad. "You didn't see the doctor like I told you to."

"I was busy."

"You know that's going to hurt like hell when the doc has to break up all that ecto gel. Especially if it completely solidifies and the bone has to be rebroken to set right."

"Yeah, I know."

"Hope her pussy was worth it."

"Shut up, Lu." Lucien held the door to the stairs for her. "And you bet your ass it was."

Their client, a frazzled-looking but distinguished older gentleman, was waiting in the hallway outside the closed-off wing. "Thank you for coming so quickly, Mr. Smok. I'm Roger Fitzhugh, the hospital administrator." He shook Lucien's hand, looking past Lucy like she was Lucien's assistant. "It's here in the NICU." He indicated the double doors beside them but seemed reluctant to open them.

"The NICU?" Lucy frowned. "You're sure you're dealing with a poltergeist? They generally attach themselves to adolescents. Sometimes prepubescent children, but I can't imagine what would prompt such activity around newborns."

"I suppose the diagnosis is up to your team. I'm no expert. But…*something* is in there, and it isn't happy."

"Is the ward clear?"

"Yes, we moved all the patients down to another level and sealed off the area."

"All right. We'll handle it from here, Mr. Fitzhugh. Thank you." Lucy opened the door, and Fitzhugh stepped back.

The air was thick with charged particles as the doors swung shut behind them, making the hairs on Lucien's arms stand on end.

"This feels like a haunting, not a poltergeist."

Lucy nodded. "That's what I was thinking."

"Are we even equipped to open a gate?"

Lucy reached into her bag and pulled out her kit. "We should probably draw some blood now and be ready to use it. I've got the catalyst."

Lucien took off his coat and rolled up his sleeve.

She watched him with a frown. "Are you sure you're up to it? I could do this one."

"You know Edgar wouldn't like it."

"Since when do you care what Edgar wants?"

"I care when he gets mad at you and treats you like shit for something I did."

"Aw. I had no idea you cared, baby brother."

"Shut up and take the blood before it gets any freakier in here."

While Lucy took the needle out of its packaging, Lucien swabbed his arm and placed it on the nurse's station for her to tap a vein and draw. The same kit was useful for attracting revenant bloodsuckers. The only difference in dealing with apparitions was the catalyst, a compound developed by Smok Biotech that reacted with the supposedly infernal component in the Smok blood to create a thinning of the spectral veil that could open a gate to the other side. Useful for sending the already dead and disembodied packing.

Lucy filled the vial and transferred the needle to the

glass tube containing the catalyst, red blood swirling into the clear liquid. "Ready to go."

"All right, let's do this."

As they moved down the corridor toward the nursery, the resistance from the malevolent spirit was palpable. Something definitely didn't want them here. To prove the point, a gurney came flying at them from a side corridor, and they jumped out of the way. It slammed into the wall hard enough to crumple the frame.

"There." Lucy pointed toward the window of the nursery as they straightened. A shadow figure stood on the other side, the darkness of its misty form pulsing with rage. She raised her voice and spoke to it. "You don't belong here. It's time for you to go."

A vibration of sound, almost subsonic, rose from a deep rumble to an ear-piercing shriek, and the glass of the observation window shattered outward.

Lucien instinctively turned and covered Lucy, flinching as a few shards struck his back.

Lucy shoved him off. "Dammit, Lucien. I can take care of myself."

"I was making sure the vial wasn't hit."

"You were being a misogynist ass."

Supplies started hurtling toward them, and Lucien ducked a tray of surgical tools. "We'd better get this done before that thing takes an eye out. You want to approach it? Be my guest."

Lucy covered her head with her jacket and darted forward, the vial in her fist. The shadow charged her, and Lucy stiffened with a jolt as it went through her, now swirling between them.

"Hit the juice." Lucy whirled toward him. "Now!"

Armed with the violet wand from Lucy's bag—designed to generate electric shocks for sex play, though Lucien really didn't want to know if Lucy ever used it for that purpose—Lucien hit the button as the spirit flung itself in his direction. The spark flared in the darkness, illuminating the human shape within. A teenage girl stood petrified in the violet glow, and for a moment he could see her face, twisted with grief and anger.

Lucy smashed the vial on the floor in the center of the spirit's form, and the ghost began to scream. The spattered liquid spread, thinning the veil where Lucien had her trapped, kept in place with repeated jolts from the wand, while the air filled with violet sparks and the smell of ozone.

The wailing sound, Lucien realized, wasn't a wordless cry. She was screaming, "No!" and holding out her arms toward him. Lucien felt sick. There was nothing he could do to stop it now. The void swallowed her up, and only a soft weeping lingered as the thickness in the air dissipated. He heard a single word in it, a name: "Emma."

Lucy pushed her hair back from her forehead, holding her hand to the top of her head for a moment. "Jesus. That was brutal. Do you think that was her name? Emma?"

Lucien shut off the wand and dropped it into the bag. "No. I think it was her baby's."

Lucy's hand dropped to her side. "Damn. That's why the NICU."

"I hate this job."

"Yeah." Lucy straightened her coat and picked up the bag. The dimly lit ward looked ordinary now.

In the waiting area, Roger Fitzhugh got to his feet as they emerged through the double doors. "Did you find it?"

Lucy nodded. "All clear."

"And…the price?"

Lucy handled the financial arrangements. Lucien had done it a few times, and it always left a bad taste in his mouth. His sister was only too happy to step in and demonstrate her superior skills—a performance for the benefit of a man who wasn't even here to appreciate it.

She considered for a moment, looking tired. "It was a garden-variety haunting, Mr. Fitzhugh. It's on the house."

Lucien studied her as they headed back out to the helipad. The fee for any consulting job was the same. The price was a soul. Lucien had always assumed it meant nothing more than a life—as if a life weren't everything—but it was the Smok reputation that mattered. Clients believed the souls were collected for hell.

Lucy noticed him watching her. "What?"

"That was uncharacteristically nice of you."

"I wasn't being nice. We got our soul. No need for another."

"Yeah, well." Lucien shrugged. "I suspect you may have one yourself. But don't worry, Lu. Your secret's safe with me."

It was just after two in the morning when Lucy dropped him off. In addition to the aches and pains, he was really feeling the drain of the night's work. It was only a few milliliters of blood, but the opening of a gate always took something out of him. And it was just another reminder that he was running out of time. If the Smok legacy was true, he would become something inhuman before he took his place in hell—what form that would take, the legend didn't say. But Lucien wasn't taking any chances. He had to finish developing the anti-transformative.

Lucien peeled out of his suit and lay on top of the covers, too tired to turn down the bed. It still smelled of Theia.

She was still part demon. That hadn't changed. But he didn't give a damn. Lucien laughed at the inadvertent pun. Whatever she was—whatever *he* was—Theia made him feel there was a reason to get up in the morning. And that, he realized, was something he hadn't felt in a very long time.

Chapter 15

After receiving a call from Leo at the crack of dawn to let her know he was back from the Hunt, Rhea went home from their impromptu pajama party. With a parting shot at Rhea about being penis whipped, Theia went back to bed and had vague dreams about Rhea's Náströnd, the Shore of Corpses in the Norse underworld where Rhea and Leo's astral projection in dragon form had rescued Leo's disembodied soul. Images of rotting corpses, reanimated and climbing from a foul primordial soup, were enough to shake her out of sleep, glad of the daylight. At the periphery of the dream's fading memory was the wounded blue wyvern diving into the hell lake pursued by the cockatrice.

Theia stood in the shower, goose bumps on her flesh despite the hot water, trying to wash away the image of those sloughing, scrabbling corpses—revenants for certain, if anything was. Revenants and cockatrices and wyverns, oh my.

"Wyverns?" Theia opened her eyes as she spoke the word aloud, the brilliant blue letters floating in the air as though the word was significant. Where had that come from? She'd thought of the creature as a dragon when she'd dreamed of it before but not a specific breed. Maybe it was something she'd seen in a video game. Or one of Rhea's books.

The doorbell was ringing when she turned off the water. Theia jumped out of the tub and grabbed her robe from the back of the door, throwing it on over wet skin as she ran to answer the bell.

Lucien stood on the stoop holding his phone. "I got the

replacement but I still couldn't call you because I don't have your number. So I thought I'd drive across town and tell you that." He grinned then cocked his head as he took in her appearance with a sideways smile. "Funny…that's just how I fantasize you."

"You fantasize about me?"

"Constantly." Lucien beamed. "Can I come in?"

"Watch out for darting cats. I'm not supposed to let Puddleglum out." She unlocked the screen door, and Lucien stepped in and closed it behind him just as the cat skulked around the corner and tried to make a break for it.

"Curses. Foiled again," Lucien said in a cartoon villain voice, grinning at the cat. He glanced up at Theia, looking slightly chagrined. "I have no idea where that came from. I think I was channeling him. Is he a warlock?"

Theia laughed. "I wouldn't be a bit surprised."

Lucien kissed her, silencing her laugh, and pulled her close. "I missed you in my bed. I think I may have to keep you there." He stepped back after a moment and glanced down at the damp marks her robe had left on his khakis. "You're all wet." He untied the belt at the front of the robe, sliding his hands inside and around her ass. "Can I dry you with my tongue?"

Now she was definitely wet. But she hadn't thought about where this might go. As fantastic as yesterday had been, she couldn't just expect him to continue his one-sided pleasuring. But she wasn't sure if she was ready to take the plunge into post-virginity immediately.

Lucien's lascivious grin turned questioning. "No pressure, of course."

"Sorry. I just…hadn't thought about what might happen next."

"Theia." He played with a strand of her hair, a wistful smile on his face. "There's no timeline. I can dial it back a bit. I know I can be a little intense." He retied her belt, making a prim little bow. "For now, how about breakfast? If you haven't already eaten, that is. There's this cute little place on Cedar Street that makes fantastic lavender scones."

Theia grinned up at him. "Now I'm starting to think *you're* some kind of warlock." She turned toward the bedroom. "Just let me get dressed. You had me at scones."

"That was kind of the last word I said, actually, but at least I managed to reel you in while I was still speaking."

They had just ordered when Lucien received a text. He frowned as he read it.

Theia watched him over her coffee cup. "Anything wrong?"

"No." Lucien looked up. "I mean, yes. Another job. Lucy's unavailable, so I have to leave now to handle it."

Theia's mouth curved into a pout. "No fantastic lavender scones?"

"Not for me, I'm afraid. I'm really sorry about this. We're not usually this busy. But you should stay—I'll settle the bill."

"Why don't I just go with you?"

"You want to come with?" Lucien glanced at the message again with a dubious look. "It's a botched resurrection."

"Botched…resurrection?" Theia blinked, not sure she was hearing right.

"Someone paid a reanimator to bring a loved one back from the dead. It literally never works. It's the monkey's paw of spells, and yet people try it all the time. Like teenagers calling up vengeful spirits in the mirror as a drunken party game, trying to resurrect the dead never goes out of style, no matter how disastrous. Of course, Smok is very good at making sure those disasters never get publicized."

The idea of witnessing the results of a botched resurrection was both horrifying and compelling. She'd seen

Phoebe and Rafe deal with the spirits of the dead before, but never the reanimated dead.

"I'm up for it, if it's not against the rules."

"There aren't really any rules—or if there are, I make them." Lucien grinned. "If you really want to come, I can tell them you're just observing as a new apprentice so they won't expect you to step in. And you have to promise to follow my directions. I'm not being an ass—I just have to be able to ensure your safety."

Theia smiled. "I do want to come. And I give you my word. I promise I have absolutely zero interest in getting in the way of a revenant. Because, you know—*actual* revenant."

Lucien grimaced. "Touché." He paid for the uneaten scones, and they hit the road.

"The client is in Oak Creek," Lucien told her as they drove through Uptown Sedona. "Nice to have something close by for a change."

"Aren't all of your clients local?"

"No, we're worldwide. I spent a lot of time on the West Coast and in Europe after college, working with our agencies there. Edgar wanted me home for the lab opening. Lucy's been handling things for him locally, but he's been trying to encourage me to take a more active role in the company."

"What about your mother? Is she not involved in the company?"

Lucien's expression was guarded. "They're divorced. The business was never her thing anyway. She kind of loathes the entire Smok enterprise. Can't say that I blame her."

"But you still do it." Theia realized it was a shitty thing to say. "I mean—"

"No, you're right. I take part in aspects of the business that I find morally and ethically…uncomfortable. I can't really justify it other than to say I feel a sense of familial obligation." Lucien was quiet, and Theia thought it better not to intrude on his silence.

He turned onto Jack's Canyon in the Village of Oak Creek and headed west.

"Ione lives a few blocks from here." Theia glanced at Lucien. "Which maybe I shouldn't have told you. You've abandoned the idea of going after Dev, I hope?"

"I already know where your sister lives. But unless Dev's demon goes on a rampage, yes, I've given up on that plan. I'm rethinking my sources."

"Your sources?"

"For information on rogue creatures. I have a few insiders who alert me to candidates in the area. And some anonymous sources." Lucien glanced at her. "That's what put me on your family's trail, actually. An anonymous 'concerned individual' tipped me off." He paused. "The same person that sent me the link to your personal genealogy research."

"Someone sent you that?" Theia frowned. Who could have been able to link to the file? It was a private upload to the genealogy site, which only immediate relatives could access without expressly having the link.

They pulled into the driveway of a modest-looking duplex. Theia wondered how the occupants were able to afford Smok Consulting's services.

"Keep behind me when we approach the subject," Lucien advised. "Sometimes they can move surprisingly fast."

"How do you…get rid of it?" Theia asked as he rang the doorbell. "Do you have to kill the revenant?"

"No, it's already dead. All I have to do is release the shade from the body." He shook his head. "It's really a cruel thing to tie a shade to a rotting corpse. It's unconscionable that anyone would do it."

A middle-aged woman opened the door. Dark circles

under bloodshot eyes made her look somewhat manic, as if she hadn't slept in days.

"Mrs. Castillo. I'm Lucien Smok, and this is my colleague, Theia Dawn. She'll be observing—"

"Thank God you're here." The woman grabbed Lucien's hand and held it in both of hers. "*Es mi abuela.* She passed on a month ago, but my mother was distraught, and she couldn't get over the loss. I didn't know she had called a *brujo* until I came home from work on Friday, and I found her sitting with Abuelita. I didn't know what to do. My husband's cousin told me about your services."

Lucien patted her hand and gently drew his other out of her grip. "You did the right thing, Mrs. Castillo. Just let us take it from here."

As soon as they stepped inside, the smell nearly bowled Theia over. Her eyes watered, and she covered her mouth as Lucien's client led them to a bedroom in the back.

"Mamá? The doctor's here." Mrs. Castillo turned to Lucien and lowered her voice. "I had to tell her you were a doctor coming to help my grandmother. She has Alzheimer's. My mother, I mean. Not my grandmother." Tears sprang to her eyes as she opened the door.

The curtains were drawn, and it took a moment for Theia's eyes to adjust to the light. On a little day bed in the shadows, two elderly women sat holding hands. But one of them had a swollen face with a grayish-blue discoloration. The swollen one began to curse in Spanish. Theia understood just enough to know that the words were shocking.

Mrs. Castillo crossed herself.

Lucien touched her arm. "What's your mother's name?"

"Rosa Campos."

"And your grandmother?"

"Lupe Ramirez. Lupita."

"I'll need Rosa to move away from the—" Lucien caught

himself. "From your grandmother." He held out his hand. "Mrs. Campos, I'm Dr. Smok. Can I speak with you?"

Rosa looked confused. "The doctor was here. Mamá was sick but the doctor made her better."

Obscenities continued to fly from the older woman's mouth—along with a terrible stench that Theia was surprised she could even distinguish next to the pervasive smell of rotting flesh.

"I just need to give her a checkup. And I have some vitamins for you." He took a bottle from his bag and emptied two pills into his hand. He turned to Mrs. Castillo. "Can you get a glass of water?"

The woman eyed the pills with mistrust. "What are those for?"

"I think it's best if she's sedated," he murmured, "before I take care of the—your *abuela.*"

Hands trembling as she stepped into the room to pour a glass of water from the pitcher beside the bed, Mrs. Castillo took the pills. "Come on, Mami. Take your vitamins and let the doctor look at Abuela."

The old woman reached obediently for the pills, but the revenant knocked them from her hand with a snarl, and Rosa began to cry.

"That's okay. I have more." Lucien shook out another two pills. "Can you come here to me?"

"You're not my doctor." Rosa began to speak rapidly in Spanish.

"She wants her granddaughter." Mrs. Castillo looked at Theia. "She thinks you're my daughter. She wants you to give her the pills."

"Me?" Theia glanced at Lucien. The smell of the decaying flesh was making it difficult not to gag.

Lucien shook his head. "You don't have to."

But Rosa had gotten up, reaching for Theia. "Conchita, be a good girl. *Dame las vitaminas.*" The revenant tugged at her hand, and Rosa tugged back. Theia swallowed bile as a layer of the revenant's skin sloughed away.

She took the pills and the water and stepped closer. "Here you go, Abuela."

The old woman took them, and Theia held the water for her, trying to ignore the rage—and stench—emanating from the revenant.

"*Puta!*" The undead woman spat the word at Theia, along with a viscous gray substance that struck her cheek.

Theia covered her mouth and stumbled back. For a moment, she was sure she was going to lose the battle and vomit.

Stepping to her side, Lucien wiped the trail of slime from her cheek with a handkerchief. "You're doing amazing," he murmured.

Rosa's eyelids began to flutter, and she leaned her head on her mother's shoulder.

"Mamá, why don't you lie down and take a little nap?" As Mrs. Castillo moved toward her mother, the revenant lunged for her, letting Rosa tumble onto the bed.

Mrs. Castillo screamed and threw her arms over her face reflexively, and the revenant sank her teeth into one of the upraised arms. Watching in horror, Theia thought incongruously how impressive it was that a woman in her nineties had died with all her teeth.

Lucien darted forward, taking a vial of clear liquid from his pocket. He opened it and flung the contents at the revenant, shouting in what sounded like Latin.

The revenant shrieked and let go, cringing and backing toward the daybed at the touch of the liquid as if it were acid.

"Lupita Ramirez." Lucien's voice projected with a deep, authoritative tenor. "You don't belong here. I command you to come out. Be free." He repeated the words in Spanish, and the revenant made an agonizing sound, a wail that seemed to encompass both misery and relief. The haunted, rage-filled eyes emptied, turning glassy and dull, and the body crumpled lifeless to the floor.

Mrs. Castillo began to sob. Mercifully, Rosa's eyes had remained closed, unconscious to the loss of her mother for the second time.

"A crew will be here shortly to take care of the remains." Lucien spoke soothingly, patting the woman's shoulder. "They should be done before your mother wakes up. It's entirely possible she won't remember any of this." He cleared his throat. "And while I hate to speak of business at a time like this, there is the matter of payment. I assume our policy regarding the timing in the case of a reanimation reversal has been explained to you?"

She nodded, wiping her eyes.

Lucien glanced at the sleeping woman on the bed. "If I can make a suggestion…it might be a mercy to let your mother make the payment."

"No, no." Mrs. Castillo shook her head vehemently. "It will be me. I've already made arrangements. My daughter will take care of my mother."

Lucien nodded and took a small vial from his pocket. "This will complete the transaction. I recommend that you take it at bedtime and go to sleep as usual."

As Mrs. Castillo took the vial, she grabbed Lucien's hands once more. "*Gracias*, Mr. Smok. You don't know what this means to my family. I haven't slept since Abuelita…" She glanced at the corpse and squeezed her eyes shut. "And now it's over. It's over."

Lucien pressed her hands and extracted himself from her grip. "You should see to that arm." He nodded to the bite mark.

Mrs. Castillo's eyes flew open, wide with terror. "It won't make me like her, will it?"

"No, no. Of course not. It's just that it looks painful."

* * *

On the drive back to Sedona, Theia was quiet, trying—and failing—to reconcile the events she'd witnessed.

Lucien glanced at her after a few minutes. "Are you okay? That was a rough one."

"What was that vial you gave her?"

"Holy water. Well, really, just plain water. Its power is in the belief of the shade. She actually left on her own, believing she'd been exorcised."

"No, I mean the other vial. The one you gave Mrs. Castillo."

"Oh." Lucien stared ahead. "I probably should have done that in private."

"*Lucien.* What was it?"

"A lethal dose of pentobarbital. It's painless."

Theia leaned back against the headrest, letting her breath out slowly. She'd wanted to be wrong. Wanted him, at least, to express some shock at the statement.

"So that's the payment. She's going to kill herself."

"Well, no. Not exactly. The payment for any of our services of this nature is a soul."

Theia's head throbbed as she turned to look at him. "What the hell do you mean, a *soul*?"

"It's my family's legacy. We…" He glanced at her for an instant before looking back at the road. "Legend says we collect souls for the devil."

"The devil. There's an actual devil."

Lucien shrugged. "I don't know. Maybe there's not even any such thing as a soul. But those are the bargains we make at Smok. And people enter into them willingly. In most cases, the designated payer lives out his or her normal life. But to reverse a resurrection, payment is due in full when services are rendered."

Sweat beaded her forehead, and Theia gripped her door handle. "Pull over."

"What?"

"Pull over! Right now."

Lucien pulled onto the shoulder of the highway, and Theia threw open the door and vomited into the dirt. Her stomach lurched so violently she expected to see it in the gravel turned inside out.

Lucien held out his handkerchief when she straightened and sat back against the seat, and Theia yanked it from his hand, careful not to wipe her mouth with the bilious substance he'd cleaned off her cheek from the revenant.

"I'm sorry. I shouldn't have brought you."

"You shouldn't have brought me? That's what you're sorry about? You just told a woman to kill herself and go to hell—and handed her the poison to do it."

"It's the job. It's why I hate it so much."

"Oh! Well!" Theia threw her hands in the air. "As long as you *hate* it."

"Theia—"

"Just take me home. I need to be alone."

Lucien pulled back onto the highway without a word.

When they arrived at Phoebe's place, he looked over at her at last, obviously wanting to say something. Whatever it was, Theia didn't want to hear it. She got out and slammed the door and went inside without a backward look.

Chapter 16

Lucien drove home, the usual dark funk that hung over him after a job magnified by a thousand. Why had he taken Theia with him? In one afternoon, he'd revealed to her every repugnant thing about himself and the Smok legacy. He was so used to letting Lucy handle the negotiations that he'd forgotten just how personal and ugly it felt—especially this one. And yet he'd done it in front of Theia without even preparing her beforehand.

Yesterday, he'd been devastated by the news of Theia's heritage, ready to renounce her. Twenty-four hours later, he'd pushed her away with the ugly truth of his own, and all he wanted to do was get down on his knees and beg her not to leave him. As if she was even *with* him in the first place.

His smashed laptop screen greeted him when he got home, and Lucien punched it again for good measure. And then punched it a third time and a fourth, imagining it was his face. The ecto gel in his arm reverberated with a sickening thud. Lucien kicked the laptop onto the floor and stomped on it. After a moment, he started to laugh at his own stupidity, dropping onto his knees on the Berber carpet and laughing until he was crying and could barely breathe. He tipped over sideways and rolled onto his back, wheezing and gasping, tears pouring down his temples into his ears.

"God, you stupid bastard." He sucked in air, holding his stomach. Honestly, he should just get himself one of those little vials of pentobarbital and put an end to it. Put himself and the rest of the world out of his misery. One fresh soul, coming right up.

It wasn't like anyone had a gun to his head forcing him

to carry out his repugnant duties. What would have happened, after all, if he'd just neglected to give Mrs. Castillo the vial and let her live out her life? Was someone going to reprimand him? Maybe Edgar would have him fired.

The idea made him laugh again, but after a moment, his laughter subsided. What *would* happen if he didn't do it? Absolutely nothing, that's what.

Lucien got up and grabbed his keys and headed back down to his car. Screw his duties. He drove back to Mrs. Castillo's house and pounded on the door.

She looked shocked to see him. His was probably the last face she wanted to see. Behind her, visible through the open bedroom door, the cleanup crew moved about, calmly carrying out their work.

"Mr. Smok? Did you forget something?"

"I did," he said. "Myself."

Mrs. Castillo squinted at him. "I don't understand."

"I made a mistake, Mrs. Castillo."

Anxiety clouded her features, and her hand flew to her uncombed hair, a gauze bandage visible on her arm where the revenant had bitten her. "Is she going to come back? I don't think my mother can handle it."

And how would her mother handle the loss of her daughter so soon after?

"No, there was no problem with the service. It was a billing error. Usually, my sister handles these details, and I didn't realize we were waiving the usual pay-on-receipt-of-services clause. I'm so embarrassed, Mrs. Castillo, but if you wouldn't mind, could I get that medicine back from you?"

"The medicine? I don't understand. Is there something wrong with it?"

"It's just that there's no need for you to use it. The bill won't come due until your natural expiration."

"My…expiration?" She was sleep deprived, and it took

a moment for the words to sink in, but when they did, her face lit up like beam of pure light. "I don't have to take it?"

Lucien smiled. "You don't have to take it."

Mrs. Castillo burst into tears and flung her arms around his neck, taking him by surprise. He indulged her, letting her weep until the cleaners emerged from the hallway behind her with the body bag to transport Mrs. Ramirez to the cemetery for reinterment.

Gently tugging Mrs. Castillo's arms from around his neck, Lucien moved her aside so they could get by. She stood watching them with her hand over her mouth, weeping quietly.

"The medicine?" Lucien prompted after the body had been loaded into the truck.

"Oh, yes." Mrs. Castillo grinned. "Of course, yes! Let me get it for you." She hurried to her bedroom across the hall from the room where the revenant had been earlier but paused in the doorway, looking perplexed. "I had it right here. Did the other gentlemen take it already?"

Lucien followed her to help her find it. "I doubt they would have even known about it. They don't deal with this end of the operation. You've probably just forgotten where you set it down."

"No, it was right here by the bed. I had everything set up for when I was going to go to sleep tonight. I didn't want my daughter to have to worry about anything." Mrs. Castillo turned and went across the hall to check on her mother and let out a sharp cry. "Mamá! Mamá, no!"

From behind her, Lucien could see the old woman lying on the daybed on her back, staring up at the ceiling with eyes that had as much life in them as a Lucite marble. Next to her on the end table was the empty bottle.

Mrs. Castillo ran to her, shaking the limp body. With a sob, she dropped to her knees and embraced her mother. The devil, it seemed, had gotten his due.

* * *

Lucien meant to drive home again, but he found himself in Phoebe Carlisle's driveway. As he sat in the car trying to get his head right, he saw Theia's face appear at the window and disappear again. After a moment, the door opened, and Theia held the screen door for him, waiting.

He stepped out of the car and moved toward her, feeling like he was drowning in quicksand. If he could just get to her, he could keep his head above the mire. There was no welcoming smile, no forgiveness when he reached her, but she let him in, and Lucien clung to her, unable to move. His body began to shake, he realized with some horror, with silent sobs.

"Lucien?" Theia's hand hovered on his hair. "What is it? What's happened?"

He shook his head, not trusting himself to speak. He felt so raw right now that if he dared open his mouth, every cry he'd kept inside since childhood would come pouring out.

"Come inside." Theia drew his arms down to his sides and led him in, steering him to the little pleather-and-wood love seat. Lucien stroked the artificial texture of the vinyl, trying to stop thinking about Mrs. Castillo's sobs. He wasn't crying tears. Not yet. Maybe he could still get himself together and start acting like a man.

He heard his father's voice saying it: *Stop crying like a girl and start acting like a man.* He'd been eight years old. He'd forgotten that day. It was like it had never happened. Until now.

"I went back. I went back to the house, and it didn't matter. Nothing matters."

"What do you mean? To Mrs. Castillo's house?"

Lucien closed his eyes and nodded. "I went to get the vial back. I thought I could make a difference and change something. I thought I could do the right thing for once. She was so happy when I told her she didn't have to take it." His voice broke, and he dug his nails into his palms. "But it was too late. Somehow, they knew what I was going to do. Someone knew. The cleaning crew. I don't know…"

He was quiet again for so long that Theia must have thought he was sleeping, and she shook his shoulder gently.

"Lucien?"

He exhaled slowly. "It was Rosa. The old woman. Someone gave it to her. They collected the old woman's soul while she was sleeping. My act of rebellion, my grand gesture… it was just a joke."

"Oh, Lucien."

"You were right about me."

"Right? About what?"

"Whatever it was you thought when you first met me. Whatever you thought about me today after what you witnessed. I'm garbage."

"You are not garbage, and that isn't what I thought." Theia held his gaze, and Lucien looked away, but she turned his face toward her with both hands. "You're a human being. You're allowed to make mistakes."

Lucien laughed and then couldn't be sure whether he was laughing at "human being" or "mistakes," which gave his laughter a slightly hysterical edge.

Theia drew him into her arms, resting his head on her shoulder, and he remembered belatedly that she was an empath. She'd known he was going to break before he did. And when he broke, it was like a crack in a dam bursting under the pressure of a lifetime of unshed tears.

He wept for his grandmother—the only connection he'd had to his mother, who'd never come back—at whose death his father had told him to "act like a man." He wept for the souls he'd collected and the lives he'd seen ruined. And he wept for himself, knowing it was puerile and self-indulgent but unable to stop now that he'd started. Every loss, every wound came back to him, multiplying the ache in his chest, until he had nothing left.

"Lucien, it's all right. You'll be all right." Soothing, meaningless platitudes, but from Theia's lips, they were life preservers tossed into a turbulent sea. She might have said anything; it didn't matter. The sound of her voice was his lifeline.

He raised his head, afraid to see in her face that she thought less of him now, but when he met her gaze, she seemed to truly see him as no one had before.

Theia brushed a tear from his cheek and leaned toward him, reaching for his mouth with hers. Their lips came together, and Lucien surrendered to that drowning feeling he'd experienced the first time they'd kissed. It was as if they'd both gone under but shared oxygen with their breath. As long as they stayed together, as long as Theia was close to him, he'd survive.

It didn't even occur to him to want more. Kissing Theia was more satisfying than most sexual encounters he'd had. Maybe satisfying wasn't exactly the word—more of a physical communion, perhaps. He wanted to keep doing it, to keep tasting the salt of his own tears on her mouth, to keep feeling the silk of her lips and the velvety texture of her tongue with his.

They ended up curled together on the love seat, Lucien resting his head on her breast. So maybe he wanted a *little* more. He grinned to himself against the soft curve beneath her cotton shirt. But he wasn't going to push it right now. He liked where they were, comfortable, not needing words. No pressure. He'd said it more than once, but it was true. He felt none when he was with her—no pressure to put on an act. Not the confident arrogance of the playboy or even the everyday simple, stupid stoicism of being a man. With Theia, he was just himself. And for the first time, that felt okay. Maybe she was right. Maybe he wasn't entirely garbage.

"So what do I do now?" He hadn't meant to say it aloud.

"Now?"

"How do I go on being Lucien Smok, heir to the Smok fortune and all that comes with it?" He shook his head. "Don't worry. Rhetorical question."

"You've already made a start. Going after rogue creatures isn't exactly playing by Smok rules."

"I collect those souls, too, though. So maybe it's just me indulging my own need to feel self-righteous. Going after people like Leo."

"You said an anonymous source gave you his name. I think I have an idea who that might be."

Lucien propped his elbow on the couch cushion. "Who?"

"Carter Hamilton. It can't be a coincidence that he crashed Phoebe's wedding at the same time you did. It would be in his interest to have someone else do his dirty work and take down my family and the people close to us."

"Hamilton." Lucien nodded slowly. "That would make sense. We've done a lot of cleanup for him over the years. He knows my father fairly well. I've never met him, but if he was looking for a way to wreak some havoc, he'd only have to go to Polly's to get information about what I do."

"What is that place, exactly? Did you really meet a client there?"

Lucien sighed and straightened. He wasn't sure why he'd lied to her before.

"Polly…is my ex-girlfriend. She owns the club. It's a hangout for unnatural people. Enhanced people. And people pay her for information. She's one of my key sources."

Theia sat up beside him. "What kind of enhanced people?"

Lucien met her gaze. "Vampires. Werewolves. Valkyries."

"Valkyries?"

"Leo used to spend time there some years ago, according to Polly. With a rogue Valkyrie."

Recognition dawned in Theia's eyes. "Faye." She paused, brow wrinkling. "Wait…she and Leo were here in Sedona years ago?"

"The club can be entered from anywhere in the world. It's sort of…timeless. Not exactly fixed in time and space."

"Not *exactly*? How does that work?"

Lucien shrugged. "You'd have to ask Polly. But I doubt she'd tell you."

"And what about Polly? Is she…timeless?"

Lucien gave her a sidelong glance with a tentative smile. "Are you jealous of Polly?"

"Should I be?"

She was. The realization made his heart do a little flip. Jealousy meant she was invested in him. In this. It meant there *was* a "this." He'd never imagined a relationship was something he wanted. The warm glow at the idea that he had one surprised him.

"There's nothing between me and Polly anymore. She's just a friend. And I suppose, in answer to your question, she is a bit timeless. The club is a sort of extension of her, a web or a net she sends out to draw in people who interest her."

"A web? What is she, a were-spider?"

Lucien laughed at the idea. "No. Polly…is a siren."

Chapter 17

It took Theia a moment, her mind stuck on the image of a spinning light on top of a police car, before her eyes widened with understanding. "An actual siren? As in *The Odyssey*? As in luring men to their deaths?"

Lucien's smile was wry. "I doubt she's ever lured any man to his death—unless he went willingly—but, yes, those sirens."

Theia wasn't sure she wanted to know what he meant by that middle bit. She was going to have to compare notes with Rhea. Which was worse as an intimidating ex, a siren or a Valkyrie? She imagined a siren's experience would be impossible to compete with—even if Theia *had* any experience.

Lucien started to say something, but his phone interrupted. "Damn. Another haunting. I'm starting to feel like Bill Murray."

Theia rose as he did. "Do you usually have this much business?"

"No. Not at all." Lucien frowned. "It's starting to seem a little weird. Like something's stirred up the dead around here."

The last time something had stirred up the dead in Sedona, it had been Carter Hamilton.

"Lucy's already on it, so hopefully this will be an easy one. As soon as we finish up, I'll give you a call. Speaking of which, I'd better get your number in here." He glanced up with a sly half smile once he'd entered the number she gave him. "So you were just kidding about me shoving the job up my ass, right? I'm going to see you there tomorrow?"

Theia laughed. "I have a final in the morning, but I'll be there in the afternoon. You can consider your ass safe."

As he pulled out onto the drive and Theia closed the door, he texted her with an emoji: a smooching heart.

An irritated meow came from the guest room, accompanied by a perturbed doorknob rattle. She'd forgotten to let Glum out after stashing him to open the front door.

Theia stepped aside for his flounce after releasing him. "Sorry, buddy. Sucks to be thumbless."

He gave her a condescending stare before trotting to his window spot and peering out belatedly after the "intruder."

As she started to text Rhea about her bizarre afternoon, her phone rang, Rhea's photo popping up on the screen. "Speak of the devil," she answered.

"And how did you know I was going to do that?"

Theia took the phone to the papasan. "Do what?"

"Speak of the devil. I found out something interesting from Ione."

"You've lost me."

"She called to check on me. I don't think she trusts me with a millionaire's house. And I happened to mention the incident with Lucien the other night—"

"*Rhe.*"

"I had to. I need to get some of the lamps on the walkway fixed and replace a windowpane, thanks to Oliver Queen. And she gave me an earful about the family Smok. Apparently, they go back to the time of Madeleine Marchant, and they're into some very sketchy things."

"I know that. That's the research I was doing at Rafe's dad's place."

"You know? Why didn't you tell me?"

"I don't know." And, honestly, she didn't, now that she thought about it. It was like she'd gotten so used to keeping things from Rhea that it was becoming a habit.

"Did you also know that Lucien has a nickname among the magical community?"

"No. What?"

"Little Lucifer."

Theia snorted. He was hardly little.

"It seems the Smok family has a reputation for making *infernal deals*. Like crossroads kinds of deals." She paused. "Theia Dawn. Are you going to tell me you knew about that, too?"

"I only found out this afternoon. I went with Lucien on a consulting job and witnessed a deal in action. It wasn't pretty."

"And that's okay with you?"

"No, of course it isn't. And I told him that and made him take me home. But then he went back to the client and tried to nullify the deal and found out it was too late. You should have seen him when he showed up here. He was absolutely wrecked."

Rhea was quiet for a moment. "You're starting to worry me."

"There's nothing to worry about."

"You're working for Smok Biotech, and you're going with Lucien on his creepy crossroads client calls."

"I haven't actually started working for Smok."

"Because it's the weekend. Are you taking the job or aren't you?"

"Maybe. Yes. So?"

"Theia, your boyfriend collects *souls*."

"So does yours."

"That's not the same thing."

"Isn't it?"

Rhea sighed. "We're not talking about Leo Ström. We're talking about Lucien Smo— Oh, wow. *LS?* You couldn't even get your own initials. You always have to copy me."

Theia couldn't resist needling her. "Actually, you're the one who copied me. I dated Leo first, if you recall."

"Ouch. I can't believe you went there. Seriously, though, infernal deals aside, Lucien doesn't exactly have a sterling reputation. I talked to Leo about that place you mentioned. Polly's Grotto? He's heard of it, all right."

"From when he used to go there with Faye."

She could almost hear Rhea's mouth drop open in indignation. "What the hell, Theia? Have your visions gotten spooky accurate lately, or are you becoming a pathological liar?"

There was a distinct chance the answer to that entire question was "Yes."

"Lucien told me about it this afternoon. Apparently, he used to be involved with Polly, the owner. He wanted me to know because he's not the creep you're trying to make him out to be."

"He dated her?"

"And she's a siren. So stick that in your Valkyrie pipe and smoke it."

"I don't even know what that means."

"Neither do I. It just came out."

"Go back to the part where Polly is a siren."

"Yes, he dated a siren. They're real. Apparently, everything is real. That shouldn't really surprise you. You're hooking up with the Chieftain of the Wild Hunt."

"Aren't you a little concerned that Lucien is popping off to visit his ex-girlfriend the siren on a Saturday afternoon?"

"She gives him information. That's how he confirmed his erroneous intel on Leo. Which he originally got from some anonymous source who's been tipping him off about our family."

There was a brief pause before they said the name together. "Carter Hanson Hamilton."

Rhea growled. "That absolute dirtball. It wasn't enough

that he sent an actual Nazi after Leo to steal his soul, now he's setting up Lucien to send Leo to hell?"

"I don't have any proof that it's him."

"It's totally him. You know you're going to have to tell Ione about this."

As much as Theia hated the idea, Rhea was right. Which meant she was going to have to tell Ione everything about Lucien.

The haunting ought to have been routine. No over-the-top *Ghostbusters*-style vanquishing, no silly beeping REM pod tech and primitive blinking flashlight communications. A haunting usually consisted of a simple soul collection. Easiest job on the books. Ordinarily, opening a portal wasn't even required. The haunting in the NICU last night had been an exception. As with Lupe Ramirez, often all that needed to happen was to convince the spirit or shade that it was in the wrong place, and it would go on its own. A forcible crossing, whether done with electrical current or by a practicing witch through spell casting, was generally considered undesirable and could be dangerous if not done right.

Lucien arrived in Litchfield Park west of Phoenix at ten after five, expecting to meet up with Lucy, who'd been in Phoenix already when the call came in. Her car was parked in front of the client's property. She'd gone in without him. Lucien swore to himself as he got out and approached the door. If she was going to handle it herself, why had she bothered to call him in on the job? He could be spending the evening with Theia.

The client, a young black man about Lucien's age, opened the door to his knock, looking frightened and harried. "You Lucien?"

Lucien paused. Something wasn't right. "Where's Lucy Smok?"

A hand reached from around the door and opened it wide. "Hi, sweetie! I'm right here." It was Lucy's voice and Lucy's body, but it was the most un-Lucy-like greeting he'd ever heard.

Lucien narrowed his eyes. "You're not Lucy. Don't bullshit me. Who am I speaking to?"

Her face broke into a grin. "And Lucy thinks you aren't the brainy one. Daisy Fox, at your service." She looked him up and down as she stepped around the client. "And you are absolutely dreamy." She stroked Lucien's cheek, and he stepped back with a shudder. "Guess you're not those kind of twins, huh?"

"What do you want, Daisy? My organization can help you without you having to resort to body theft."

"I doubt that. Besides, this is infinitely more fun." Daisy stroked Lucy's hands over her body before turning around to go back into the living room and flopping into an armchair like she owned the place.

Lucien addressed the client as he closed the door. "What happened?"

"My fiancée was acting weird—like your sister is now—and I worked out that she was possessed. So I called you people on the advice of a lawyer friend. Your sister showed up and tried to reason with the spirit. Next thing I knew, Sherrell—that's my girl—had collapsed, and the ghost was in your sister."

Across the room, Daisy beamed at Lucien out of Lucy's face.

This wasn't a simple haunting. It was a step-in, a forcible takeover of a living person by the deceased, unwilling to give up a life on the physical plane. And the shade had apparently hopped into Lucy when she'd attempted to compel it to release the body it occupied. As with a demon possession, this shade seemed to have the ability to move through the ether—and through hosts—at will. It was a rare shade that had such control, and Daisy's didn't fit the profile. Someone else was controlling it. They had a necromancer on their hands.

"Where's Sherrell now?"

"She's upstairs resting. She doesn't remember any of it. But I can't get this lady to leave. I mean, your sister. Or *not* her. Whatever it is."

"So Daisy Fox isn't someone you know?"

"Never heard of her."

"And when did this start, Mister…" He'd forgotten the client's name. Bad form.

"Mitchell. Jesse Mitchell." He held out his hand, and Lucien shook it. "Sherrell came home from work early yesterday acting funny. I thought she was sick. She didn't let on she wasn't Sherrell until this morning. That's when I called my friend. He represents some unusual clients, and I figured he might know what to do. He gave me your number."

That wasn't the usual method of client referral. Neither was the referral for the reanimation of Lupe Ramirez.

"Did your friend happen to explain how we work? I mean, he told you about the cost?"

Jesse stuck his hands in his pockets and swallowed before he nodded. "Your office explained it to me. I agreed to the terms. Your sister gave me a finger prick to sign the agreement." Traditionally, contracts for souls were signed in blood, but that was really just for show. They only needed a drop of blood, impressed with the signatory's thumbprint, to seal the deal.

Lucy-Daisy sighed loudly from the living room. "You boys are boring me to death." She laughed at the pun.

Lucien ignored her for the moment. "Thank you, Mr. Mitchell. I'll take care of the rest. It may take me a little while to get her to leave, but we'll get rid of her."

"Stop talking about me in the third person. It's very rude."

Lucien walked into the living room. "You're lecturing me about manners? You've violated at least two people intimately in the last forty-eight hours. That, Ms. Fox, is exceedingly rude."

"*Violated.* That's a very strong word. Ask our Jesse here. His girl is none the worse for wear."

"Just because someone can't remember what happened to them doesn't mean doing whatever you like with their body is okay. That's what violation is."

"You think I don't know what violation is? You think I don't know what it's like to wake up somewhere and not know what happened?"

"I don't know anything about you, Daisy. Why don't you tell me why you're doing this?"

"Why don't you go fuck yourself? I don't need you to condescend to me."

"Mr. Smok?" Jesse held out his phone with the browser open. "I found out who she is."

Lucien took the phone. A picture of a smiling young Navajo woman appeared. Lucien read the headline aloud. "Body Found in Phoenix Dumpster Identified as Daisy Fox, Missing From Window Rock Since April."

"Congratulations." Daisy gave them a slow clap. "You know how to use the internet."

Lucien handed back the phone. "I'm sorry that happened to you, Daisy."

"I don't need your pity, either."

"What do you need?"

"I've pretty much got what I need. Maybe some less stuffy clothes would be nice." Daisy rose, glancing out the window. "That my car? The black convertible?"

"You're not going anywhere with Lucy's car or Lucy's body." Lucien blocked her path to the door. "Why don't you tell me how you were able to step into her? She's not exactly inexperienced with people in your state."

Daisy laughed, an unnerving sound coming from Lucy's mouth. Not that Lucy didn't laugh, but it was usually a very dry laugh, indicating how deeply unamused she was by something.

"Did you have help?"

The laughter stopped. "What do you mean by help?"

"Is someone controlling you, Daisy?" If a necromancer was responsible, it was probably her killer—or at least someone with access to Daisy's bones. "Is it the person who hurt you?"

A flash of rage distorted Lucy's features. "He's not going to get me to give up this body, and neither are you."

"He will, Daisy. If he induced you to enter Sherrell, and he helped you hop from Sherrell to Lucy, he can make you do anything. But I can help you. I can make him stop."

"How can you help?" Lucy's face crumpled, another expression he'd never seen on his sister. "He took my body. I tried to get back in. I couldn't get back in."

A disturbing idea occurred to him. "Are you saying your body was still alive when you left it?"

Tears were streaming down Lucy's face. "He gave me a drug. Said it was just going to make me feel good. And then suddenly I was outside and I couldn't get back. He'd put something around my neck. Like a collar."

The necromancer had used a blocking object, something the shade couldn't cross to reenter her unconscious body.

"He said he wouldn't do anything to me—to my body—as long as I did what he asked. And I did. I went where he said. And now you're telling me my fucking body is a corpse!"

"You didn't know." Lucien touched Lucy's arm, and Daisy flinched. "I'm so sorry, Daisy."

Daisy jerked away from him. "So now he doesn't have anything on me and I don't have to give this one back."

"I'm afraid that's not how it works. He probably kept...a

souvenir. A small bone is all he would need. That's how he could continue to dictate your actions. When you jumped into Lucy, was it a conscious thought? Or did you just find yourself here?"

Daisy shook her head, turning and looking around as if trying to find a way out. "I don't remember." She turned back to Lucien, her expression pleading. "Can't I just keep it? Can't I stay? I don't want to go."

Before he could answer, before he could even tell her it would be okay if he released her, that she could go where she pleased, Lucy's body collapsed.

Lucien caught her before she hit the ground. "Daisy?"

Her eyes fluttered erratically. "Fuck. *Me.* Goddammit."

Lucy was back.

She opened her eyes in a squint and glanced around. "Little bitch jumped me without warning. Did you vanquish her?"

"No."

"No?" Lucy pushed away from him, getting to her feet. "Then where the hell did she go?"

Lucien straightened. "Someone else appears to have forced her out. She was pleading to stay."

"Well, isn't that special?" Lucy gripped her head. "Ow. She gave me a damn migraine."

"I've got some ibuprofen." Jesse hurried upstairs to get it.

Lucy watched him go. "We should probably check on his girlfriend. Make sure the shade didn't just get pulled back into the original host."

"I doubt that's the case. Looks like you were the target. Daisy knew who you were. I think this whole thing was staged for our benefit. Whoever's controlling the shade was obviously trying to get our attention, letting us know we're vulnerable to their magic."

"Speak for yourself. She just caught me off guard."

Lucien folded his arms. "Lu. You've never been caught off guard in your entire life."

Jesse reappeared with the pills and a glass of water.

"Thanks." Lucy downed the pills. "If you don't mind, Mr. Mitchell, I need to look in on Sherrell. Just to make sure the problem is fully resolved."

Jesse nodded. "She's upstairs in the first bedroom."

Lucien nodded to Lucy. "I'll handle it. You take care of the business arrangements." He was being a coward, passing the responsibility of soul collecting back to Lucy after one attempt to do the right thing. But this wasn't a pay-on-receipt situation. There was time to remedy things if he found a way to later.

Lucien paused at the top of the stairs. Was that what he wanted to do? Was he going turn everything on its head and refuse to collect souls? The idea made him slightly heady. But the anxiety that followed immediately overshadowed the feeling. If he refused to fulfill the earthly duties of the Smok heir—what would it mean for the infernal ones?

Chapter 18

Lucy's post-step-in headache was still severe, so Lucien left his car and drove her back to Sedona in hers.

After several minutes, he glanced over at her, eyes closed as she leaned back against the seat. "You awake?"

Lucy scrunched her eyes together. "Unfortunately."

"I wanted to talk to you about something that happened at the job I went on earlier today. The reanimation reversal."

"Yeah, that sounded like a fun one."

"I gave the client the requisite dose for the payment, and she was prepared to pay in full that evening, but something happened to it. She found it in her mother's room. The old woman had taken it."

"Wasn't the old woman the one who was reanimated?"

"That was *her* mother. Rosa was the one who hired the reanimator. She has Alzheimer's, so someone must have taken advantage of her. She couldn't have had the presence of mind to think about how to bring her back from the grave. And now she's dead, too. I think the cleaning crew gave the meds to her."

Lucy opened her eyes in a squint. "The cleaning crew? They wouldn't even know what it was."

"Normally, I'd agree, but the client swore she'd put it in her own room in preparation for taking it that evening, and the old woman was still knocked out from the sedative I had to give her in order to vanquish the revenant." Lucien had meant to tell her about driving back with the intent of giving Mrs. Castillo her reprieve, but the story worked without the extra detail. Lucy would just assume the client had called him later. God, he really was a coward.

"Maybe the client's lying. Maybe she chickened out and didn't want to pay. It wouldn't have been the worst decision to give it to an old woman with Alzheimer's, after all."

"That's what I told her when I was there, but Mrs. Castillo was insistent that the payment was hers to make."

"I can't imagine why anyone from the cleaning crew would interfere in that. I suppose we can call the contractor tomorrow and ask." She closed her eyes again, and Lucien drove the rest of the way in silence, but his conscience was still nagging him as he dropped her off at her villa.

"Hey, Lu?"

She was already out the door, but she turned and leaned into the passenger window. "Yeah?"

"Have you ever…let a client off the hook on a deal like that?"

"Off the hook? You mean like the ghost girl the other night? Pro bono?"

"Sort of. I mean for the pay-on-receipts. Have you ever told them they didn't have to pay until the normal expiration of the contract?"

"Why would I do that?" Lucy peered at him with a suspicious expression. "Lucien. Did you tell that woman she didn't have to pay?"

"It didn't seem right. I drove back after I got home, and I asked for the pentobarbital back. I told her there had been a clerical error. You should have seen the joy in her face."

"We don't do this for joy."

"Why the hell *do* we do it?"

"You know why."

"Because of the curse."

"The curse?" Lucy laughed—the unlaugh he was used to hearing. "We do it because it's business. We offer a very important, needed service for a fee. Everyone goes into the agreement knowing full well what they're agreeing to. No one forces them to sign." She straightened and frowned.

"This is that little empath's influence, isn't it? She told you it wasn't fair and said you were a bad man, so you defied centuries of protocol, jeopardizing our entire operation for some pussy."

"Don't talk about her like that."

"I notice you're not denying it. You'd better straighten up, Lucien. Edgar indulged your rebellious phase, and he turns a blind eye to the mystery archer who just happens to have all the same client information we do. But you start messing around with the business and he's going to rain down hell on your head."

Lucien laughed, copying Lucy's sharp sound of disdain. "What's he going to do, put me over his knee?"

"I'm not kidding, Lucien. Do *not* fuck with the business." Lucy slapped the hood of the car as she went around it. "And get your own damn ride home. This one's mine, and it's staying right here."

It was after ten by the time he got a car. He really wanted to see Theia, but he was bone tired. He'd have to call her and tell her he'd see her tomorrow at the lab. He had the driver take him home.

Lucien undressed on the way to the bedroom, looking forward to at least sexting with Theia for a few minutes before he passed out. She'd left him a message with pretty much the same conclusion he'd come to about the late hour and asking him to call when he got in. With his phone in his hand, he climbed into bed—and nearly sat on a brand-new laptop someone had placed there.

He smiled tentatively. Had Theia gotten him a gift? He opened the cover, which triggered some kind of automatic video messaging system, and found himself staring at his father, seated at his desk.

"Lucien."

"Edgar. I'm not really dressed for face time."

"Are you entertaining?"

"Not at the moment."

"Then put something on and sit down."

Lucien grabbed his robe from the bathroom and returned, trying not to let on that his stomach was in knots. For Edgar to want to talk to him in real time, face-to-face, he had to be in deep shit. Lucy had ratted him out.

Edgar was dressed in a conservative suit, as if he'd been conducting business at this hour, his steel-gray hair meticulously styled. "As you know, Lucien, being born a Smok comes with great responsibility."

"I know that—"

"Don't interrupt." Edgar's expression didn't change, but his voice dropped instantly into a deeper register. That tone had instilled fear in Lucien as a boy. It wasn't doing a half-bad job of it now. "I've been giving you space to grow up, to grow into these responsibilities. My father was so much harder on me. There was no sowing wild oats or running around like a spoiled adolescent doing as I pleased. I had to grow up fast. But I've never wanted to be hard and inflexible like my father. I've striven to give you and Lucy a better upbringing."

It was all Lucien could do to keep a straight face at the idea of Edgar as warm, loving patriarch.

"But there comes a time when a man has to take responsibility for his actions and to earn his keep. I'm not going to be around forever, and you're nearly twenty-five."

"Edgar—"

"I've spoken with the bank about your trust, which is slated to be fully under your control on your birthday." Which it almost certainly wasn't going to be now. "I hadn't planned to do this quite so soon, but a business opportunity has presented itself that makes the timing ideal. I'm prepared to start turning the business over to you." Edgar's mouth curved upward into what Lucien supposed was his idea of a warm, fatherly smile. "Think of it as an early birthday present."

Lucien had been concentrating so intently on Edgar's tone and facial expressions that he hadn't really been listening— because he'd thought he knew what was coming. But this was definitely not it.

"You... I'm sorry. What?"

"I've made arrangements for the day-to-day operations to fall to your sister. She really is the brain of the organization, and she's been handling much of it already. That will free you up to be the public face of Smok International and all our subsidiaries, which of course includes any and all business of a sensitive nature. I'd like you to meet with some of my colleagues tomorrow afternoon to get the ball rolling."

"I don't understand." Lucien struggled to follow. "You're turning the company over to me? Now?"

Edgar gave him that bizarre smile again. "Don't mention anything to Lucy until I have a chance to talk to her in the morning. I want to make sure she doesn't see this as some kind of a step down. The arrangement actually is quite favorable for her, but she's liable to overreact. She's very much like your mother in that regard."

"So... I'll be..."

"The chief executive officer of Smok International, with primary responsibility for the Smok Biotech division. Congratulations."

The knots in Lucien's stomach turned into a confusing mix of elation and anxiety. The company was his. He'd never dreamed Edgar would give up control of even the slightest bit of it so long as he was healthy and his wits were still sharp. The business opportunity he was willing to relinquish it for must be something astounding.

A million thoughts whirled through his head. He could change things now from the top down. If the company was really his to control, he could put a stop to the questionable practices that had bothered him all his life. He could actually help people, make their lives better. And he could make Smok's mission one that permanently removed the predatory elements they dealt with instead of rewarding them. No more turning a blind eye to abuse and mayhem. No more little girls trapped in blood slavery, considered expendable.

Edgar was still smiling. "I thought you'd be pleased. We'll go over all the details tomorrow, but there is one small condition I'd like to discuss with you before I make it official."

Lucien's mind was still lost in grand daydreams. "Condition?"

"I understand you've been keeping inappropriate company. Now, what you do for *recreation* isn't my concern. If you want to keep that what's her face, Polly, on the side, it's none of my business. Keep a dozen Pollys."

"I'm not seeing Polly anymore. You don't have to worry about me embarrassing you or the company."

"As I said, you can do what you like on your own time, in private. But I want you to stop seeing Theia Carlisle."

"Theia Dawn," he said automatically, before the meaning of his father's words struck him in the gut. "Wait. What are you saying?"

"You know perfectly well that the Carlisle sisters are the direct descendants of Madeleine Marchant. I don't have to tell you what harm that unsavory witch has done to this family. We've managed to turn the situation to our advantage over the centuries, but we do not forget where we come from, Lucien. And that will become even more apparent to you once I begin to show you the inner workings of the company. But I will not do so unless I have your solemn oath that you will sever ties with the girl completely. This is nonnegotiable."

Chapter 19

Lucien was dumbstruck. There was no way he was going to give Theia up. He needed her. More than he wanted to. But it was equally clear that Edgar wouldn't be swayed by any argument Lucien could make. When Edgar made up his mind about something, it was made up for everyone around him.

"Do I have your word, Lucien?"

"I… Can I think about this?"

"There is nothing to think about. If you refuse this one condition of mine, the company and all its holdings will go to Lucy. Your trust fund will be cut off. You will never see a penny of it. And Lucy will be under a legally binding oath not to turn around and give you a pity allowance after my death."

A moment ago, Lucien hadn't given a damn about the company other than the thorn it had always been in his side. Then he'd had an instant to reimagine it as his own before Edgar had taken it away again. But he'd never imagined being cut off completely. He wouldn't even begin to know how to survive by himself. For all his talk of wanting Lucien to become a man, Edgar had made him dependent on the company and his money, making sure he knew nothing about the details of living an independent life. Lucien felt like a fool.

"Edgar, I think if you met Theia—"

"I said this is nonnegotiable, Lucien. But if money alone doesn't sway you, perhaps you need a little bit of incentive to come to your senses and make a rational decision. I've sent you something via email. Look it over and get back to me tomorrow. I'll set up the meeting and send you the invite. If you don't show up on time, I'll assume you've made your decision, and I'll send someone to collect my property and revoke your access to Smok Biotech and any of our holdings. Good night, Lucien."

Edgar's parting shot had been straight to the heart. Lucien couldn't lose access to Smok Biotech's labs. He needed the research data on the anti-lycanthropy project. He needed the cure. Maybe if he went to the lab right now and downloaded everything he could onto an external drive... But Edgar would have thought of that. Lucien wouldn't be surprised if his access was temporarily suspended.

He pulled back his fist reflexively, preparing to punch the screen of the new laptop, but managed to draw his arm up short. This might be the only thing he had to his name by tomorrow. He couldn't afford to have a temper tantrum.

His phone buzzed, and Lucien picked it up, forgotten on the pillow after finding Edgar's face staring at him. Theia wanted to know where he was.

Theia.

He could have everything he'd ever wanted—financial security, respect, power and the real possibility of effecting change in the world. Or he could have Theia—and lose everything he'd ever known. It shouldn't even be a contest. He should have been able to give Edgar his answer without hesitation: Theia was enough, she was everything, and Edgar could go fuck himself.

An email notification popped up on the laptop with a message from Edgar. He'd promised Lucien some additional incentive. What the hell could he possibly say in an email that would make a difference? But maybe Lucien shouldn't be hasty to make a decision. Maybe for once in his life he should weigh the evidence and come to a reasoned conclusion before making up his mind. It couldn't hurt to sleep on it.

The message notification on his phone chimed again. Everything okay?

Lucien typed in a response, his thumbs shaking.

Sorry. Took me forever to get home. Had to drive Lucy back from the job site. Long story. She wouldn't let me keep her car and I had to wait for a pickup.

He sent the message and watched Theia's typing bubble before writing another.

I really wanted to see you tonight, or even just talk for a bit, but I'm about to drop. Do you mind if we talk in the morning?

Her response came quickly enough, no sign that she was suspicious.

I totally understand. We'll see plenty of each other tomorrow. But I miss you already.

God, he missed her—like an essential amputated limb he hadn't even known he had until it was cut off. Talk about maudlin.

Miss you, too. Good night.

Theia sent a little heart emoji that made his actual heart twist.

Lucien turned off the phone, not wanting to allow himself to be distracted in case Theia texted again. He was going to read Edgar's email and give it due consideration, whatever it was. And then he was going to get some sleep.

He'd find a way to make the right decision tomorrow. He just needed fortitude.

He opened the email and found that Edgar had sent him an attachment that looked remarkably similar to the one his anonymous source had directed him to containing Theia's genealogy research. If that's all it was, it wasn't incentive at all. He already knew about Theia's bloodline.

He breathed a sigh of relief. The scale had tipped toward Theia, and just that realization made it possible. He could do this. He could walk away from Smok's hold over him entirely. He could learn how to do something respectable for a living. He had some biotech knowledge, after all.

But that reminded him of the reason he'd painstakingly educated himself about the lycanthropy research. If the legend turned out to be not just a legend, he might become what he'd always despised. And he wasn't sure how much time he had left. Without Smok, Lucien might become a monster.

He'd been scanning the document idly while his mind raced, when something caught his eye. This wasn't Theia's research after all. At least, not solely. Someone had made annotations.

The Lilith blood phenotype isn't simply a magical strain giving those with the dominant gene special abilities. Lilith blood is specifically designed to trigger paranormal abilities in those the Marchant-descended women choose to mate with. More than that, it seeks out such dormant abilities and acts as a pheromone, drawing in the unsuspecting mate. It is how Rafael Diamante Jr. became an avatar of Quetzalcoatl. It is how Dione "Ione" Carlisle controls her familiar, the demon within Dharamdev Gideon. And it is what led the immortal Leo Ström to Rhea Carlisle, one of the twin pair, released from the bond with the Valkyrie only to become bound to a descendant of Madeleine Marchant. It is the Lilith blood that makes these men surrender their human selves to these innocent-seeming women. And every one of the men ensnared becomes the embodiment of the beast: the serpent, the dragon, the snake—Lilith's companion. Together, the Carlisle sisters are the Whore of Babylon, riding on the back of the seven-headed dragon of the apocalypse.

Chapter 20

There was a problem with Theia's new access card when she arrived at the lab. When she came back down, the security guard at the front desk confirmed that it wasn't authorized for access to the floor where the Smok lab was situated.

"I guess something must have gotten mixed up in the system. Can you call Lucien Smok for me and tell him Theia Dawn is here?"

The guard dialed upstairs. "There's a Theia Dawn here to see Mr. Smok." After listening for a moment, she hung up, regarding Theia without expression. "Mr. Smok has left orders to revoke your access."

Theia wasn't sure she'd heard right. "My access... What?"

Someone spoke from behind her. "The job offer has been rescinded."

Theia turned to see Lucy, sharply dressed as always, giving her a cool, smug smile. "I suppose this is your doing."

"Not at all. Can't say I'm displeased about it, though."

"Why would Lucien rescind the offer? That doesn't make any sense. I just saw him yesterday. I talked to him last night."

"I'm well aware of the time you spend together. And I'm also aware that you got him to make a stupid mistake yesterday that resulted in an innocent woman's death. If you want to know why he's rescinded the offer, you can probably start there."

"That's ridiculous. I didn't make him do anything."

Theia took her phone out of her bag. "I'm calling him right now to find out what's going on."

Lucy shrugged, arms folded. "Be my guest."

The phone rang once before rolling over to voice mail. Which meant he'd declined the call when he saw her name. What the hell was going on?

Lucy was smug. "Looks like he's busy."

Theia's hand curled around the phone at her side. "I want to know what this is about. Did something happen on the job you two were on yesterday evening?"

"Something always happens on a job. It's an unpredictable business. But we left a satisfied customer, as always."

"Oh, really?" Theia lowered her voice. "Someone was satisfied to sign away their soul?"

Lucy frowned, uncrossing her arms. "This is why it's a bad idea to bring outsiders in. You don't understand the nuances of these issues, and you aren't meant to. But this is not something you can just stand here in the middle of our lobby and talk about as you please."

"It's not exactly your lobby. This is a university building, and I happen to be a student here as well as faculty."

"That can change."

"Excuse me?"

Lucy turned and walked toward the exit. "If you want to have a candid discussion about the change of plan, follow me."

Theia paused, glancing back down at her phone. She could send Lucien a text and just wait here. He couldn't be completely cutting her off. Something had happened, and if she could just talk to him, they could work it out.

Lucy turned back at the door. "This is the only offer you're going to get. If you don't leave voluntarily, security is instructed to send for the campus police to escort you out."

Theia's mouth dropped open. They couldn't just kick her out of a university building. Could they? What if she'd been expelled from the graduate program? She could at least get some answers from Lucy—whatever grain of truth there might be to them—and try to reach Lucien again later. Dropping the phone back into her purse, Theia pressed her lips together and followed Lucy through the door.

Lucy walked her out to the parking lot. Maybe Theia was being a sucker, and Lucy wasn't going to tell her anything after all. She hesitated at the edge of the lot as Lucy pressed the button on her key fob and the convertible beside them beeped in response.

Lucy nodded toward the car. "Get in."

"Where are we going?"

"We're not going anywhere. It's the only secure place to talk."

Theia opened the passenger door reluctantly and slipped inside, leaving it open a crack.

Lucy got in beside her and reached across to close it. "I'm not kidnapping you, for God's sake. I'm trying to avoid being overheard."

"Overheard saying what?"

She fixed her gaze on Theia, the same startling pale eyes as Lucien's, her expression grim. "The reason Lucien isn't responding is that our father made him an offer last night that he couldn't refuse."

"What kind of offer?"

Lucy's mouth twitched. "He's turning over the entire enterprise to Lucien immediately, something we didn't expect for years to come."

Theia knitted her brow. "What does that have to do with my working for Smok Biotech?"

"It's not about you working for Smok Biotech—though I can't stress enough what a really stupid idea that was. It was a condition of the offer. Edgar insisted that Lucien stop seeing you."

Theia's eyes smarted as if there were smoke in the air.

"He offered Lucien control of the company if he stopped seeing me?"

"Not just the company." There was that twitch again. "Everything. He either stops seeing you or he loses it all, cut off without ceremony."

Theia raked her hands through her hair, trying to process this. "I have to talk to him. He doesn't have to do this. And he doesn't want to. I'm sure of that."

Lucy's expression was cold. "I'm not here to help you jeopardize Lucien's livelihood. I just wanted you to know so you'd stop trying to contact him. You can't change his mind—Lucien needs Smok Biotech more than you can possibly understand—and you won't change Edgar's."

Theia frowned. "I don't believe you."

"That's your problem."

"I mean about why you're telling me this. Why not just wipe my memory like you threatened to? You could probably wipe Lucien clean out of my brain, couldn't you?"

"Do you want me to?"

"*No*, I don't want you to. I want to know why you chose to tell me the truth about what's going on with Lucien—if it's the whole truth—instead of just taking the easy way out. Making sure I'd never bother you again. There has to be a reason you're telling me this."

Lucy looked out through the windshield. "Lucien said you were intuitive."

"Sometimes."

She was quiet a moment before taking a preparatory breath. "There's something wrong with all this. Edgar retiring without warning, giving Lucien sole control of the company. I didn't see it coming. The way he's always talked about Lucien, I half expected him to eventually give the company to me after he got tired of waiting for Lucien to grow up. He's given me all the financial responsibilities—I've already been handling them, but he's officially making me the CFO—but the company will be Lucien's." Lucy paused. "And there's a silent partner."

"Meaning what?"

"Meaning my father has signed over a percentage of the company to an investor who doesn't want to be publicly connected to it. I suppose a secret partner is a better word for it. He wants to benefit from our success and meddle in the business without anyone holding him responsible."

A chill ran up Theia's spine as Lucy spoke. "Who is this secret partner?"

Lucy gave her a sidelong eye roll. "It wouldn't really be a secret if I shared it with you, now would it?"

"What if I guessed?"

Noncommittal, Lucy waited with an expression of mild interest.

"Would it happen to be Carter Hanson Hamilton?"

Lucy's dark brows lifted. "I guess you really *are* psychic."

"Not exactly. It's just what I'd expect of him. I suppose you know our history?"

"Who doesn't? The murder trial was highly publicized."

"He also tried to steal my sister Phoebe's soul and have her killed while he was in prison last year, and he sent a Nazi who was obsessed with Norse mythology after Leo Ström. The creep kidnapped me and unleashed a *draugr* on Rhea."

Lucy's eyes registered sudden understanding. "So that's what was up with that. We got an alert from one of our staff psychics that someone was using one of the holy relics from the Third Reich to raise the dead, but it was handled before we had a chance to investigate." She studied Theia. "So Ström sent the Nazi's soul to Náströnd, I take it?"

"And destroyed the *draugr*, yes."

Lucy laughed. "My baby brother has more in common with that Viking than he thinks."

"Baby brother?"

"Technically, I was born the day before he was—11:58 p.m. I ought to be the heir, but our father is a traditionalist. Which is why I can't imagine him agreeing to a partnership with Hamilton. We've consulted for him in the past, but Edgar could never stand him. Said Hamilton was an opportunistic amateur who didn't respect the limits of power. This whole thing came completely out of the blue, and it has me worried. And Hamilton has already sent me inappropriate emails. I don't know what he thinks is going to happen, but if he imagines for one minute that I'm one of the perks of his partnership, he's going to be sorely disappointed. If he so much as looks at me, he's going to lose his balls."

Lucy seemed to realize she wasn't alone in the car, and she drew herself upright. "At any rate, he's a problem, and I don't like problems. Whatever he has planned for Smok International, I intend to be a thorn in his side. But don't think I'm not pleased as punch about Lucien dumping you. I'd hate for you to make the mistake of thinking that this cozy little conversation means we're friends. And Lucien has nothing to do with this. I'm not going to mention to him that I've had any contact with you, and I'm not going to try to persuade him that he's making a mistake."

"Fair enough." Theia would find a way to get Lucien to talk to her. She opened the door, since it looked like the conversation was over. "Thank you for telling me. You didn't have to."

"I didn't do it for you. Lucien has enough on his plate to deal with. He doesn't need you complicating things."

Theia paused with her hand on the door. "Has it occurred to you that Carter might be using necromancy on your father?"

"You mean with a step-in?" Lucy shook her head. "No. He's definitely himself, even if his actions are unusual. A step-in wouldn't be able to fool anyone for a prolonged period of time. And I've talked to him at length."

Theia nodded and got out but turned back once more before closing the door. "Don't underestimate Carter Hamilton. One thing you can be certain of is that he has a plan. And he's obsessed with other people's power."

Chapter 21

Theia had left him another message. He ought to block her number if he was serious about this. And he *had* to be serious about this. She was dangerous to him. Even without the role her blood might play in the fulfillment of the Smok curse, being with Theia meant losing access to Smok's labs. And even if Lucy was willing to defy Edgar's wishes and allow Lucien access to the research, it was useless without access to the scientists working on his cure.

Until now, developing the anti-transformative had been a fail-safe, something to fall back on in case the legend turned out to be true. If, at some distant point in the future, his father's death triggered what lay dormant in Lucien's blood, Lucien would simply be able to take a pill and suppress the infernal transformation. But the warning his father had sent him about Rafe, Dev and Leo rang true. Which meant Theia's interest him—his very attraction to her—was fated. It was the Lilith blood that wanted to bring forth the devil in him.

Lucien turned off his phone, unwilling to sever the ties completely. Which was a bad sign, and he knew it. But he wasn't ready. Not yet. What he needed now was a distraction.

Polly had brought in a good crowd this evening. As Lucien threaded his way through it, he discovered why. Polly had booked a performer. To anyone unfamiliar with the clientele that frequented Polly's, it looked like an erotic dance performance. But the anemic-looking blonde was obviously a bloodsucker groupie, and it became apparent as she worked the pole and stripped down to her G-string that she had tracks in the less visible places that vampires with discretion preferred for feeding. The purpose of the striptease wasn't to titillate sexually, it was to arouse the vamps. And once she had, they came to the stage—not to put dollar bills in her G-string but to taste.

She clearly got a sexual charge of her own out of it. Lucien looked away in disgust as the bloodsuckers crowded around, dipping their fangs into the marks at the undersides of her arms, beneath her breasts, inside her thighs, and sucking greedily. The donor moaned and crooned with pleasure and finally climaxed loudly, and the crowd cheered.

"Not your thing, baby?" Polly smiled down at him, dressed tonight in poison-green silk with long aquamarine locks to match. She could easily have swum out of a pre-Raphaelite painting.

"Blood porn? No. Never. But then you know that."

Polly slipped into the seat opposite him, managing to give him a sympathetic look. "I haven't forgotten. If I'd known you were planning on making an appearance here again so soon, I'd have moved the performance to another night."

"No, you wouldn't, but it's sweet of you to say so." Lucien downed his third bourbon.

Polly raised an eyebrow at his empty glass and signaled one of her staff to bring him another. "Anything bothering you? You usually don't drink alone these days."

"I'm celebrating." Lucien tried to smile and felt like he couldn't remember how. He was an alien pretending to be human. He gave it up and raised his glass after the waiter refilled it. "You're looking at the new CEO of Smok International."

Polly took the bottle from the waiter and picked up the glass he'd set in front of her. "Congratulations." She watched Lucien over the rim as she sipped. "Do I detect a note of dissatisfaction with your good fortune?"

"You haven't asked if Edgar's kicked the bucket." Lucien took another drink, and Polly refilled it. "He hasn't, by the way. He just decided out of the blue to retire and turn the whole thing over to me."

"And there's a catch, of course."

With a nod, he drank again. "No dirty Marchant blood allowed."

One green eyebrow twitched. "You mean Carlisle blood, I take it."

"Same thing."

"You like this Carlisle girl. A great deal."

Lucien shrugged and emptied his glass.

"Sorry, sweetie. I told you no good would come of that association, but I hate to see you like this."

The suckfest on stage was getting louder. They were practically having a vampire orgy right in the middle of Polly's Grotto. The donor had been lifted into the air on her back—crowd surfing—so they didn't have to crouch to feed. Lucien was starting to wish he'd brought his crossbow.

He glared at Polly. "How far are you planning to let them go? They're going to bleed her dry."

Polly waived her hand dismissively. "They know the rules. She knows her limits. This isn't her first performance."

"No doubt. She's reaching another one of her limits right now, from the sound of it."

Polly reached across the table to take Lucien's hand even as she refilled his drink. "This thing is really eating you up. I wish I could do something to help."

Lucien laughed. "Is that an offer?"

Polly smiled knowingly. "There's always a standing offer for you, baby." Her thumb rubbed against his palm, a suggestive stroke and press.

"You're doing the silent song tonight, I see."

Polly's smile didn't waver. "We've always been so very much in tune."

He could take solace in her as he had before, both of them knowing it was only solace. Knowing she had any number of lovers and didn't need him one bit. Instead, she wanted him. He couldn't help being flattered. Lucien let his thumb move along the webbing between her thumb and forefinger.

The sweet scent of violets wafted toward him through the smoky air. The same scent Theia's skin had as he'd pressed his lips to it.

"Lucien?"

He jumped at the sound of Theia's voice.

Lucien pulled his hand out of Polly's—a bit forcefully, because she resisted—and turned to look up, mortified. But it wasn't Theia. It was her more colorful twin. Rhea stared ice daggers into him with Theia's gray eyes. And the Viking stood behind her, arms folded and fists clenched like he was resisting punching Lucien in the face.

Rhea turned her ice daggers on Polly. "Who the hell is this?"

"This is Polly. She owns the—"

"Oh, I've heard of Polly. Polly the siren. Nice. Jerk." Rhea turned back to Lucien as Polly raised her eyebrows with amusement. "Theia's sobbing her eyes out trying to figure out what she did wrong, and it turns out it's because she's not some tarted-up sex siren."

Polly's eyes narrowed.

"Theia didn't do anything wrong."

Rhea's gaze shifted, fixed over his head at the stage. "Holy shit." She looked to Lucien once more, her gaze now more fire than ice. "Is this what you're into? Live sex shows? Theia totally dodged a bullet with you, asshole. Come on, Leo. Let's go."

"It's not a sex show," said Lucien. "They're…" What was the point in finishing that thought, though, really? He took a drink of his topped-off bourbon.

"They're drinking her blood," Polly offered helpfully. "I believe your erstwhile immortal friend here has seen a similar performance a time or two." Polly smiled at Leo. "Isn't that right?"

Leo's face turned bright red, and he ran his fingers through his untidy reddish-blond hair in a nervous gesture that was amusing given his usual demeanor.

Rhea glowered, looking up at him. "Leo?"

"A long time ago," he muttered. "With Faye."

Lucien snorted. He'd drunk just enough to be extremely incautious. "I've heard a few things about you and Faye." He could feel Leo's eyes on him without looking up.

Leo took a step closer to the table, the awkward moment having apparently passed. "Care to elaborate?"

"Talked to a few Valkyries," said Lucien. "To hear them tell it, you were something of a kept man." He picked up his drink again. He'd lost count of which number this was. "Kept on a leash."

The glass spun out of his hand so fast, it took Lucien a moment to realize Leo had knocked it from his grasp.

While Lucien was still contemplating the unexpected speed, Leo grabbed his collar in both fists and hauled him from his seat. "Why don't you say that to my face?"

Rhea shifted her feet, boots crossed at the ankle as she bit her lip. "Leo, let's just go. He's not worth it."

Lucien met Leo's eyes and smiled. "Kept. On. A. Leash."

"Oh, shit." He heard the words from Rhea before he found himself flat on his back on the table with Leo's fist in his face. He wasn't really feeling it. Which meant he'd had way more to drink than he wanted to admit.

He slithered out of Leo's grasp and hit the back of his head on the table as he dropped to the ground. That smarted a little. It would smart more tomorrow. Lucien scrambled up and dashed past Leo, heading for the door, but Leo caught him by the arm—the arm Lucien had forgotten to see the doctor about. He heard the snap before he felt the thick pop of the solidified ecto gel stretching and bending.

Leo let go of him, looking slightly nauseous. Rhea's eyes were wide, and even Polly looked a little green—notwithstanding the evening's wardrobe choice.

"What?" Lucien stared at them, swaying slightly. He wasn't sure if it was the blow to his head or the booze. And then he glanced down and saw his arm pointing the wrong way at the elbow. And a bone sticking out of it. And chartreuse gel oozing from it like an ectoplasmic emanation. Or putrefaction. He wasn't sure which one of those things made the blood rush out of his head before he dropped.

Head swimming, he was dimly aware of being carried off the floor to a back room while Polly spoke.

"I'd happily let him stay here for the night, but I have a business to run at the moment, and I think he needs medical attention." She seemed weirdly far away.

"Yeah, I'm sure you would be *thrilled* to." Rhea's voice, dripping with sarcasm. "Which is precisely why he's going with us."

"He's not our problem," Leo muttered under his breath.

"You *are* the one who knocked…*that*…out of his arm." Polly again. "Violence is strictly forbidden in the Grotto, as I'm sure you're aware. But I'm willing to overlook the infraction if you'll see that Lucien's taken care of. I suggest you call Lucy. No doubt she'll have experience with… whatever that is."

"I think she gave him some kind of shot the other night when it was broken," said Rhea. "Let's just call her, Leo. We can hand him over to her and be done with it. Her number's in his phone under Bitch."

Lucien giggled.

Someone was digging in his pockets. He'd left his phone at home so he wouldn't be tempted to check Theia's texts.

"It's not here," the Viking growled.

Lucien made a dismissive motion with his arm, trying to indicate that he didn't have the phone, but his arm evidently didn't quite do what it was supposed to, and everyone groaned.

He opened his eyes, focusing on Polly frowning down at him. "I'll get an Uber," he tried to say, but it didn't sound like that, either.

"Get Anubis?" Rhea glanced at Leo. "What is he talking about?"

Leo looked baffled. Lucien started to laugh. That's when he realized he was insanely drunk and that he was going to regret all of this, and he didn't care.

Rhea's disapproving expression made him laugh harder. "Okay, let's just get him outside. I'll call Theia. Maybe she has Lucy's number." For some reason, this made Lucien laugh even harder.

With a growl of disgust, Leo hauled Lucien off the couch he was lying on, one arm braced under Lucien's unbroken one. Polly showed them the back way out of her private suite into the alley, and Lucien stumbled along with Leo, giggling like an idiot.

Rhea walked ahead of them to the parking lot, her phone in her hand. "Thei? We have a bit of a situation here. Lucien's been injured. Again. Do you have Lucy's number? He doesn't have his phone on him." There was a brief pause. "Okay, well, you don't have to yell. And Leo didn't do it. I mean, he did, kind of, but it wasn't his fault."

A cheerful chirp and flash of taillights announced that they'd reached Rhea's little red car, and Leo opened the door and shoved Lucien into the back.

Rhea glanced inside dubiously while Lucien tried to fold his legs into it, half reclining. "He'd better not puke in Minnie Driver." She spoke into the phone again as she got behind the wheel. "Just give us his address, then. We'll drive him home and he can call Lucy himself." Rhea listened for a moment. "Oh, for God's sake. Fine. Then we're coming to you."

Someone was operating a jackhammer in the next room. Lucien groaned and tried to cover his ears, only to find his right arm screaming with pain like someone had stuck a knife through it.

"What. The. Fuck."

"Lucien?" The jackhammering came again. Except it probably wasn't a jackhammer but someone knocking on his door. "Are you awake?"

He rolled onto his side so he could cover one ear and press the other to the pillow. "No."

The door opened, and light flooded the room. Lucien moaned in protest.

"I brought you some extra-strength aspirin." It was Theia. He could smell violets. Though he supposed it could be Rhea. Except she wasn't swearing at him. It was Theia. "Figured you might want it. For a number of reasons."

Without opening his eyes, Lucien held out his hand, and Theia placed the pills in his palm. He swallowed them dry before realizing she was holding a glass of water. She set it beside him on the nightstand. His mouth felt like he'd been sucking on gauze. He was probably going to need to sit up and drink that. Eventually. Maybe when he was dead.

Theia was still hovering. "I didn't know if I should take you to the emergency room. I figured they wouldn't know what to make of that…stuff."

Lucien grunted, hoping it was an acceptable answer.

"Lucien, can you just talk to me for a minute? Like you give a damn that I'm here?"

Reluctantly, he opened one eye. And felt like the biggest

asshole alive. Theia's eyes were red and puffy, like she'd been crying for hours. Probably all night and then some.

"I'm sorry." It was the only thing he could think of to say. Because he was. Sorry to his bones. Sorry he wasn't strong enough to stand up to his father. Sorry that he knew what he knew about her—and that he'd let it define his actions. Sorry that he'd ever met her, because how was he ever going to be normal again without her?

"I tried to call you. I texted you a dozen times."

"I know."

"Acting like I don't exist so you don't have to deal with your decision to choose money over me is a shitty thing to do. Can you just tell me to my face that you don't want to see me?"

Lucien sat up, clutching the bed to try to keep it from spinning. "No, I can't."

"You can't tell me to my face."

"I don't want to." The look on her face made Lucien's heart hurt. Dammit, hearts were stupid. Even stupider than heads, which in his case was pretty damn stupid. *Shut up, heart. Shut up.* "I don't want to because I don't want it to be true. But it is."

The pained look in Theia's eyes turned hard. "Okay. Well, I'm glad we cleared that up. I'll call you a cab." She slammed the door before he could say anything else, and the reverberating echo, like rocks smashing together in his head, made it impossible.

After a moment, Lucien realized he was in the master bedroom, which had a bathroom attached. He rolled out of the bed and made his way to the toilet, bracing his left hand on the bed for balance. He had to use the left hand to aim, too, which was awkward.

As he made his way back through the bedroom, he paused with his hand on the doorknob. What was he going to say to her? What the hell was he going to do?

Reflected in the full-length mirror in front of him was a painting hanging over the bed: John Collier's *Lilith*—the redheaded nude with the secretive smile—in the embrace of the snake. Maybe it *was* his fate. Maybe he should stop running from it. Leo and Rafe Diamante and Dev Gideon seemed perfectly happy with their lot. Maybe he could embrace the devil inside him and everything would be okay.

And maybe hell was real, and he would find himself dragged down into it, unable to escape Madeleine Marchant's curse.

His arm throbbed, and his head was pounding. And his goddamn heart hurt. He opened the door, ready to tell Theia that he was an idiot, that he was prepared to defy his father's wishes, and he didn't care if he was penniless and hell-bound so long as he was with her.

Theia stood by the open front door at the end of the hallway. "Your cab is here. Hurry up. I don't want Puddleglum to get out."

Chapter 22

The cab pulled out onto the drive, and Theia let the edge of the curtain fall. She was done crying over Lucien. He could go to hell for all she cared.

Rhea had told her about Polly and how Lucien had been having no trouble at all getting over Theia. It hardened her resolve. Let the siren have him. Theia had been ignoring all the omens, all the warnings, all the dreams. Now she didn't have to, because fate had decided for her.

With Carter's help.

Theia frowned. It was past time to talk to Ione. There was something happening here that was bigger than having her heart stomped on. Might as well bite the bullet and do it face-to-face. She still had Ione's shawl from the reception to return.

Theia texted her sister to tell her she was coming by with the shawl and headed out.

Ione was in a considerably better mood than she'd been after the wedding. Which of course Theia was going to ruin by bringing up Carter again. After dropping off the shawl, she lingered in Ione's garden, trying to figure out how to broach the subject while Ione trimmed her roses, but, as usual, her big sister managed to be one step ahead of her.

"Rhea says you have a new job. When does it start?"

Theia sniffed a cluster of tea roses. "It fell through, actually."

"That's too bad." Ione deadheaded a limp rose with her pruning shears. "You and that Smok boy looked pretty good together."

Theia groaned into the rose petals. "Why do you always know everything before I tell you about it?"

Ione gave her a cryptic smile. "I have my witchy ways."

"Nice. You're doing magic divination about my love life. Who isn't?"

"Rhea, for one. She says you won't let her read your tattoos."

Theia stepped back from the rosebush with a glare. "She told you about Lucien."

"She was a little worried about you. I'm sorry it didn't work out."

"That's kind of what I came to talk to you about."

"Oh? I thought you came to bring back my shawl." Ione gave her that look again that said Theia was fighting a losing battle if she thought she could ever put one over on her big sister.

"I don't suppose Rhea mentioned anything about Lucien's hobby."

"She did say something about an archery incident."

"Did she happen to tell you that someone's been feeding Lucien information about us to get him to target Leo and Rafe and Dev?"

Ione scowled. "It's *him*, isn't it? That's what he was doing at the wedding. Letting us know he had us in his sights."

Theia inspected another rose before broaching the rest of it. "I talked to Lucien's sister yesterday and found out Carter has signed on as a silent partner with Smok International. Lucy says he has some kind of influence over her father—I'm betting you and I can guess how—and the whole thing has her worried."

"Lucy?"

"Lucien's sister. They're twins. She kind of hates me. But I think she hates Carter more."

With a sharp snip of her shears, Ione managed to deadhead a happily blooming rose. "What does he want with a pharmaceutical company?"

"It's more like parapharmacology. I can't really get into the specifics. I signed a nondisclosure agreement. But suffice it to say, there are…magical applications. The company also has a consulting arm that cleans up after magical accidents. They cleaned up your place."

"*My* place?"

"After you, uh, let Kur out that first time."

Ione blushed but shook her head. "That was Rafe's crew."

"The construction crew was Rafe's. The cleaners were contractors. From Smok."

Ione's eyes darkened. "Which Carter now owns part of."

"Which means he has a potential foot in the door of every magical household in the world."

"Lovely."

Theia stepped away from the roses. "I have to drive to Flagstaff, so I'd better get going. I just thought you should know."

Ione walked her to the garden gate, frown lines etched into her forehead.

Theia turned back after opening it. "By the way, congratulations, Mrs. Gideon." She winked and gave Ione a kiss on the cheek.

Ione's eyes widened before narrowing into a glare. "I told him not to tell you. And it's Ms. Carlisle, thank you very much. I'm not changing my name."

Theia grinned. "Of course you're not."

Lucien gritted his teeth as the doctor extracted the last of the gel.

Fran gave him a disapproving look from behind her rimless glasses. She'd been treating Lucien's mishaps for most of his life.

"You know this wouldn't be this painful if you'd just called me the day after it happened."

"Yes, I know. Yes, I'm an idiot. Yes, I deserve every ounce of pain I've got coming."

Fran glanced over the top of her lenses. "I wouldn't go quite that far. But it is going to be painful, unfortunately. And not just right now. It's not possible to restore the bone fully since you've let this gel degrade. I'm removing as much as I can, but you're likely to retain some residual gel in the joint, which will probably cause some chronic stiffness and inflammation."

"You mean I've managed to give myself arthritis before I even hit my midtwenties."

Fran shrugged apologetically. "That's about the size of it."

"Fantastic."

The doctor straightened, holding up the large syringe full of fluorescent gray-green sludge. "That should do it. As for the break, I think we can avoid a full cast and keep it immobilized with a splint. As long as you promise not to get into any more fights until it heals."

"Yeah, I think my fighting days may be over."

"I heard you're taking the helm at Smok. Congratulations. I never thought Edgar would retire. Certainly not this early." Fran glanced up as she adjusted the straps of the splint. "How does Lucy feel about all this?"

"I don't know. I haven't spoken to her."

"Do you think that's wise? I mean, she is still the CFO. Not to mention your sister."

"She'll get over it." Lucien's response was a bit terse, but it seemed a little inappropriate for Fran to comment on family business. He supposed she saw the two of them as almost like family of her own, having treated them since they were kids. And she was also his shrink.

Fran was quiet as she finished and packed up her bag, and Lucien felt like a jerk. It was becoming a familiar feeling.

"Thanks for making the house call." He lifted his arm gingerly. "It still hurts like hell, but honestly, it feels at least fifty percent better."

Fran's warm smile was back. "That's what Edgar pays me for." She studied him for a moment. "Have you been sleeping well? You look a little wan."

Lucien laughed. He was born wan.

"There's been a lot to get used to. And I drank more than I should have last night."

"If you need a prescription for a sleep aid, I can write one up." She took out a pen. "Or a refill on your antidepressants or antianxiety meds."

"Thanks, but I think I'm good."

After she'd gone, Lucien discovered a message waiting for him from Edgar. He was being summoned: a command performance with the board of directors to meet the new financial partner—none other than Carter Hamilton. Nothing like being thrown into the deep end with the sharks. The informal meeting with Edgar's inner circle the day before had been tedious enough. This was the part of the business he'd never wanted to inherit. Lucien was beginning to think he'd made a very bad bargain.

His first official appearance as CEO would be with his arm in a sling. Not exactly the picture of confidence he wanted to project. He was the last to arrive. Lucy sat at what was usually Edgar's right hand, but Edgar stood behind the chair at the head of the table, waiting to turn it over to Lucien. Lucy's expression was stoic. Not that stoicism was anything new for her. Edgar gave Lucien a big, pretentious smile. It was all for the benefit of the board. Lucien was sure Edgar had never smiled at him genuinely in his life.

After Edgar introduced him and the board politely applauded, Lucien took the CEO's seat while Edgar moved to a seat among the other members. To Lucien's left sat Carter Hamilton in the flesh, polished and overeager, like a slick, blond, high-end car salesman. He seemed innocuous enough, but something about him raised the hairs on the back of Lucien's neck. Maybe it was the overdone tan that put Lucien in mind of a grifter politician.

After the preliminary business was out of the way and niceties had been exchanged about Lucien's place in the firm, Edgar turned to Hamilton. "As you know, Carter Hanson Hamilton has thrown in his lot with the Smok enterprise. He'll be working closely with Lucy in restructuring our executive operations." Edgar paused and laughed. "I should say *your* executive operations. As of today, I'm officially stepping down from active participation in the company." Surprised glances were exchanged around the table. "Carter, would you like to say a few words?"

Unnecessarily, Carter pushed back his chair and got to his feet. "Thank you, Edgar. I'm thrilled to be a part of the Smok family. I see a new, even more prosperous tomorrow for Smok International, and I'm delighted to be able to work with the lovely Lucy Smok on making our plans come to fruition."

Lucy's mouth curved into a smile, but her eyes weren't participating.

As Carter spouted a few more lines of inane corporate babble and the board began to discuss the day's business, Lucien's mind wandered. What was he even doing here? He could be with Theia, curled up in bed and nursing his hangover. Instead, he was becoming his father, the last person he'd ever wanted to be.

The meeting was over before Lucien expected it, and he started guiltily, wondering if he'd actually fallen asleep with his eyes open. The board members were approaching him to shake his hand and apparently to try to cozy up to him with more corporate babble and flattery.

Carter was the last to greet him personally. Though the other members had casually taken Lucien's left hand without comment, Carter made a point of reaching for the right and stopping short.

"My apologies." He offered his own left hand instead. "Tennis accident?"

Lucien shook his hand, annoyed by the unnecessary firmness of Carter's grip and the way he pulled Lucien in toward him like an insecure ape trying to assert dominance. "Archery. It's a hobby." For some reason he felt the need to add, "Crossbow."

Carter was still gripping his hand. "Ah, are you a hunter, Mr. Smok?"

"Like I said, it's a hobby." Lucien pulled back on his arm, and Carter finally released him. Lucien resisted the urge to wipe his hand on his slacks.

"I'm more of a racquetball man myself. I have a court reserved every Wednesday at 10:00 a.m. on campus. Perhaps we could meet tomorrow and…" Carter glanced at Lucien's sling. "Oh, right. Sorry. Maybe another time when you're feeling up to it." Carter turned to Lucy, who was packing up her briefcase. "Lucy, why don't you meet me there tomorrow? It will give us a chance to discuss strategy."

Lucy paused and glanced up at Carter as if he'd just suggested joining him in a naked mud bath. "I have some other commitments, so I afraid I can't…" Her words trailed off, and she stared openmouthed as Carter turned and started talking to one of the other members of the board without listening to her response.

As the board members filtered out, Lucien turned to go, but Edgar tapped him on the shoulder.

"If you don't mind, Lucien, I have some details to go over with you. Can you stay a few minutes?"

Lucien glanced at Lucy, who was heading out the door. He couldn't remember the last time he'd been alone in a room with Edgar. He was a grown man, and the idea actually made his stomach churn with anxiety.

"Can it wait?"

Edgar's dark brows drew together in disapproval. "No, Lucien. It cannot wait. Have a seat."

Lucien returned to the table reluctantly, hesitating at the chair he'd been sitting in before. Deciding it would be a gesture of respect to leave it for Edgar, he took one on the side, leaving a gap between them.

But Edgar remained on his feet. "You may have some questions about the timing of my announcement. I've already spoken to Lucy about it, but I thought you should know." He clasped his hands behind his back and paced around the table.

"Know?"

"I'm sure you're aware that I've used Smok's patented medication for some years to supplement my youthfulness. It turns out that prolonged use has some rather unfortunate side effects. Not surprising ones, really, when it comes right down to it." Edgar stopped pacing and turned to face Lucien. "Quite simply, things are falling apart. Rapidly. Both body and mind. I was very lucky to run into Carter Hamilton recently. He's in remarkable health for his age, as it happens, and has never used a drug." He crossed to the window and looked out at the mountains, perfectly framed. "I'm not well, Lucien. But Carter is extraordinarily well. He's agreed to share the secret of his good health with me in exchange for majority interest in Smok's holdings."

Lucien had known Edgar was older than he looked. Even as a small child, he'd been aware that his father was quite a bit older than the parents of his peers, but it was never spoken of. Lucien and Lucy's mother hadn't been his father's first wife, but they were the only children Edgar had fathered. Lucien had always suspected it was why his mother had left after performing the job she'd presumably been recruited for—producing an heir. For all he knew, she'd been paid for it.

"Why step down as CEO?"

Edgar turned, his brow creased with annoyance. "What?"

"I understand making a bargain with Carter Hamilton for whatever his secret is, but once you've done that, why not continue to run the company?"

Edgar's expression was stiff. "That wasn't the bargain. The company is yours. Stop whining about it."

"I'm not whining. I'm just curious."

"You're trying to squirm out of your responsibilities as always. Don't think I didn't notice your lack of interest and participation in the meeting today. And I wasn't the only one who noticed. You can't rely on Lucy to do everything for you your entire life, Lucien. You're a man. Act like one."

Lucien's face burned. There was no retort he could make to any of that, because it was true.

"If there's nothing else…" He got to his feet, eager to be anywhere but here.

"There is, in fact, something else." Edgar's expression was grim. "We need to discuss the legacy bequeathed by Madeleine Marchant."

The name, as always, sent a chill down Lucien's spine. "So there is one, then."

"Of course there is one. Why on earth do you think I've been prolonging my life?"

Lucien had assumed it was the reason anyone would: fear of dying. "I hate to state the obvious."

"You think it's vanity? That I'm afraid of looking old?" Edgar shrugged. "I suppose there's some truth to that. Age means frailty, and I cannot afford frailty. But more than that, my continued longevity means that Madeleine's payment can be deferred. As Smoks, we deal in souls. Not the least of which are our own."

Lucien had a sinking feeling he understood. "You've bargained your soul."

"Not mine, Lucien. Yours."

Chapter 23

The pain in Lucien's arm intensified. "What do you mean, mine?"

"You know the story. Every seventh generation is required to serve in hell. I found a way to skip a generation—staying alive."

Lucien wasn't following. "But according to the family tree, yours is the sixth generation of Smoks since the last to serve."

Edgar shook his head. "I've let you believe I was far older than I am so that you could get used to the idea of being the one to bear the curse. I'm not the first Edgar Smok. That was my father. Nevertheless, my lifespan was extended well beyond the time that my service was to come due, so the duty passed to my offspring. I know it seems callous of me, but you must understand that it was a decision I made many years ago, long before you were born."

Lucien was the eighth generation. Edgar had cheated, selling Lucien out—selling Lucien's *soul*—to avoid the Smok fate.

Everything made sense now. His father's distance and coldness. Even the way Edgar had let Lucien get away with everything short of murder despite the gulf between them. It hadn't made sense that Edgar wouldn't be harder on him given the lack of warmth in their relationship. Lucien had pushed every boundary, trying to find out just how far he could go before Edgar would step in. But he'd only done so when Lucien had started seeing a Marchant descendant.

"You realize my staying alive also benefits you, Lucien."

y, when I tried to report for my first day of

an his hand through his hair. "Dammit. I'm so
ean, not about Lucy—although that, too—but
About all of this. It just happened so suddenly,
n't know what to do."

glanced at him. "And do you know what to do

nestly?" Lucien sighed, wishing he could give her
swer she deserved, but he hadn't yet worked it all out
head. There was still the issue of the Lilith blood. He
n't sure if that was separate from the legacy. He shook
head. "No. But I know that I hate not being with you."
Theia kept her eyes on the road. "Well, that's something,
guess. So where am I driving you? I assume you had a
ar in the parking lot."

Lucien shrugged. "I can get another one."

Theia laughed, though not humorously. "Wow. Your life
is something else."

"It is, isn't it? Where were you heading?"

"Me? I just finished my last final and was on my way
home. To my place, I mean. My apartment here in Flag-staff."

"I haven't seen your place."

Theia threw him an annoyed look, the point of her bob
swinging against her cheek with the quick movement of
her head. "Well, yeah. Shortest relationship ever. Even for
me." The word *relationship* made the little blip of hope at-tempt a comeback.

"There are some things I'd like to talk to you about."

"Things like Susie the siren?"

"Polly the—" Lucien stopped himself, reddening. "I'm
not seeing Polly. She's not a factor in this."

"And what would 'this' be?"

Lucien let out a choked laugh. "How the hell does it
benefit me?"

"Because this isn't a 'pay on receipt of services ren-dered' transaction. The bill only becomes payable upon
my death. So the longer I live, the longer you can go on
about your life. In that respect, we're both very lucky that
Carter Hamilton came along. The Smok family may lose a
little power, but a Smok will remain the public face of this
company. You're free to enjoy a long, full life." Edgar in-clined his head. "But only the span of an ordinary human
life. That was the deal. So you see, I can't prolong the in-evitable indefinitely. My time runs out when yours does.
And vice versa."

Lucien swiveled away from him. "And what happens,
exactly, when the bill comes due? Say I die an old man,
seventy years from now. Are you saying there won't be
any consequences until then? No physical effects from the
curse in our blood?"

"Do you see any in me?"

Lucien swiveled back reflexively at the question.

"For all intents and purposes, you are fully human, just
like the rest of the Smok family. The change comes, as I
understand it, once the soul is delivered—which occurs
without it having to leave the body. A sort of transmogri-fication."

"You're saying I'm going to turn into some sort of mon-ster on my deathbed and get sucked down into hell."

Edgar frowned. "You always see the worst in every-thing. I hardly think *monster* is the preferred term. As far
as I know, you won't look any different. You'll simply *be*
different. Most likely, youthfully restored. I expect you'll
look much as you do now."

"Only I'll be a demon reigning in hell."

Edgar had on one of those smiles again. "Better than
serving in heaven, as the saying goes."

"And yet you've spent decades making sure you never had to."

"Naturally, you make *me* out to be the monster. I've been the villain of your entire life. You have no idea of the sacrifices I've made for you. Am *still* making for you." Edgar waved his hand in the air in irritation, as if he couldn't articulate what he wanted to say. Perhaps his mind really was going. "That's enough. Go home."

Lucien had plenty to think about as he left the building. If Edgar was right about the terms of the Smok legacy, it could change everything. If shifting into something inhuman no longer loomed on the horizon, the threat of the loss of Smok Biotech was meaningless. What he had to consider was whether he could survive without the rest of what the Smok empire offered: power, money, a good life—everything he had access to now. He still had hopes of doing some good with that power, of changing how Smok operated and putting a stop to its complicity in allowing evil to prosper and proliferate. He was doubtful that anything would change with Lucy at the helm. She was too pragmatic.

There was also the fact that his fate, like Edgar's, was only postponed. But it was hard to see something that was so many years away as the looming threat he'd always feared. Would defying Edgar affect that eventuality in any way? Could he even trust anything his father said? After all, Edgar had sold Lucien's soul to the devil.

Having left the boardroom with an increasing feeling of hope, he was already cycling back toward pessimism and mistrust. Maybe he *should* have Fran give him some meds.

He was so deep in the vicious circle in his head when he reached the parking lot that he stepped off the curb without looking. A horn blared, wheels screeching, and Lucien found himself just centimeters away from the hood of a silver hybrid. Angry at himself, he directed the anger at

the car and slammed his ⌐
out the driver.

Through the windshield, ⌐
at him in disbelief. Both of the⌐
Theia's shocked expression turn⌐

She lowered the window and ⌐
you look where you're going?"

Lucien took his hand off the hood ⌐
the car, realizing how much better he fe⌐
at by Theia—having any interaction wi⌐
know. I think I'm probably an idiot." ⌐

"You got that right."

The driver of the car behind Theia honked a⌐

Theia glared. "Are you going to move or just s⌐
being an idiot?"

"Can I get in the car and be an idiot?"

Her mouth twitched, resisting a smile. "Depends on ⌐
idiotic you plan to be."

Lucien smiled. "I never plan. That's the genius of m⌐
idiocy."

The horn honked again, longer this time, to let them know the irked driver meant business and would honk again, by golly.

Theia's expression didn't change, but the lock on the passenger door of her car clicked open. Lucien wasted no time in taking her up on the tacit invitation.

He slipped in and closed the door. "Thanks for not running me down."

"It was touch-and-go there for a minute." Theia pulled out onto the main drive. "It's going to be awkward running into each other on campus like this. Although Lucy said she might fix that for me by making sure I got kicked out of my graduate program if I didn't leave you alone."

"She what? When did she say that?"

196

"Yesterda⌐
work."
Lucien ⌐
sorry. I m⌐
about me⌐
and I di⌐
Thei⌐
now?"
"H⌐
the ar⌐
in hi⌐
was⌐
his⌐

"This would be me trying to figure out some very complicated things about who I am. And who you are."

Theia glanced over again and nearly rammed the car in front of her as it stopped when the light changed. She hit the brakes forcefully. "Who *I* am?"

"The Lilith blood."

"I thought we'd already discussed that. I thought you were okay with it."

"That was based on the information I had at the time. I have more now."

"So you want me to drive you to my *home* so you can tell me what else you don't like about me in my own personal space. I don't think so."

Lucien reached for her hand on the steering wheel, and she flinched but didn't pull it away. He felt a million times stronger, a million times surer of himself, at the touch of her skin.

"I want to figure us out. If you'll give me a chance. I can't promise where the conversation will end up, but I think we deserve to have it. We don't have to go to your place, if it makes you uncomfortable, but I'd like to talk to you somewhere private. We could just sit in the car, I guess."

Theia went through the intersection. "I have gourmet doughnuts at home. I think we might need them."

What she'd dreamed about and feared, her worries about the dark prince—everything Lucien told her about the Smok legacy while she nervous-ate three artisanal doughnuts confirmed her suspicions that it was all coming to pass. He was the one. And fate had brought them together, as surely as it had Phoebe and Rafe, Ione and Dev, Rhea and Leo. She'd just kind of hoped her fate wasn't really going to be this dark.

Theia leaned her head against her fist with her elbow

propped on the back of the couch, trying to digest Lucien's words along with the doughnuts. "So according to your father, you won't descend to hell for sixty or seventy years."

"Barring some kind of accident or disease. It was the first time he spoke to me about any of this, and given his ulterior motive in staying alive as long as he can, I have no reason to disbelieve him."

"And Carter is going to help him do that."

"Apparently, he has some secret to the fountain of youth."

"Yeah, it's called feeding on the life energy of other people. How do you know he isn't planning to feed on yours?"

"That would be detrimental to Edgar's agenda. He's not going to do anything that would shorten my life." Lucien smiled ruefully. "For the first time, my father is actually rooting for me to succeed at something."

Theia returned the smile, but Carter's involvement was worrisome. He certainly wasn't doing anything out of the goodness of his heart. She was pretty sure he didn't have one. Maybe the secret to his longevity was that he'd had his heart removed and kept in a crypt somewhere, magically preserved—and magically preserving *him*.

"So what happens if you don't honor your father's wishes? Does that change things?"

Lucien breathed in deeply and exhaled. "I'm not sure. Given everything he told me, I don't see how it could. Except for one possible unintended consequence."

There was always an unintended consequence. "Which is?"

"It's the possibility that completely aside from Edgar's manipulation of the legacy, some other factor would trigger it." Lucien looked at her pointedly. "You."

"Me?" Before the protest was even out of her mouth, the connection became obvious. "You mean my blood."

"The theory is that it's what drew us together. That's why I tried to break it off with you so completely and so suddenly, without having the decency to tell you what was happening. I'm not proud to admit this, but I was scared. I was afraid that if I saw you again to tell you about Edgar's ultimatum, to try to explain to you that he'd forced my hand because of the anti-lycanthropy research, that you'd seduce me."

Theia couldn't help the surprised titter of laughter. "Seduce you? I've never seduced anyone in my life."

Lucien smiled. "But you have." He reached for her hand and wove their fingers together. "Everything about you seduces me every time I see you. You seduced me from all the way across the room that first moment at the reception."

"By choking on a grape."

Lucien shook his head, still smiling. "My God, woman. I've never seen anyone choke on a grape so seductively in my life."

Now she was laughing out loud. He stopped her with a kiss that, once again, took her breath away. Theia melted into him, moaning softly at the connection she'd somehow managed to convince herself wasn't real. It lent credence to the idea that it could be the influence of the demon strain in her blood, called home by Madeleine's curse—but if it was, more power to it. Something that felt this right couldn't be bad. Except…

Theia let out another moan, this time in frustration, and pushed herself away from the firm plane of his chest.

Lucien's strikingly pale eyes searched hers. "What's wrong?"

"I want this—you have no idea how much—"

"I think I have some idea." He dipped his head toward her.

She put her fingers against his lips as he tried to move in close again. "But I don't want to turn you into something you don't want to become." She shrugged helplessly and let her fingers fall.

Lucien's brow furrowed. "So now the thing we're afraid is drawing us together is going to be the thing that keeps us apart?"

"We have to think this through. We have to be sure about what we want."

"I don't want to think anymore. I'm tired of thinking. I want *you.*"

"But doesn't that back up your theory? You came over here conflicted, depressed, wanting to tell me why this wasn't going to work—" She stopped midsentence and glared at the insistent shake of his head. "I could tell that was what you were thinking, Lucien. Don't deny it. I could feel it."

Lucien let go of her hand and launched himself off the couch with a one-armed shove. "So now I'm just some stupid pawn who doesn't know his own mind. Is that what you're saying?"

"That's not what I'm saying at all. I just want us both to be clear about what we're doing, why we're doing it and whether we're prepared to accept what might happen." She fixed him with an unflinching gaze. "Are you?"

Lucien clenched his fist in the hair at his forehead. "How can I know that, Theia? How can anyone know they're not going to die tomorrow? What I know is that I feel like my guts have been ripped out when I'm not with you." He gave her a helpless little attempt at a smile. "I'm not prepared to go through life without my guts. Don't make me."

Theia rose and wrapped her arms around his neck, and Lucien unclenched his fist and slid his good arm around her waist. Their bodies fit together like a set. His feelings for her were powerful and real—so strong that she had to make a conscious effort to separate them from her own. This wasn't about blood for either of them.

"If it's what you want, Lucien…" She took a breath of certainty. "It's what I want."

He bent to kiss her again, but something vibrated between them.

Lucien laughed. "That's not a phone in my pocket, I'm just happy to see you." He retrieved the offending device. "Let me just turn off…"

Watching the swiftness with which Lucien's smile dropped away felt like stepping off the sea floor in the shallows into a bottomless drop.

She withdrew her arms. "What's wrong?"

"My father… Lucy found him unresponsive on the floor of the boardroom. He's in the hospital."

Chapter 24

Lucien was quiet as they drove to the hospital. Lucy was already there, hovering in the waiting room as they stepped off the elevator.

She threw Theia the side eye as she hugged her brother. "What's she doing here?"

"I was with her when you called."

"Well, that didn't take long. Did you walk straight out of the boardroom into her car?"

"Pretty much, yeah."

"Convenient, then, that Edgar's unconscious and can't disown you."

Lucien stepped back and held her at arm's length. "Watch yourself, Lucy. This has nothing to do with Theia."

"Then I repeat, *what* is she doing here?" Lucy jerked her arm out of Lucien's grasp as he started to answer. "It was a rhetorical question, asshole." She paced away from them, facing the doors to the ICU.

Theia spoke quietly to Lucien. "Do you want me to go?"

"No. No, please stay. I need you here." He took Theia's hand, and Lucy made a derisive noise as she glanced over. "How did this happen?" he asked her. "Do the doctors know anything?"

Lucy sighed and folded her arms but didn't turn. "They think he's had a stroke. They said he has an unusual amount of plaque buildup in his arteries for his age." She glanced at Lucien. "Of course, I didn't tell them…" Her voice trailed off as she eyed Theia once more.

"You can say whatever you want in front of Theia. She knows about everything."

Heat flashed in the pale blue of Lucy's eyes. "Oh, well, isn't that just *swell*, Lucien."

"Edgar said he talked to you about his health problems. All he told me was that his health was deteriorating rapidly, and the partnership with Carter Hamilton was going to give him the opportunity to remedy that. Do you know anything more?"

Lucy turned toward them, regarding Theia icily. "You really want to talk about this in front of her?"

"Yes. She has experience with Hamilton."

Lucy's expression was slightly less hostile as she acknowledged it. "I suppose that's true." She dropped onto one of the awkwardly upholstered hospital waiting room chairs. "He was supposed to give Edgar an amulet. I assumed he already had and that everything was settled."

"Was there an amulet on him?"

"No."

Lucien considered. "Edgar seemed a little off when I left him, like he was exhausted by talking to me. I had the impression that whatever Hamilton was going to do for him, he hadn't done it yet."

Lucy pinched the bridge of her nose. "Do you think we should contact him? I hate the idea. He gives me the creeps. But maybe he can still reverse whatever's happening."

Theia was tempted to answer, to tell them that where Carter was concerned, they should run—fast—in the opposite direction. But this was their father, not hers.

"The deal's already been struck," said Lucien. "He'd just be fulfilling his end of the bargain."

"That's kind of what I'm worried about." Lucy sighed, staring up at the ceiling. "I'm not positive, but I have a sneaking suspicion that Edgar offered Hamilton more than just a controlling interest in the company." She leveled her eyes on Lucien. "I think he promised him me."

"*What?*" Lucien dropped onto the chair next to her, letting go of Theia's hand. "What are you talking about?"

"I don't know that Edgar meant it in quite the mercenary way it sounds. But I believe he thought Hamilton and I would be an obvious match and that promising me to him was merely a formality, because I would see the wisdom in such a 'merger' myself." She rolled her eyes. "And would apparently find Hamilton irresistible."

Theia had to swallow hard against the urge to retch. Not an uncommon reaction around the subject of Carter Hamilton, but this time it seemed clear it was Lucy's reaction she was picking up on. She certainly couldn't blame her.

Lucien put his hand on his sister's shoulder. "Hamilton's not coming anywhere near you as long as I'm around."

Lucy let out a sort of wheezing sound that seemed to be a laugh. "That's really sweet of you, Lulu, but I'm a big girl. I think I can take care of myself." She gave him a wry smirk. "I know the Russian martial art of Systema."

"I'm serious. If this was part of the deal Edgar made, I'm not standing for it."

Lucy's smirk turned into a glare. "Lucien, take the out when it's offered to you. If you don't stop patronizing me, I'm going to punch you in the throat and they're going to have to check you into your own room."

Theia had to look away to hide a smile. She could imagine Rhea saying the same.

"The point is," said Lucy, "I don't think we have a choice. We're going to have to call Hamilton eventually. He owes Edgar, and if he's withholding what he owes, he may find himself on the receiving end of one of my throat punches himself."

The elevator opened behind Theia. As she turned to move out of the way, she found herself face-to-face with none other than Carter himself.

He smiled, showing his overly white, perfect teeth. "Ms.

Dawn. What a pleasant surprise. Though not an entirely unexpected one."

Theia sneered. "It's not mutual."

Lucien rose and came to stand between them. "Hamilton."

Carter offered his hand, but Lucien put his in his pocket. "Terrible news about Edgar. How are you holding up?"

"We're just waiting to hear from the doctor."

Lucy rose behind them. "We've already had some interesting news. My father's health is exceptionally deteriorated. I believe you and he had an arrangement for you to share the secret of your good health with him. Why wasn't that done?"

Carter moved past Lucien to take Lucy's hand in both of his. "I can only imagine how hard this must be for you. I did offer to share my health regimen with Edgar, but I fear he may be beyond a few protein shakes and a low-fat diet at this point."

Lucy yanked her hand from his grasp. "Cut the crap, Hamilton. You were supposed to give him an amulet to safeguard him against something like this. Where is it?"

Carter frowned, casting a glance at Theia. "Are we divulging the Smok secrets in front of outsiders now? Has she signed an NDA?"

"As a matter of fact, she has," said Lucy. "So you can answer any and all questions related to the business in front of her. I'll take full responsibility."

"Will you? What an interesting development." He reached into his inside suit pocket and pulled out a small square box. "As it happens, I do have the amulet. It isn't a magical cure, however. It would have been better for Edgar to have had it on him before this ischemic event befell him, but it may prolong his life. As to the quality of that life, I can't make any guarantees. There was a ritual involved that would have imbued Edgar with the strength of the magic behind the amulet. We were supposed to meet this evening, but life happens swiftly, doesn't it?"

He opened the box and lifted out a length of gold chain with what looked like a gemstone charm dangling from it—black sapphire—set in ivory. Only Theia was pretty damn sure it wasn't ivory. Carter had used the bones of his victims to make his charms when he'd attempted to steal Rafe's power. She shivered and hugged her elbows.

Lucy held out her hand, but Carter didn't offer the amulet. "I think we need to come to some kind of an understanding about what this is worth."

Lucy frowned. "What do you mean, what it's worth? You own a controlling interest in Smok International. That was the deal. That's what it's worth."

"This deal took several months of negotiation, and it involves a number of complex elements. If you haven't already reviewed your father's copy of the contract, I suggest you do so in short order." Several months. So he'd been wheeling and dealing from behind bars, knowing he had someone in the DA's office to make his entire conviction go away—and knowing when. "The upshot is that, as the controlling interest in the company, I do have certain rights. And certain privileges." He dangled the amulet in the light, admiring it. "And this particular bit of magic wasn't easy to come by. But you are correct in saying that it was a large part of the deal."

"Then give it to me, or I'm going to have to contact our lawyers. And trust me when I say they will be going over every line of that contract with a fine-tooth comb."

Carter gave Lucy a look of admiration. "I've heard you like to play hardball. I like that in a woman."

"I don't really care what you like in a woman."

After setting the amulet back inside the box and closing it, Carter held it out to her. "I look forward to sparring with you. Consider this a gesture of good faith."

Lucy took the box, but Lucien stepped in and put his hand over hers. "Are you sure you want to do this, Lu?"

"I told you, I can handle myself."

Lucien gave Carter a dismissive look. "Can I speak with my sister in private a moment, Mr. Hamilton?"

"Certainly. I'm sure Ms. Dawn and I have some catching up to do."

Theia stared him down. "No, I'm sure we don't."

Carter grinned, like some spray-tanned ghoul, and strolled away from them down the hall.

Lucien ignored him, intent on Lucy. "You can't give this to Edgar without reading the fine print in that contract."

"He needs it, Lucien. And, frankly, *you* need it. I'm not going to have Edgar dying on me and you following him." Her voice wavered, just the slightest bit, in what Theia was sure was a rare display of emotion toward her brother.

"But you heard him. The required ceremony hasn't been done. It's not going to restore him to health."

"But it will keep him alive. And right now, that's the best we can do."

That much turned out to be true. After Lucy found a nurse who promised to put it on Edgar when Lucy managed to work up some impressive tears, telling the nurse it was a religious symbol that she didn't want her father to die without, the doctor emerged with good news. Edgar had stabilized.

Lucy and Lucien were allowed to see him briefly, but only one visitor at a time. While Lucien went in, Theia sat awkwardly beside Lucy in the waiting area, keeping a wary eye on Carter, who, for the moment, was maintaining a respectful distance.

"So." Theia cleared her throat. "Are you planning to wipe my memory or have me kicked out of the university after this? Or both?"

Lucy exhaled, her head against the seatback and her

eyes closed. "I reserve the right to do either at a later date if you intend to interfere in any way with how Lucien runs the business."

"I have no intention of interfering."

"You've already interfered, Theia. Your entire existence is an interference." She opened her eyes. "Lucien said he told you everything. Does that include the things he's done in the name of business over the years? Neither of us are innocents."

"I have some idea."

"You have no idea. And I suppose he told you about his suicide attempts and the fact that he's on antidepressants."

"No, he didn't. But it's not like I've never taken antidepressants before. Who hasn't?"

"You're almost adorably naive." Lucy wasn't smiling. "Almost. The only thing Lucien has ever done with any enthusiasm—besides drink and screw an endless parade of women—is his special project at Smok Biotech. He may not need it now. Maybe Edgar will hang on, and everything will be hunky-dory. But ask yourself what he's going to do without his research to keep him focused. And without his outlet of hunting rogue creatures. It's not an inexpensive hobby. How long will it be before he begins to resent you for taking everything away from him?"

Theia smoothed her hand along the seat's upholstery, studying the seams. "Are you saying that even with your father incapacitated, Lucien will be cut off if he continues to see me?" Lucy's momentary silence made her glance up.

"You are really something. I'm sitting here in the hospital with my father's life hanging by a thread, and you're conniving how to benefit from his misfortune."

Theia blushed, realizing that was exactly how it sounded. "I'm sorry. That's not what I meant. Of course I hope he recovers fully." She would have said more, but Lucien returned, looking grim.

He bent to give Lucy a kiss on the cheek, which seemed to alarm her.

"What's wrong?"

"He's stable, but he's barely there. He can't communicate. He doesn't respond when I speak to him—he just stares vacantly. If he survives, he's going to need around-the-clock home care."

Lucy's expression matched his. "And the amulet will keep him like that."

"Until I die, presumably."

She swore and shoved herself out of her chair, heading straight for Carter at the other end of the waiting area. "This is exactly how you planned it, isn't it?"

Carter remained seated, smiling up at her calmly. "How's that?"

"You never intended to keep up your end of the deal. You held on to that amulet until Edgar's body gave out on him, until all it would do was keep him alive as a living poppet."

"I think you're letting your emotions get the best of you, my dear. Totally understandable under the circumstances. But it might do you some good to go home and get some rest."

The tension in Lucy's body was clear even from where Theia was sitting. Lucy was holding back a well-deserved ass kicking with everything she had. Theia couldn't help rooting for her to fail in her endeavor to resist the impulse.

Lucy stared down at him, jaw clenched. "If anyone should go home, Hamilton, it's you. If you know what's good for you, you will get up and walk out of here right now before I do something I'll regret."

Carter rose with leisurely grace. "I can see that you're upset, so I'll give you and Lucien some privacy. And some time to decide how to proceed with Edgar's health care. Just let me know if there's anything I can do to help."

After nodding to Lucien and Theia on his way to the

elevator, he turned around to observe Lucien while waiting for it to arrive. "You look a little run-down, Lucien. You might want to take extra care with your archery. I assume it's also how you came by that fading black eye." He glanced at Theia, deliberately holding her gaze though he was still talking to Lucien. "You'll need all your strength for your other…pastimes. In my experience, the Carlisle women are absolute wildcats in bed."

The elevator opened before Theia could think of a snappy retort to put him in his place, and Carter stepped inside and faced them for one last parting shot. "But of course, you wouldn't know that yet, would you, Lucien? You've fallen for the delicate unspoiled fruit. Let me know how it goes if you manage to pierce that delectable untouched skin. Absolutely anything could happen."

Theia's face blazed, and Lucien launched himself toward the elevator with a snarl, but the doors closed in his face.

After giving Theia a disbelieving look, Lucy broke the awkward silence that followed. "If she's a virgin, what the hell did I walk in on the other day?"

Lucien turned to give her a sardonic, James Spader smirk, his eyebrows raised suggestively. "Creative chastity."

As Theia drove back to her place later, Lucien pushed the point of her bob behind her ear, letting his fingers linger at her nape. "Thank you for coming with me tonight. And for putting up with that odious piece of garbage."

Theia shrugged. "He doesn't bother me. His game is intimidation and trying to make everyone around him feel inferior. He's what would happen if an internet troll stepped out of the comments section into your living room. He deserves exactly the same consideration."

Lucien smiled at the thought of an in-person block button. "You know I'm not bothered about you being a virgin, either. I'm not concerned with…"

"Piercing my tender flesh? Being the first to pluck my delectable flower?" She gave him a quick sideways grin.

Lucien laughed. "Jesus. That guy. Who talks like that?"

"I was going to say a Neanderthal. But that would be an insult to Neanderthals." Theia slowed at the turn toward her apartment. "Rhea's going to look in on Puddleglum for me, so I was planning on staying in Flagstaff tonight. But would you rather be alone? Do you want me to drive you home?"

Lucien shook his head. "I most emphatically would not rather be alone. Lucy says she'll call me if anything changes, but the doctors don't expect it to. And for obvious reasons, neither do I."

Theia glanced at him. "Did you and Lucy talk about what you're going to do? I mean, are you…"

"Going to let my father live out the entire span of my life being spoon-fed pureed meat from a blender and wearing a diaper?" Lucien sighed. "I wish I knew the answer to that. It was his bargain to make. He sold his soul as surely as he sold mine. I have every right to live a full life before I pay the bill he racked up. I just wish that felt better to say than it does."

They climbed into bed with little fanfare, Theia in her underwear and a T-shirt and Lucien in his boxers, planning only to sleep. The splint and sling would make anything else difficult anyway. And making out didn't seem quite right with Edgar in the condition he was in. Although if Edgar remained in that state indefinitely, Lucien would have to get past that.

Despite their plans, Lucien couldn't help kissing her good-night, and the kiss turned into more. Not a lot more—he could tell she shared his apprehension about what might happen if they went any further—but he was content with moving slowly with Theia. Something he'd never considered in his life. He'd been other women's first—or other girls', anyway, in high school—but looking back, he was fairly sure he hadn't exactly been a great first experience. He wanted to do this right with Theia. Especially if it turned out to be the only time they could be together. If he was going to turn into some inhuman creature and join the seven-headed beast of the apocalypse afterward, he was damn well going to make it good for both of them.

He lay awake after she'd fallen asleep, his head too loud to find stillness, and got up to go to the bathroom after an aborted attempt to quiet it.

As he washed up by the glow of the electrical switch that served as a built-in night-light, Lucien glanced in the mirror over the sink. The shadows made his face look odd. Was his hairline receding? Laughing at himself for being paranoid, he switched on the light, but his laughter died as his eyes adjusted to the brightness. Two small, bony protrusions were erupting beside his widow's peak. Lucien touched the top of his head and confirmed his worst fear. He was growing horns.

Chapter 25

His hand, as he pushed back his hair to see closer, felt stiff and awkward. His fingers were hard to uncurl, as if he were an old man with severe arthritis. He brought his hand down in front of him. The fingernails were lengthening as he watched—long and curved and pointed. He was growing claws. He could feel it in the hand in the sling. As he nudged the fabric off his arm, his shoulders ached, and he rolled them back—and saw another protrusion at his shoulder blade. Lucien ran his fingers over the growth. It was leathery, and it was expanding.

Panic started to set in, and Lucien sat on the edge of the tub trying to breathe. There was a prototype of the anti-transformative at the lab. But how the hell was he going to get there? He couldn't risk calling a car and having something happen while he was in it that couldn't be undone. Maybe he could take Theia's car. He could slip out while she was sleeping, get to the lab and shut this whole process down in less than twenty minutes. The dosage hadn't been perfected yet, but they'd been successful in reversing the shift in the animals they'd bred for the lab. It was almost ready for human trials, and there was no time like the present.

But it was becoming quickly apparent that he was running *out* of time. He needed a thumbprint to get into the refrigerated case where the serum was stored, and his thumb was turning scaly. Maybe the retinal scan bypass would work. He rose and saw his reflection in the mirror. His eyes looked wrong. They were still the same pale blue, but the pupil was a vertical slit. The horns positioned above them were small but obvious. And from behind his back, a pair of leathery, webbed wings in brilliant blue were unfurling.

A loud crash woke Theia from a dream about the Carter-cockatrice gloating at Edgar Smok's bedside. Theia rolled over to see if Lucien had heard the noise, but he wasn't in bed. Across the hall, light was visible under the closed bathroom door. Maybe he'd dropped something.

"Lucien? Are you okay?" When she didn't get an answer, she threw off the covers and hurried to the door. "Lucien?" It was locked, and only silence emanated from behind it. Theia rattled the doorknob. "Lucien, answer me. Are you all right?"

Lucy's words came back to her. *And I suppose he told you about his suicide attempts.*

"Lucien!" Glancing around for something heavy, she spied the stone doorstop behind the front door and ran to grab it. With a few sharp blows, she'd broken the doorknob, latch and all.

Theia expected to find Lucien collapsed on the floor. Instead, the room was empty. A light breeze blew the thin window curtain inward through an empty frame above the bathtub, fragments of one of the sliding panes scattered in the tub. Theia scrambled onto the edge of the tub and looked out. There was nowhere he could have gone. They were on the fifth floor. The parking lot below them was undisturbed.

Lucien's clothes were still in her bedroom. So was his phone.

He was still using the same password, thank goodness. She selected Lucy's number, but the call rolled to voice mail after a single ring. Why would Lucy decline a call from her brother with their father in intensive care?

A moment later, a text message came through with the answer.

Sorry, Lulu, I'm exhausted. Edgar's condition hasn't changed. I've gone home to get some rest. Consider this permission to bone your girlfriend.

Theia quickly responded.

This is Theia. Lucien's disappeared. I'm worried.

She waited several minutes, but there was no indication that Lucy had read the message. Maybe she'd turned off her phone. After leaving a more detailed text about what had happened, Theia checked the contacts. Lucy's address at a luxury resort in Sedona was listed. Hopefully she didn't have more than one place she was staying.

After throwing on jeans and sandals, Theia took a quick walk around the complex before getting into her car to see if there was any sign of Lucien, but she found nothing. She drove by the lab first—where of course she couldn't get in—and checked the hospital, both in the ICU and at admissions to see if Lucien or a John Doe had been brought in. Nothing.

It was four thirty in the morning when she arrived at Lucy's resort. The room number was a villa with a private entrance. Theia expected her to ignore her knocking, so she kept at it until at last she heard movement inside.

"Lucy?" She shouted against the door as she continued pounding. "It's Theia. Lucien's missing. Open the door."

"Maybe he's just sick of you" came the reply from the other side.

"Can you just open up?"

"It's four thirty in the morning, Theia."

"And I'm going to stand out here pounding on your door until you open it, so you might as well get it over with before I wake the adjoining villas."

There was silence for a moment followed by the clunk

of a dead bolt. The door opened, and Lucy peered through the crack, the security latch stretched across the gap, her face in shadow.

Theia squinted into the darkness. "I replied to your text."

"Yeah, I saw it."

"Aren't you the least bit concerned? Lucien went out a five-story window in his boxers without leaving so much as a broken twig at the bottom where he ought to have landed."

"Maybe he just climbed down. He's always been a good climber."

Theia sighed. "Lucy, you obviously know something. Is he here? Is he having some kind of a breakdown?"

"No, he's not here. I don't know where he is. But I wouldn't be surprised if he's having a breakdown. I'm considering one myself."

"Did you get some news about your father? I went by the hospital to see if Lucien was there. They said Edgar was sleeping and hadn't had any visitors."

"Edgar isn't sleeping. He's in a catatonic state. He will probably never sleep again—or do anything else—thanks to Hamilton and his amulet. And apparently we were all wrong about what that means."

"Wrong how? What do you mean?"

Lucy leaned her forehead against the door frame and sighed before unhooking the security latch and stepping back to hold the door open.

When Theia entered, Lucy went to sit on the couch. The lights were off, but the pale predawn glow through the sheer curtain illuminated Lucy's features. Her usual neatly styled hair looked tousled above her braid. Of course, she'd just been woken up at four thirty in the morning.

Theia sat on the edge of the chair opposite her. "So what did you find out?"

Lucy chewed on a cuticle. "You'll appreciate this. You're into genetics. Lucien and I are monozygotic twins, like you and Rhea. We're identical, not fraternal. But apparently, our original fertilized egg had an extra X chromosome, and when our tiny little blastocyst split, Lucien took the Y chromosome with him. Hence, identical twins but different sexes."

It was unusual but not unheard-of. "Makes sense. You two do have an extraordinary resemblance."

"The upshot," said Lucy, "is that it turns out we're both cursed by dear old Madeleine Marchant. And the amulet, it seems, has the effect of rendering Edgar effectively dead as far as the curse is concerned. So, lucky us, it kicked in early this morning."

"What do you mean, *it kicked in*?"

Lucy stretched her arm along the back of the couch to switch on the lamp beside her. In the glare of the compact fluorescent bulb, her pupils contracted. Into vertical slits. And what Theia had taken for tousled hair was the result of two small but distinct garnet-colored horns. It looked like a clever Halloween costume—novelty contact lenses and carefully applied spirit gum under latex horns. But Theia had seen enough magical transformation to know it wasn't.

"Yeah," Lucy agreed to words Theia hadn't said. "Kinda leaves ya speechless, doesn't it? Of course, my first reaction was a bit more audible. And I demolished my bathroom mirror." She held up her bloodied knuckles. "My martial arts training took over, and I tried to kill the mirror demon, but it punched me back."

"Shit."

"Yeah, that was the next thing I said. Plus a few other choice expletives."

"And this just happened to Lucien, too. In my bathroom."

"It would seem so."

"Did he come here?"

"No. I haven't heard from him, except a phone call I ignored because I was freaking out. But I guess that was you."

"Yeah." Theia pushed her hair out of her eyes, as if it would make Lucy's appearance go back to normal. "But how did he manage to crawl out my bathroom window and disappear from the fifth floor?"

Lucy sighed and stood. "I imagine with the help of these." A pair of ruby-red webbed wings unfolded at her back, extending from her shoulders at least three feet in either direction, bony segments between the webs terminating in black claws. "Ruined one of my favorite shirts. I'm not pleased."

"Well, this is—wow." Theia shook her head. "Lucien and I were afraid that if we—if I—if we consummated the relationship, it might trigger the transformation. Carter Hamilton intimated as much."

"And did you?"

"No. Now I'm starting to feel pretty stupid about that."

Lucy retracted her wings and sat back on the couch. "If it's not too personal—oh, hell, of course it's personal, but I don't really give a damn. Is there a reason you're still a virgin at age…"

Theia swallowed. "Twenty-two. For a while I thought it was because I was unfuckable." She dismissed the notion with a shrug. "But really, it was my dreams. My visions. I kept seeing an alliance with a dark prince, and it scared me, so I kept pushing guys away."

Lucy laughed. "And then your dark prince comes along and you miss your window of opportunity."

"I like to think the window's still open. I mean—you don't think he flew…to the underworld?"

"To hell? Well, *I* didn't. But maybe he's still the one who has to pay the soul price. He did grab that Y chromosome in the zygote lottery. Who knows? I have a feeling, though, that this isn't the final transformation."

"You think…"

"I expect the full dragon experience is yet to come."

"What about Smok Biotech's research? Lucien said the lycanthropy suppressant was months away from clinical trials, but maybe it could inhibit your trigger."

"My trigger? And what do you suppose triggered this? Obviously, it was Edgar's collapse. I think it's a little late for suppressing genes."

"That's not what it does. I mean, obviously, much of the research was geared toward isolating the gene responsible for the shift and finding a way to shut it off. But what Lucien was working toward was developing a drug to manage lycanthropy. Like you'd manage diabetes."

"Turning into a dragon is not diabetes."

"No, but it's a condition that can be managed, and a response to a trigger that can be suppressed. Like inhibiting serotonin or norepinephrine reuptake in antidepressants. We just have to pinpoint the right neurotransmitter."

"God, no wonder Lucien's into you. You sound like a biology textbook. I'm pretty sure he jerked off to those as a kid."

"My point is that there may be a simple fix to this. But we have to find Lucien. Do you have any idea where he would go with no clothes and no wallet?"

Lucy shrugged. "I don't know. Maybe to Polly?" Lucy seemed almost apologetic, as if she cared whether the idea was hurtful to Theia. "That's where he's always gone in the past when he's been in trouble. Sometimes she gives people sanctuary at the Grotto. And she has contacts who could hide him. We've used them for safe houses. She doesn't like to divulge her list, but she'll hook people up with what they need. For a price."

There was always a price.

Rhea and Leo were asleep in Phoebe's room when Theia stopped by to grab some clothes. And Leo, apparently, slept in the nude. Well, they both did, but Theia had seen Rhea naked plenty. Facedown on the bed with his arm across Rhea protectively, Leo displayed a nice little half-moon above the sheets. Theia took a picture for trotting out later to mess with Rhea.

After tiptoeing to the dresser and sliding open the drawers as quietly as she could, Theia turned around with a pair of Phoebe's capris and a clean T-shirt to find she'd disturbed Rhea anyway.

Rhea rubbed her eye with a fist, looking crabby. "What time is it? What are you doing here?"

"I'll tell you when you wake up. Go back to sleep."

Puddleglum appeared and jumped onto the pillow above Rhea's head to announce that it was time for breakfast. Whoever slept in Phoebe's bed, apparently, was the designated server.

Rhea sighed and slid out from under Leo's arm. "I'm up, you philistine."

With her eyes half-open, Rhea fed Puddleglum while Theia brewed a pot of coffee.

Rhea shuffled to the breakfast bar and slouched onto a stool, yawning. "How's Lucien? What's the word on his dad?"

"That…is a complicated story."

"Of course it is."

"You can go back to bed."

"Shut up. Just tell me."

"Edgar is in a vegetative state. Probably thanks to Carter Hamilton. And Lucien…took off."

"Took off?"

The coffeemaker beeped, and Theia waited until she'd poured them each a cup. "He went into the bathroom in the middle of the night, apparently developed secondary dragon characteristics and flew out the window."

Rhea nearly choked on her coffee. "You pulled an Ione,

didn't you? You screwed his brains out and turned him into a dragon. You little minx."

"No, I didn't."

"Of course you did. Just own it."

"I *didn't.*"

"Come *on.* What makes you think it wasn't you?"

"Because I haven't had sex with him."

Rhea nearly snorted coffee through her nose. "Right. Because you're saving yourself for marriage." Her mocking grin faded slightly as she took in the serious expression on Theia's face. "You… Theia… You've *had* sex before."

Theia didn't respond. Which was response enough.

Rhea set her mug on the bar with a bang, sloshing coffee over the top, her mouth hanging open. "You've never had sex and you never told me?" Her shocked expression turned to aggravation. "I can't believe you don't tell me things. Our whole lives, I thought we were open books to each other. We shared everything. Who *are* you?"

The equilibrium Theia strove to maintain, like an internal level that kept her on an even keel, not buffeted by the stress of other people's confusing emotions or intrusive visions, suddenly snapped.

"Do you realize that I've never had anything private, never kept a secret—from any of you—for most of my life? Everybody always assumed that whatever you did, I did, like I wasn't a whole person, I was just half of a twin set. I never needed to act up. I'd get in trouble in school—and at home—for things you'd done. People never asked my opinion on anything, just filled in what they thought I was thinking. Thought I'd like whatever you liked. I always got birthday and Christmas presents in your favorite colors, books and video games that were on your wish list. Doesn't that bother you? Didn't it ever drive you crazy when people acted like we were interchangeable?"

Rhea, for once in her life, was at a loss for words. "I…

got you in trouble on purpose, stupid. Because you were Miss Perfect. And now I find out I was living with a creepy pod person the whole time."

"Very funny."

"That's me. The hilarious one. See? People know that about me. We're totally different. No one thinks you're funny at all."

Theia growled and threw her hands in the air, dropping onto the stool beside Rhea to drink her coffee in resignation.

"Sorry." Rhea nudged her with her elbow. "It never bothered me because I was always trying to live up to your image. When people thought I was you, it made me look good." She took a sip of her coffee and muttered into it, "I *may* have given certain people the impression that you were a total slut in high school, though."

"Nice."

"So what are you going to do about Lucien? Do you want me to send Leo after him?"

"What is he, a bloodhound?"

"No, I just figured…" Rhea considered for a moment. "No, I guess he can't just automatically find magical people. He hunts down murderers and oath breakers."

Theia swallowed a sip of coffee. "I'm going to go talk to Polly."

Rhea swiveled on her stool to stare at her. "Are you sure that's a good idea?"

"You think I can't handle talking to his ex? You talked to Faye plenty of times, if I recall correctly."

"Polly didn't seem like that much of an ex the other night. And Faye's different." Rhea lowered her head over her mug. "We have an arrangement."

Theia paused with her cup halfway to her mouth. "*Have* an arrangement? What arrangement? I thought she released him from his bond when you broke the Norns' curse."

"She did. She just…sometimes we…the three of us get together and…"

Theia had tried to take another sip of coffee, and she nearly choked on it. "Oh. My. God."

Rhea sneaked a glance from the corner of one eye, a mischievous grin on her face. "You're such a prude. *Virgin.*"

"I am *not* a prude. I just don't… I thought you said you were just experimenting in college."

"You, of all people, should know how experiments go. You have to do it multiple times to see if you can duplicate the results."

"Wow." This was a whole new side to Rhea she'd never suspected. Apparently, Theia wasn't the only one with secrets. "Regardless, that is *not* happening with Polly. I don't need to conduct any research on that subject."

Rhea shook her head. "That's a shame. I mean, a *siren,* come on."

Theia concentrated on her coffee. "So, anyway, I'm going to go talk to her and see if Lucien sought sanctuary with her or maybe is hiding out someplace she knows about. Lucy says Polly keeps lists of information on people in the magical community."

"Well, that doesn't sound at all shifty."

"She also exacts a price for information, so I'm not sure what that's going to be."

"I can think of one."

"Enough with the threesomes, you perv."

"You just assume I was talking about a threesome."

"Weren't you?"

Rhea grinned. "Well, yeah, but it's rude to assume." She got up to refill her coffee. "In all seriousness, though, I don't trust this siren chick. Who knows what she's going to want? If she's going to be offering Faustian bargains, you're going to need backup."

"I don't think she deals in souls. Lucy would have said so—that's her thing, after all."

"I suppose there's that. But I'm going with you."

Theia sighed. "If we both go, she'll want a payment from you, too. She's not going to hand out information to whomever I happen to bring along."

Rhea set the pot on the warmer. "I'll stay in the car, and you can signal with a text if you need help."

"*No.* Will you just let me do this myself, please? Now I'm sorry I told you."

Rhea took a sip of coffee, looking sullen. "Keeping secrets, being all virginal, doing things by yourself—you are the worst twin. I want a new one."

"Oh my God. You pain in the ass."

Rhea smiled. "That means I'm going."

"Fine. You're going. But you *are* staying in the car."

"Cool. We'll take Minnie."

Theia hadn't considered the fact that she was going to face Lucien's super-hot ex-girlfriend when she'd chosen the navy capris and white T-shirt. She felt awkward as she got out of the car in the parking lot of Polly's Grotto. For that matter, what if no one was here at this hour? It wasn't like Polly actually lived in the club. Was it?

The door was locked. Theia stood in front of the entrance, trying to decide what to do. Should she knock? Maybe she should call Lucy and find out what the protocol was. Or maybe she should stop being a baby and suck it up and try the door.

Before she could psych herself up, one of the doors opened on its own. Polly probably had a camera on it. No turning back now.

Theia took a deep breath and went inside. The door swung shut behind her.

Chapter 26

As her eyes adjusted to the dim interior, she realized the place wasn't empty. A woman with long platinum-white hair that clearly wasn't white with age was seated in a semi-circular booth between two unearthly pale young men on one side—who seemed to be a couple—and someone Theia could only describe as a human tiger on the other. The naked tiger-man growled.

"Now, now, Giorgio. Don't be rude." The white-haired woman stroked his fur. "Polly's is open to everyone who finds their way in. Particularly tasty little demon-blood girls." She extended her hand toward Theia. "Don't be shy. Giorgio won't bite. Without my permission. And Raul and Rocco only bite boys."

Theia approached the booth, feeling decidedly under-dressed. Polly was draped in a white silk gown that looked like it belonged to some femme fatale from the 1940s, designed to show off her curves.

Theia reached over Raul and Rocco, who were paying her no mind—and appeared to be giving each other hickeys, though Theia suspected they were sharing blood—and took Polly's hand to shake it, but Polly simply held hers with her fingertips, looking Theia up and down. "I'm Theia Dawn—"

Polly stopped her. "I know all about you, sweetheart. Even if I hadn't already met your twin—who's waiting in the parking lot to come to your rescue should I turn out to have an appetite for human flesh—I make it my business to know about everyone who matters. What I don't know is what you're doing here. If you've come to make a fuss over Lucien, I'm afraid you're wasting your time. I offered him my bed, knowing he wasn't getting his needs met with you—no offense—but he refused."

Theia wasn't quite sure what to say to that, but she breathed a little sigh of relief. "Nice to know I matter, anyway."

"You and your sisters have more power than you think. So long as that power doesn't threaten mine, you matter, but you're of little consequence to me. Now what is it that's brought you into my cozy grotto?"

Theia wanted to remove her hand from Polly's, but yanking it away seemed rude. "I'm generally a good judge of whether someone's lying to me or not, so I'm going to assume from your question that Lucien isn't here."

Polly's frosty-white eyebrows rose. "And why would he be here? Don't tell me you've lost him?"

"I think you know how I lost him."

"If you mean his transformation, yes, I am aware. But not because he's been here. What made you think he would be?"

Her fingers were really beginning to feel awkward in Polly's grasp. "I was told he might come to you for sanctuary."

"Sanctuary." Polly smiled, amused. "Lucien would never need to take sanctuary with me, though I would certainly give it if he asked." Her smile turned mischievous, and her eyes literally twinkled. "One must always ask the right question if one is to receive the right answer."

So they were playing word games. She supposed it made sense.

"Do you know where Lucien is?"

Polly's expression gave nothing away. "I do not." She'd answered in the negative, but Theia had the impression that there was more to it than the simple reply. And she was still holding Theia's hand.

"Do you know of anyone who does?"

"I know of someone who may have the answer." Now they were getting somewhere. Maybe.

"Will you tell me who that someone might be?"

The siren curled her fingers around Theia's and drew her closer across the table. "What's the answer worth to you?"

"What do you usually charge?"

Giorgio roared, and Theia jerked back on her arm and nearly fell sideways into the laps of Raul and Rocco when Polly didn't let go. But Giorgio, it seemed, was laughing.

"I don't *charge*. I merely expect. It's a courtesy. I see Lucien hasn't explained how I operate, so let me make it easier. I like shiny, pretty things." She held up her other wrist, a charm bracelet sparkling with gemstones of various shapes and sizes.

Theia bit her lip. "I don't think I have anything shiny."

"Oh, sure you do. Lots of shiny things. Everyone does. I once had a choker made of irises."

Theia thought she meant the flowers, but after a significant glance from Polly's glittering eyes, the meaning became clear. Her own widened. No way in hell was she giving this nutjob an eye.

Polly laughed. "Those were from desperate men, as I'm sure you can imagine. People generally pay what they're willing to give up. From you, I think…" She studied Theia intently, as if trying to decide, though it was clear she had something in mind from the start. "Yes, a drop of blood would make a lovely trinket."

This was starting to bring to mind monkeys' paws and Faustian bargains. "Where would the drop of blood be taken from?"

Polly laughed. "Smart girl. Just a finger prick. Nothing life threatening and no need to maim anything. You'll barely feel it."

"And what are you going to do with it?"

Polly's expression turned unfriendly. "That's a very rude question. Do you ask everyone you give a gift to what they're going to do with your gift?"

This wasn't exactly a gift. It was more like extortion. But Theia knew better than to say so out loud.

"Let me put it another way, then. Will this 'gift' give you any power to harm me?"

"Oh, you *are* a smart girl." Polly's affable smile was back. "No. It won't affect you in the least. It will simply be my trinket to do with as I please, when I please." She took a pin from her gown—which certainly didn't look as if it were holding any pins—and drew Theia's index finger toward her. "Are we agreed?"

"This is the only price you're requiring? No hidden follow-up or extras?"

"Nothing at all." Polly placed the pin against Theia's finger.

"And you'll tell me who knows where Lucien is?"

"I'll tell you the name of someone who *may* know. That's the best I can do. Not knowing where he is myself, I can't speak in certainties. I can only give you likelihoods."

This was starting to seem like a bad deal, but the pin had pricked her finger before Theia could back out of it.

Polly touched the drop of blood, transferring it from Theia's fingertip to her own, and released her. "Marvelous. I think I'll have to wear this one on its own. It's much too nice to be crowded by a bunch of ordinary charms." The red drop solidified on her finger into a sparkling, faceted gem. Polly tucked it away into her cleavage and glanced over Theia's head toward the door. "Your vivacious twin is getting anxious."

The door swung open in the same leisurely fashion as before, and Rhea, facing the parking lot, whirled around. She took a step inside, peering into the darkness.

"I'm over here, Rhe. You didn't have to come after me. I'm fine."

"You've been in here forever."

Polly laughed. "If she'd been in here forever, you'd have perished long ago."

Theia sucked at the still-bleeding finger and pressed it to her thumb to stop the blood. "The name, please?"

"Of course," said Polly. "Lucy Smok."

Theia blinked at her. "Is this some kind of joke?"

"Not at all."

"You don't think I'd thought of that? That Lucy wasn't the first person I went to?"

"It's hardly my fault you didn't specify whom you'd already spoken to. You asked me who would be most likely to know where Lucien is. And that is Lucy."

Theia wanted to strangle her. "Lucy is the one who told me to come see you. That's why I'm here."

Polly shrugged. "That's unfortunate. You might have led with that. Nevertheless, Lucy Smok is the most likely person to be able tell you where Lucien is. If she chooses not to, that's her business."

Rhea marched toward the booth. "People like you love to play games of semantics. Come on, Thei, you're wasting your time with her." She grabbed Theia's hand and turned her toward the door.

"People like me?" Polly's voice hinted that Rhea had gone too far, and Theia tried to pull her toward the exit without saying anything else, but Rhea paused and turned around.

"You immortals. Like the Norns. Creatures above it all who like to mess with mortals, making sketchy deals where everything's fine print."

"Forget it, Rhea. Come on." Theia tugged her toward the door, afraid it might close on them at any moment and lock them in.

"For your information," said Polly as they reached the exit, "I do *not* make sketchy deals. I provide information honestly."

"Oh, really?" Rhea shook Theia's hand off her arm. "My sister asked you a simple question, and you gave her a bullshit answer because it fit the semantics of the question. That's not my definition of honesty."

"Your sister seems to have a pretty good grasp of semantics, and she considered her question carefully. Do you think you could do better?"

"*Rhea.*" Theia shook her head, but once someone pissed Rhea off, there was no dissuading her.

"In the interest of *honesty*," said Polly, "Theia has already asked me directly if I know where Lucien is, and the answer is no. But if you have another question, I may have another answer."

"And what did Theia give you for it?"

Polly took the gemstone from her cleavage and held it up in the light. "A drop of blood. Isn't it pretty? I wouldn't mind a matching set. They would make lovely earrings."

Rhea glanced at Theia. "You gave her your blood?"

"It was just a drop. A finger prick. She swore it wouldn't give her any power over me or cause me any harm. What she said rang true."

"Fine." Rhea stepped forward, holding out her finger.

"Rhea, don't. She's just playing with us."

"I have a question," Rhea said stubbornly.

Polly smiled, producing her pin from nothing once more. "Ask first. Present your gift after."

"Are you working with Carter Hamilton to harm my family or Lucien's family?"

Damn. Rhea was good at this. It hadn't even occurred to Theia that Polly might be in cahoots with Carter. But it ought to have. She was the one who'd hooked Lucien up with his anonymous source.

Polly seemed to be trying to formulate an answer. Rhea had definitely hit on something.

Rhea folded her arms. "Are you going to answer the question or not?"

"It's not a simple question."

"I think it's a very simple question. Yes or no?"

"I would never do anything to harm Lucien." Polly threw a pointed look at Theia. "Or anyone he cares about."

"But you *are* working with Carter."

"I *work* with no one. I provide information. Carter Hamilton bartered with me for certain information that he was free to do with as he pleased. But if he's used that information to harm Lucien…" Polly frowned. "I would be extremely unhappy with him."

"Well, he has." Theia returned to the booth. "He made a deal with Edgar to become a silent partner of Smok International, promising Edgar an extended life. And then withheld what he'd promised until giving it to him would only prolong Edgar's suffering."

"Mr. Hamilton isn't known for his scruples, but Edgar did make the deal. Though I don't see how he's harmed Lucien."

"You don't see how? Because Edgar is in this limbo state between living and dying—this state that Carter drove him to deliberately—Lucien is transforming into a demon. You probably know Lucien better than anyone. How can you not see that as harm to him? He's been afraid of this happening his entire life. And if I can't find him, he'll probably end up in hell. If he isn't there already."

"And you have some magical means of keeping him out of hell?"

"No, I don't," Theia admitted. "But if anyone can, I would think it would be a direct descendant of Madeleine Marchant. And I intend to do everything in my power to find a way."

Polly studied her. "Being an inhuman creature isn't the worst fate. As you and your sisters have discovered, there are strengths in having unnatural blood. Lucien has always feared his power—trying to deny it, trying to run from it. I think that's a mistake. But if this transformation has been forced on him early and Mr. Hamilton is responsible, he's forfeited any remaining good will he may have had with me. I did, in fact, put him in touch with Lucien. I now regret that. At the time, I thought it would cheer Lucien up to have some new targets."

"Targets like my boyfriend," said Rhea.

"Another thing Mr. Hamilton misled me about. I wasn't aware that Leo Ström had been made mortal. I was led to believe that despite having been released from his mistress, he was still a Hunt wraith."

Rhea uncrossed her arms. "So let me get this straight. People come to you for information because you've got the goods on all things supernatural, and in the past week or so, you've let this one narcissistic, two-bit necromancer give you easily debunked information and use you to bring harm to someone who apparently means a great deal to you. Do I have that right?"

Theia cringed as Polly's glittering eyes began to smolder. Beside her, the tiger-man growled low in his throat, and they'd finally gotten the attention of the lovebird vamps. Raul and Rocco slid out of the booth without being asked, stepping back and giving Polly a wide berth as she emerged from it.

She came to stand face-to-face with Rhea, who, to her credit, didn't flinch. "Are you maligning my reputation?"

"I think you're doing a pretty good job of that all by yourself."

Theia put her arm out in front of Rhea as if to stop a physical fight. "Carter Hamilton is an expert at telling people what they want to hear. He's done his best to ruin more than one excellent reputation in this town. Just ask my sister Ione."

Polly narrowed her eyes at Theia. "And just what does that have to do with me?"

"You might consider that he's deliberately undermining your reputation for his own gain as part of his larger plan."

"What larger plan?"

"He envies everyone's power. He wants it all for himself."

Polly's expression softened slightly, and she laughed. "You think he has his eye on my little grotto?"

"And your good name. They go hand in hand, don't they?"

The siren's expression hardened again. "He's in for a big surprise if he thinks he can unseat me." Without warning, she grabbed Rhea's hand and stabbed her finger—to Rhea's squeal of surprise—taking her drop of blood. "You've gotten your answer. Time for you little witches to go."

Theia turned Rhea around and hurried her to the door before she could get them in any worse trouble. She suspected it was only the finger in Rhea's mouth that kept her from running it.

Polly spoke once more before they reached the exit. "Ask Lucy where Lucien would go if he didn't want to be found via electronic means."

Theia paused and looked over her shoulder.

"Electronic," Polly repeated.

Theia nodded. "Thanks."

Chapter 27

Rhea held her pricked finger off the steering wheel as she drove toward Phoebe's place. "What was that about 'electronic means'?"

"I think she meant somewhere without cell phone service or Wi-Fi."

Rhea's shoulders rippled in a little shudder. "Sounds like hell to me. Do you know someplace like that with meaning for Lucien?"

"No, but I think Lucy must." Theia glanced at Rhea's profile. "Thanks, Moonpie."

"Oh, God. I'm Moonpie again. What did I do now?"

"I think you riled her up to the point that she was mad enough to actually give me some helpful information."

Rhea grinned and gave her a sidelong glance. "By the way, did you see how riled up 'kitty' was? And I do mean *up*."

Theia groaned. "I'm never going to be able to look at Puddleglum the same way again."

Rhea couldn't stop giggling about "Bad Kitty" on the drive back to Phoebe's. She climbed into bed with Leo when they arrived, and Theia put in her ear buds to drown out any embarrassing noise that might ensue and dragged out Rafael Sr.'s archives, carefully rereading everything. She'd missed any hint of a curse the first time, so maybe she wasn't looking in the right place.

She combed through deeds and bills of sale in French, in which she was far from fluent but could get the gist of. Lists that looked like maybe instructions for household staffs and bills of lading—things she would have been fascinated by at any other time—and finally stumbled upon something promising after several hours of eyestrain: the declaration of Madeleine's guilt, attested to by Philippe Smok, Vicomte de Briançon.

Seeing the words on paper made her shiver. This was Madeleine's denouncement by her own employer, who, by Lucien's account, had done it for personal gain. It made it seem a great deal more real, even if she couldn't read much of it. Theia stroked her fingers over the ancient ink. At the bottom of the page was what she thought at first was a smudge. But on closer inspection, she was convinced it was the symbol of the black moon—the mark of Lilith.

She stroked the ink of her tattoo—one she'd gotten because of a dream. She'd thought it would protect Rhea from the danger the dream had foretold if she had the tattoo she'd seen on Rhea on her skin instead. Of course, Rhea had already tattooed herself with the symbol. And the dream had actually been about Leo and not danger at all. Trying to outsmart her dreams was a fool's errand.

Theia looked back carefully through some of the daily minutiae she'd skimmed over. Had she seen the symbol on something else? Sure enough, there it was on what she'd taken for a bill of lading—with what looked like a partial signature at the bottom that could have been "Madeleine." Were these Madeleine's own words?

The antiquated syntax was difficult to understand. Time for her translator app, even if it would only give her an imperfect understanding of it.

Painstakingly, Theia typed in one line at a time and copied the translations into her notepad. It seemed to be an exhortation of some kind. Theia pieced it together and came up with an approximation.

Mind what you have wrought. Seven daughters born and seven lost. The great lady will birth them again anon. And from every seven born and gone among your house will the Devil reap a son.

It was the curse Madeleine had spoken against the house of Smok.

After Lucy ignored her call and texts, Theia returned to the villa.

This time Lucy opened the door promptly and sighed. "What now? I haven't heard from him. I would have told you if I had."

Theia wasn't so sure about that. "I spoke to Polly. She didn't have any information except to tell me to talk to you and ask you where Lucien would go to avoid electronic communication."

Lucy squinted at her, obviously sensitive to the light. "Electronic?"

"Someplace off the grid. Is there somewhere you went when you were kids that might have special meaning for him? Somewhere he'd feel safe?"

"Around here?" Lucy reached up to scratch her head but stopped with a grimace as she evidently remembered what was making it itch. "We didn't spend much time around here when we were children. Although..."

"Although what?"

"There was this one time when Lucien said he was going to run away from home. Edgar was mad at him about something. I think it was right after our grandmother died. The family doctor had been at the funeral, and Lucien snuck into the back of her car. She was going to some vacation home she owned, and he ended up at her cabin. When she realized she had a stowaway, she let him stay for a day or two before she drove him back. Lucien never told Edgar where he'd been, and Fran didn't give him away. Lucien only told me about it later."

It sounded promising.

"Do you know where it is?"

"I don't, but I can get the address from Dr. Delano." Lucy was already dialing. "Hi, Fran. No new developments. I just wondered—this is going to sound like an odd question, but do you have the address of that place you used to have in the White Mountains?" Lucy listened for a moment. "You do? That would be great, thanks." She ended the call and glanced at Theia. "She still owns it. She's texting the address to my phone." Lucy forwarded it to Theia when it came through. "Seems like a long shot, but here you go."

"Thanks." Theia paused. "Do you want to come with me?"

Lucy laughed and partially unfurled her wings. "I don't think so. Not until I figure out what to do about all this myself. Lucien may have the right idea."

It was just an hour before sunset by the time Theia reached the turnoff for Heber-Overgaard, but among the towering pines lining the two-lane highway that wound up into the mountains through logging country, it was already dusk. She was stuck behind a logging truck on the gradual incline, and it was nearly dark when she found the gravel road that led to the lakeside cabin. It was slow going after that, and Theia was starting to get the creeps driving so deep into the woods. Maybe she should have waited until morning.

But just as she was seriously considering finding somewhere to turn the car around, the headlights illuminated a log cabin in a small clearing—although "log cabin" seemed too rustic a name for it. It looked like a stately old homestead, as though someone had traveled west, stopped here before reaching the other side of the mountains and let the trees grow up around them until the place had been forgotten.

Theia stopped in the ruts of an old parking spot overgrown with weeds and got out, using the flashlight app on her phone to approach the cabin. Every horror movie cliché ran through her head. Why in the world had she driven here alone? She checked the cell signal. She'd definitely entered a dead zone.

There were no lights on inside the cabin. Theia tried the door and found it unlocked. She took a deep breath and opened it. The cabin smelled long unoccupied.

"Lucien?" Her voice came out in a raspy whisper, like she was trying to shout in a dream. The eerie feeling that maybe this *was* one of her dreams came over her. She cleared her throat and tried again. "Lucien, are you here?"

Something moved in the darkness. Theia pointed the light toward the sound, but whatever it was moved swiftly out of the beam. What if Lucien wasn't here and she'd startled some wild animal? Or an ax-wielding maniac? Just as she was about to call out again, the figure in the dark spoke, and the rough whisper made the hairs on her arms stand on end.

"Why did you come?"

"Lucien?"

"Not anymore." He squinted against the beam of light as she turned it on him, and she caught the flash of something bright blue before he rushed her and snatched the phone from her hand and shut it off. He was standing just inches in front of her now, and all she could see was the preternatural glow of his eyes. "You shouldn't have come."

"You shouldn't have run off without telling me what happened."

"Should I have come back to bed and touched you like this?" A claw stroked her cheek, and Theia jumped. "You see? I disgust you."

"No, you don't, you idiot. You're just scaring the crap

out of me by hiding in the dark in a cabin in the woods and acting like you're an ax murderer."

"You should be scared."

She was beginning to adjust to the darkness. His dim shape in the shadows just looked like Lucien. Except for the wings peeking out over the tops of his shoulders, slowly rising and falling with his breath.

"Who are you, Jeff Goldblum? Stop being dramatic."

"*The Fly.* It's a good analogy. I'm not Lucien anymore. I'm like Seth Brundle becoming the fly—Brundlefly." He paused. "*Smokdragon.* Has a nice ring to it. Actually, 'Smok' means dragon in Polish." He seemed to be getting his sense of humor back.

"Except the Brundlefly was a monster. You're not."

"Give me a few days." He stroked her with his claw again, running it down her arm, but this time she was prepared and didn't flinch. She might, in fact, have gotten a little aroused. "How did you find me?"

"I asked Lucy. She didn't have any idea where you'd go at first, but then I…went to see Polly, and she told me to ask the right question."

Lucien's eyes narrowed. "You went to Polly? What did you give her?"

"A drop of blood."

"Theia." He shook his head. "God, I wish you hadn't done that."

"She promised she wouldn't use it to hurt me, and I can read people pretty well. Their emotions give themselves away when they're lying. She was telling the truth."

"Of course she won't use it to hurt you. Because now you'll never be able to hurt *her.* Any harm that comes to her will be felt by you and all her gammon. You'll come to her aid. That's how she protects herself. It's why she surrounds herself with those creatures. They all belong to her gam."

"Her…what? Her gam?"

"It's what they call a pod of whales or dolphins. A gam. From gammon. That's what Polly likes to call the ones who give her 'trinkets.'"

"Are you one of these…gammon?"

In the dark, she could just see the sadness in his smile. "Of course I am."

And Rhea had given the siren a trinket, too. It was something Theia would have to worry about later. Right now she was more concerned with Lucien.

"So what are you planning on doing, hiding in the woods and living off squirrels?"

"I was thinking possum. More meat." His smile was less sad and more amused. "But as it turns out, Fran has a propane-powered freezer full of meat, and the pantry is fully stocked." Lucien stroked her arm again, seemingly unaware he was doing it. "If you're hungry, I can whip something up."

Theia's stomach growled to announce that apparently she was.

"I'll take that as a yes." His hand slipped down to hers, but he seemed to remember himself as she intertwined her fingers with his, and he let go with a jolt. "As you see, I won't be making anything complicated, but I think I can handle a spoon and a pot." He turned and moved swiftly through the darkness into the kitchenette, as though he no longer needed light to see.

Theia followed, feeling for furniture and banging her knees on the corners of things along the way.

She rubbed her arms as she watched Lucien fill a pot with water and light the burner under it on the stove. "So there's gas at least. No electricity?"

"There is, but it's shut off when the place is empty, I guess. Sorry. Luckily all the appliances use propane." He glanced at her after taking a box of couscous down from the shelf. "Are you cold?"

"A little bit, yeah."

He shook his head. "My senses are all out of whack. Maybe I can light a fire later." He slipped off the robe he was wearing and held it out for her. "Go ahead, take it. My core temperature is higher now."

Theia put on the robe. Though it had been snug on Lucien, it fit her well enough, but she had to roll up the sleeves. He was wearing nothing but his boxers, which made for a nice view of his abs as he stirred the spices into the water. It also gave her an excellent view of his brilliant blue wings when he turned around.

Lucien caught her staring. "Freakish, aren't they?"

"That's not the word I was thinking of."

"Oh? What would you call them?"

Theia smiled. "They're kind of sexy, actually. Lovely color."

Lucien laughed sharply. "Right. So sexy. Just like the scales on my fingers and the horns on my head."

"I don't mind."

"How are you going to feel when I get further and further from human?"

"How do you know you will?"

"It's how the curse works."

"I'm not sure you know how the curse works. Have you read it?"

Lucien stopped stirring and stared at her. "Have I *read* it?"

"Because I have. Rafe's father's archives on the Covent—they're magical. Every single item that's been tagged and inventoried over the centuries can be conjured up from its listing."

"And you *saw* Madeleine Marchant's curse? In writing?"

"I held it in my hands and touched the ink."

Lucien whistled. "So what does it say? Will the gates of hell open and swallow me up?"

"Well, that's the thing. It's not so specific about details. It's more…poetic. I think she meant for your ancestors to spend years trying to work it out until the first son was transformed."

The water had started to boil, and Lucien turned back to the stove to put the couscous in. "So it's useless, in other words."

"Not if we can figure out what the words mean. I saved the whole thing on my phone. We can take a look and try to decipher it."

"Theia, there's no magic cure. The drug Smok Biotech is working on might have done something to prevent this, but it's too late. It's happening." He put the lid on the pot and turned off the heat to let the grain absorb the water. "If you want to do something useful with your phone, set the timer for five minutes. Forget Madeleine's stupid poetry."

She decided not to push it and let the subject drop.

When it was ready, Lucien dished up the couscous and served it with a bottle of water. "Sorry. I may have misled you about my culinary skills. There *is* plenty of food in the freezer, but this is actually all I know how to make, to be honest."

Theia laughed. "It's fine with me."

They took their meal into the great room, and Lucien set about trying to figure out how to light a fire in the fireplace while Theia sat on the couch to eat. Lighting fires, it seemed, wasn't part of his skill set, either, and after the fifth or sixth match failed to do anything but incinerate the balled-up newspaper he'd tucked into the logs, he bellowed in frustration. Surprising both of them, his outburst expelled a blast of blue flame—luckily aimed right at the firewood. In an instant, they had a cozy blaze.

Lucien straightened and grabbed the bottle of water he'd given Theia and drained it. "That was…" He shrugged after a moment. "Weird."

"Did it hurt?"

"No, but it dried out my throat. I feel like I've been in a stadium all night screaming." He did sound a bit gravelly. Which only added to his allure. He sat beside Theia. "I forgot to ask you how Lucy was handling things. She and Edgar have always been—well, *closer* isn't the right word, because Edgar doesn't really do close, but let's say less acrimonious than Edgar and I."

"She's handling it about as well as you'd expect. I mean, she didn't run off and hide in the woods, but she's staying close to home."

"Why would Lucy want to hide?"

Theia paused with a forkful of couscous. "You don't know? I thought maybe you two had a magical twin connection, and you could feel it. But I guess you're a little preoccupied with what you're feeling."

"Feel what? What happened?"

"You're not the only one who was struck with the curse. Lucy assumes it's because you both shared an egg."

Lucien was stunned. "She's shifting? She's…" He indicated his horns and claws. "Like this?"

Theia nodded, eating the bite of couscous. "Pretty much exactly like that. Not so much with the claws but the horns and the wings. Only her color is red."

"It never even crossed my mind that something could happen to Lucy." Lucien tried to brush his hand through his hair and cursed as his claws hit his horns. "So I guess it's a package deal. Edgar sold both our souls, and he didn't even know it. I suppose we'll both end up in hell."

"Unless we can work out what Madeleine's curse means and see if there's any way around it."

Lucien frowned, contemplating his food. "I know you mean well, but I really wish you'd drop it. I've spent the last twenty-four hours trying to come to terms with the fact that this is actually happening to me. I don't want to think about magical cures or spend my time chasing false hope." He met her eyes. "I'd pretty much resigned myself to never seeing you again. And then you show up here. And I can't pretend I'm unhappy about that fact. As much as I dread losing my humanity and becoming something even more grotesque—and as horrified as I am at the prospect of you witnessing it—all I want now is to spend the time I have left with you. Just being with you. Not fighting this."

Theia set her bowl on the steamer trunk that served as a coffee table and reached for Lucien's hand. He hesitated, claws tightly clenched inside his fist, but finally relented.

"And I'm here for that. I won't bring it up again." Which didn't mean she wouldn't keep pondering Madeleine's secrets. She just wouldn't mention it.

Lucien leaned toward her and kissed her chastely, but Theia *wasn't* here for that. She'd had enough of chastity.

She moved her other hand to Lucien's neck, thumb against the rough stubble at his jawline, and kept him from pulling away as she deepened the kiss. He wasn't difficult to persuade. He also tasted of mint. Theia laughed softly against his lips, and Lucien drew back slightly, a puzzled smile on his face.

"What's funny?"

"You brushed your teeth before I got here. You heard me coming, and you brushed your teeth."

He smiled, a hint of color to his cheeks that wasn't reflected firelight. "Maybe I just like clean teeth."

Theia shrugged off the borrowed robe. "Be quiet," she murmured and climbed over his lap, knees balanced on the couch cushions. The fabric of the long skirt of Phoebe's she'd changed into before heading out stretched to accommodate the position, but Lucien pushed the hem up higher, his hands against her thighs, abandoning self-consciousness.

The luminescent blue of his eyes was almost white.

"You're bossy tonight."

Theia rested her forearms on his shoulders. "No, I'm not. I just know what I want."

"And what would that be?"

"To stop wondering what it would be like for you to fuck me."

Chapter 28

The unexpected bluntness of that word on her tongue, so matter-of-fact, so sensually charged, sent a buzz of electric energy through him, straight to his groin. He hadn't considered that she'd want this. Not now. Not when he looked like *this*. But the delivery of that little word had certainly said otherwise. And her eyes said she wanted him completely.

He hadn't realized his hands had kept sliding, gliding up along the smooth plane of her skin beneath the skirt. His thumbs brushed lace. Cautiously, he let his claws slip beneath the elastic at the crease of her thighs to see how she'd react.

A little gasp escaped her. Not shock. Arousal. She rose slightly so his hands could encircle her hips.

Lucien pulled her closer, settling her more firmly in his lap, where she couldn't miss the hardness of his erection inside the cotton boxers. Theia rocked into him. He could feel the damp heat between her thighs. He moved his hands from her hips and brought them up to her waist beneath the T-shirt.

"Do you want these hands on you?" His voice was rough with desire. "When they're like this?"

In answer, Theia pulled the T-shirt over her head and moved his hands up higher. "They're your hands. Why wouldn't I?" She hooked her arms around his neck and kissed him, and Lucien forgot about his hands and his horns and his wings.

Kissing Theia, as always, was like happily drowning. Tasting her, drinking her in, forgetting to breathe, her soft moans vibrating against his tongue like they were coming

from him. He stroked his palms across the hard peaks of
her nipples through the bra, careful not to snag his claws in
the lace, and her little noises became more insistent in his
mouth. He tried to unhook the bra anyway and got himself
caught, but before he could ruin the moment with anger at
himself, she reached back and unhooked it for him, tear-
ing the lace away from his claw to slip the garment off.

Cock straining against his boxers at the touch of her
skin, he moved his hands back to her breasts. Perfect and
petite—he could cover them entirely in each hand. But
he didn't want them covered. Lucien withdrew his mouth
from hers, ignoring her moan of protest, and brought her
up higher on her knees, dipping his head to circle one taut
nipple with his tongue to the accompaniment of her increas-
ingly melodic sighs of pleasure until she let out a breathless squeal as he sucked the nipple into his mouth. He loved
making her breathless.

She returned the favor with a sudden dip of her hand into
the opening of his boxers to encircle his cock. The damp
nipple slipped from his mouth as he let out a soft groan.

"Are we really doing this?" he breathed against her.

"Of course we're doing it."

It dawned on him that all he'd brought with him to
the cabin were the boxers, taking wing in a panic as he'd
thrown himself out her bathroom window, somehow thinking he might land on the ground. He'd soared high, ex-
hilarated even as he was horrified, not knowing where he
was going until he'd reached the pine forests of the White
Mountains and remembered Fran's cabin.

"Theia." The word came out part groan of desire, part
lament. "I don't have any condoms."

To his surprise, she just laughed. "Don't worry. I bought
some on the way here."

Lucien's eyes widened, and he stifled another groan as

she stroked his cock. "You came up here looking for me, knowing what you'd find…and you brought condoms?"

A sexy, self-confident shrug rippled downward from her shoulders with a little motion that jiggled her breasts. Here she was, sitting in his lap, skirt pushed up to her waist, topless, his cock in her hand, and she was nonchalant about the fact that she'd come prepared to lose her virginity to him despite the fact that he was becoming a monster.

He couldn't help but laugh, delighted and amazed by her. If he lost his humanity in the morning, at least he'd have this one ordinary, extraordinary night with her.

Lucien tucked her hair behind her ears with a stroke of the claws on his index fingers. "God, I love you." The last word caught in his throat as he realized he'd said it out loud. He drew back, mortified. "Sorry, I meant—"

"Lucien." Theia put her hands on his shoulders and held his gaze. "It's okay. Don't panic. I love you, too."

He kissed her to avoid looking her in the eye any longer. He'd never said those words to anyone. He'd been in love with Polly once, his first real love, but he'd known better than to tip his hand by saying so. Polly didn't do exclusivity, and she sure as hell didn't do love. And now he'd just blurted it out to Theia like an amateur.

And she loved him back. At least tonight.

Lucien slid her off his lap and scooped her up in his arms to carry her to the large sheepskin rug in front of the fire. "Where are the condoms?"

"In my bag on the front seat of my car."

"Be right back."

He dashed outside and found the bag, digging through it to find the box so he wouldn't have to fumble for one when he got back inside. With his prize in hand, he headed back into the cabin to find Theia casually naked and lying on her belly, ankles crossed in the air behind her.

Oh, what the hell. Why not say it again?

Lucien grinned. "Have I mentioned that I love you?"

"I think you may have, yes." She swung her feet and recrossed them.

"Good. Just checking. I might have to say it a few more times." He stripped off his boxers, and Theia watched with an approving eye. "You still want to do this?"

Theia laughed. "If you don't get down here and fuck me instead of asking me that question repeatedly, I'm going to start getting mad."

He dropped to his knees beside her and felt his wings partially unfold, tipping back to balance his new center of gravity.

Theia followed the motion with her eyes, and Lucien cringed, but she looked curious. "Can I see them? All the way?"

"Right now?"

"Will it affect…anything else?"

Lucien laughed. "I think I can maintain two opposing states." He rolled his shoulders and unfolded the new bones he hadn't had the day before, letting the wings extend to their full width.

Theia rose onto her knees to face him. "Can I touch?"

Lucien nodded, and she reached up to stroke the top edges of each wing, fingers following the curve of the bone as far as she could. It was a curious, energizing sensation, a new erogenous zone, making his abs tighten and his erection stand up even straighter. When she let go, instead of sinking back onto the carpet, Theia lowered her hips to sit on her heels and took hold of his cock. While he balanced on his knees with his infernal wings stretched wide, Theia took him into her mouth.

Lucien stroked a claw lightly along her shoulder, tracing the curve of her spine to the dip before her pert bottom, trying to breathe steadily and keep it together, but the touch drew a voluptuous moan from Theia that nearly made him lose it.

He grabbed her by the hair a bit abruptly and pulled back, inspiring a less sensual sound of protest from her as she let go.

"Sorry." Lucien softened his grip and brushed her hair back into place with a sheepish grin. He folded his wings behind his back and lowered himself to the carpet, drawing her with him, his mouth against her throat. "If you want me to fuck you, darling, we're going to have to slow down." It was the sort of thing he might have said a week ago—in an entirely different tone—to keep her at arm's length, like a verbal talisman to ward off emotion he couldn't handle. But this time the word *darling* was a little prayer of devotion.

He rolled her onto her back and kissed her mouth, making sure she'd heard it the way he meant it, before moving down to the hollow of her throat, her collarbone, the slope between her breasts. Teasing each nipple with his tongue until she was arching toward him and pulling him closer with pleading moans. Tracing the contours of her breasts with his claws and reveling in her delightful shiver as he made his way farther down. And at last parting her legs and coaxing her open with his tongue.

Theia whimpered as he teased her clit, her fingers curled in his hair and her hips tilting upward to give him better access. He wanted to make her come as he had the first time he'd tasted her, but her whimper had turned into whispered words: "Please fuck me, Lucien."

It was all he needed.

He scrambled for the condom packet and ripped it open only to realize he couldn't handle the latex with his claws. "Shit."

Theia saw his predicament and took it from him, sitting up to unroll the condom over his cock. "Teamwork," she said with a wink, and Lucien framed her face with his hands and kissed her, trying to understand how he'd gotten this lucky. If it was fate and blood and demons and curses that had drawn them together, he no longer cared.

He eased her back down to the carpet, still kissing her as he brought himself between her legs. Using his fingers was out of the question.

"You sure?" he asked one more time.

Theia rolled her eyes. "Jesus. Are you going to make me sign an NDA?" She wrapped her legs around his hips. "I'm sure. And I'm not made of china, I'm just getting older by the minute."

Lucien laughed—something he'd never expected to do at a moment like this. Time to get out of his own head. Theia moaned softly as he entered her, her crossed ankles at his hips urging him on. Every motion of her body, every sound she made said she wasn't interested in his attempt to be gentle. He soon forgot to be, rocking and grinding with her as he pumped his hips, their bodies perfectly in tune, rolling with her after a moment so that she was on top. Theia rode him without hesitancy, hands beside his head as she tilted her pelvis to just the right angle to bring herself to orgasm.

He watched her nipples tighten as she picked up speed, soft moans rising in pitch until she arched her back and cried out, hips locked against his, the cry becoming soft and melodic and a little wistful as it died down. Lucien gathered her to him and kissed her throat.

"You're amazing," he murmured.

Theia gave him a shaky giggle. "I had a little help."

"A *little*?"

She laughed as he rolled her onto her back.

Lucien winked. "I'll show you little." He let go of all restraint and fucked her with abandon, letting himself vocalize while Theia crooned encouragement, hooking her ankles behind him once more. The heat of the fireplace warmed his back, and sweat was making their bodies slippery. The climax burst out of him joyfully, and without meaning to, he flung out his wings as he came inside her, dimly recognizing that she was reaching a crescendo of sound herself, coming again on the heels of his climax.

It didn't occur to him until they lay panting beside each other, relaxing in the afterglow, that her second orgasm had come with the spreading of his wings. He chuckled to himself.

Theia rolled onto her side, resting her chin on one arm against his chest. "What?"

"I think you're fetishizing me. You just want me because of my wings."

"Shut up. I can't help it if you're even hotter as a demidemon."

"You're a wing freak. Admit it."

"Oh my God." Theia slapped his chest playfully. "I need to use the bathroom." She climbed to her feet. "Tell me it's not an outhouse."

"No, there's a genuine bathroom upstairs. Nicely appointed, too. First door on the right." He watched her go with a smile, admiring the way her body moved, perfectly at home in her nudity as she trotted up the stairs. He had to laugh at how stupid he'd been, fearing that she'd bring the demon out of him, that she'd entered his life to fulfill the curse. The curse had been triggered by something utterly unrelated to Theia—that Lucy was also affected was proof. And who knew? Maybe Theia was right. Maybe there was something in Madeleine's words that held the key to suppressing this. Maybe the Smok Biotech serum could control it. All was not lost. He'd had sex with a daughter of Lilith, and the world hadn't ended.

Lucien sighed with satisfaction. He'd probably better clean up. It would be awkward if Fran showed up, alerted by Lucy that he was squatting here, and found him naked on her sheepskin rug with a used condom discarded beside him.

A twinge went through his knuckles as he picked up the condom to throw it away, and Lucien flexed his fingers. Had his claws gotten sharper? He didn't remember them curling over quite so much. A pang struck his gut just as another twisted along his spine.

"No." Lucien stared in horror as the scales that covered the tips of his fingers moved up his hands.

It was Theia, after all.

Chapter 29

Theia took her time washing up, savoring the ache between her legs. For an event that had been given such a buildup—the hype beginning before she'd even hit puberty—losing her virginity was remarkably unremarkable. She wasn't magically changed. *Nothing* was changed, really—thanks to her personal experiments with penetration, there had been no proverbial cherry popping to speak of—except that she now belonged to this not-terribly-exclusive club.

And yet it had been far better than she'd imagined. Feeling Lucien inside her, being physically closer to him than she'd ever been to anyone—as close as they could get—had given her a connection with him she couldn't explain. She still felt him there, nestled in the sensitive folds of her body. She could smell him all over her, could still taste the salty-sweet drop glistening on the tip of his cock.

She licked her lips at the memory, smiling at her reflection as she washed her hands, hair a little cockeyed, eyes shining. She was, as Rhea would call it, stupid in love. Theia dried her hands, leaving her hair mussed, and headed back down, looking forward to falling asleep in front of the fire in Lucien's arms.

She slowed on the stairs. Lucien stood facing the fireplace, wings half-erect and shoulders slightly hunched, staring at his hands.

"Lucien? Are you okay?"

He cringed visibly at her voice—*cringed*—and didn't turn. "You need to go." His voice was rough, as though he'd been stoking the fire with his breath.

"What do you mean, go? I'm not going anywhere unless you're coming with me. Why don't we just sleep here tonight and figure out what to do in the morning?"

"There's nothing to figure out. There's nothing to be done. I want you to leave."

Theia came down the last few steps, her chest tight with anger not entirely her own. "We are *not* doing this. Whatever you've fixated on, it's your depression talking to you."

"It's not depression, goddammit." Lucien whirled around.

Theia couldn't help but gasp. His hands were curled into reptilian forelimbs, blue scales covering his arms and his abdomen. And his face…his face was drawn and inhuman. Still a human-shaped mouth and nose, but no longer the pale ivory flesh—it was leathery and taut and brilliant blue.

"Lucien…"

"No. I don't know who I am, but I'm not Lucien anymore. There's no Lucien. I'm a monster. And I want you to go."

She moved toward him, reaching for him, and he snarled, making her hesitate. "Lucien, I'm not going. I love you."

"Then there's something wrong with you. And if you won't go, I will."

"No—"

He'd moved so quickly that she was still staring at the place he'd been, her hair blown across her face by the breeze he created as he passed by her. Theia turned, and he was at the door.

He paused, his hands too gnarled to turn the knob, and lifted his head. "Tell Lucy I'm sorry." The door exploded outward as he rushed it and leaped into the air, and Theia ran after him just in time to see brilliant blue wings flapping in the distance.

"No. No, this isn't fair." Tears rolled down her cheeks as she stared up into the empty sky, stars twinkling over the pines as if nothing were wrong. She couldn't even call Rhea for comfort, and she was freezing, and the ache in her cunt was compounded by its emptiness. She went back inside and found the robe, curled up in it on the couch and sobbed.

Eventually, her swollen eyes and stuffy nose forced her up in search of tissues, and she saw the wide-open gap where the door had been. Anything might get in. What the hell was she going to do now?

"Thanks a lot, Lucien, goddammit!" she yelled into the emptiness. "You could have just asked me to open it for you." But she wouldn't have. And he'd known it. She started crying again, and then got mad at herself and at Lucien and Madeleine Marchant and Edgar Smok—and why not throw God in, even though she didn't believe in him—and then really full of white-hot murderous rage at Carter fucking Hanson Hamilton.

A light appeared through the trees in the distance—two lights, headlights—accompanied by the rumble of an engine. Her heart leaped for an instant until she realized Lucien hadn't left in a car. So who the hell was this?

The car came closer, a silver Range Rover, driving a little too swiftly over the gravel for her taste. Theia stepped back inside, tightening the belt on the robe and glancing around for anything to use as a weapon. All she could find was the poker by the fire, and she brandished it as the Range Rover came to a stop in front of the house.

A woman got out, middle aged with short salt-and-pepper hair.

She stared at the broken door lying on the ground and back at Theia. "What the hell happened to my door?"

Theia lowered the poker. "Are you… You must be Fran."

"I know who *I* am. Maybe you'd like to tell me who you are?"

"I'm Lucien's…" The poker slipped out of her fingers and clattered onto the floor. She wasn't Lucien's anything.

"You're the Marchant girl." Fran closed the door of the

Range Rover and came toward her. She stopped in front of Theia and took stock of her tearstained, puffy face. "Oh, honey. I'm so sorry."

Theia had effectively broken into her house, stolen her robe, eaten her food and had sex on her rug, but she flung herself into Fran's arms, undone by the sincerity of her emotion.

"Come on. Let's get you inside. Your feet must be frozen." Fran led her to the couch, and Theia sank onto it, unable to protest. The older woman produced a box of tissues from somewhere, and Theia blew her nose while Fran went outside and dragged the door upright to inspect it. She glanced at the hole in her house. "The frame is cracked, but I think I've got some extra screws in the kitchen. We can put this back up, at least overnight until I can get a carpenter up here."

She propped the door against the wall and went to get the screws, returning with a toolbox. "Come on, give me a hand."

Theia dried her eyes and came to hold up the door while Fran screwed the hinges back onto the frame. It closed, albeit with a little wobble.

"All right, honey. Let's get some hot chamomile into you and you can tell me what happened."

Fran listened as Theia relayed the events of the past twenty-four hours, frowning at the mention of Lucien flying away. "And I suppose his arm was no longer splinted."

"Splinted? No, it wasn't. I'd actually forgotten it had been. I guess the transformation healed the bone."

"It may have made him feel invincible, like a shot of adrenaline, but I doubt the break has healed." Fran sighed. "That boy is as stubborn as his father. Worse."

"You've known Lucien a long time, I guess."

Fran studied Theia's face for a moment, as though trying to decide whether to trust her. "You love him."

"Yes."

"He hasn't had much of that in his life, I'm afraid." She took a sip of her tea and exhaled. "I've known Lucien longer than anyone in his life. I was at his birth."

"You were the attending physician?"

She met Theia's eyes. "I'm his mother."

Theia blinked in surprise. "He didn't tell me."

"He doesn't know." Fran combed her hair back with her fingers with the same gesture Lucien used. "Edgar insisted that I sign a nondisclosure agreement."

"Oh my God. These people and their NDAs."

Fran smiled sadly. "I knew what I was getting into when I married him, but I somehow thought I could, I don't know, soften him. That fatherhood would soften him. When I realized what he'd done to escape the curse for himself—leaving it to Lucien—I was furious. I told him I wanted out. That I was taking my babies and leaving him. And he reminded me that I'd signed a prenup that relinquished any claim to his offspring. I tried to stick it out for a while, but I just couldn't. It was soul crushing. So I left, but Edgar's lawyer insisted on the NDA. If I ever wanted to see my babies again, I could never tell them who I was."

"That's barbaric."

"That's Edgar. I couldn't live with him, and I couldn't live without ever seeing my children again, so I agreed. And he 'graciously' hired me as the company's doctor, which included treating the children when they needed it. I lived for their bouts of croup and strep throat. Isn't that horrible?" She shook her head, remarkably unfazed by it. "But I tried to give them affection and guidance from the perspective of a caring family doctor. Especially Lucien. Lucy has always been pragmatic and resilient—not to mention headstrong. But Lucien feels things very deeply."

"He does," Theia agreed. "It's what I love about him."

Fran squeezed her hand across the table. "You may be

the first person to see that about him outside of Lucy and myself. No wonder Lucy's impressed with you."

"Impressed?" Theia laughed. "She hates my guts. She was going to drug me and wipe my memory to get me out of Lucien's life."

"She doesn't hate you at all. She just loves her brother. She's very protective." Fran shrugged. "She's had to be."

"I take it you know what's happened to her—that the curse has hit her, too."

Fran nodded. "But only partly. It hasn't progressed as it has with Lucien, and we may have some luck with the anti-transformative serum."

Theia looked down at her teacup. "Lucien's progression is my fault. It's my Lilith blood. We finally…" Theia blushed, waving her hand vaguely. "And then afterward, that's when it happened."

"No, honey. I don't think it had anything to do with you. It was Edgar. He's died."

"Died?" Theia raised her head, shocked. "I'm so sorry."

Fran pursed her lips. "I'm only sorry it hastened Lucien's transformation."

"But how? I thought the amulet was supposed to protect him."

"Someone removed it." Fran's eyes darkened. "And I'm quite sure it wasn't anyone on staff at the hospital."

"Carter Hamilton," said Theia.

"It would seem so."

"So it's too late. There's nothing we can do." Theia had lost him.

"There may be something. I remember Edgar talking about a loophole years ago. Beyond his personal cheat, that is."

"A loophole?"

"I've been through Edgar's papers at the office and the house, and so far I haven't found anything. But I know he had other places he kept things. Safes in other houses he owned. It could be anywhere. There's supposed to be something in Madeleine Marchant's own words, an addendum to her curse."

"You mean the riddle?"

"The riddle?"

"It's part of the text of the curse. She'd magically disguised it as a household list."

"How do you know that?"

"I found it," said Theia. "I translated it. At least as far as I could. I've got it on my phone."

She got up and found her phone in the great room. "Here it is." She showed Fran the first part she'd translated, the text of Madeleine's curse on the house of Smok. "I couldn't make out all the words that followed, but it seemed to be written as some kind of cipher, like she wanted someone to figure it out."

"'And from every seven born and gone among your house will the Devil reap a son.'" Fran sighed. "That's pretty much self-explanatory, I'm afraid. Every seven generations, the eldest son of the Smok family has inherited the curse and taken his place in hell."

"I know, but the part after—see here? I think it reads, 'The harvest will materialize…' But then I couldn't make out the next bit. After that, I got 'must the seventh son be bound to be free.'"

Fran took the phone from her and studied the original. "'The harvest will come to fruition when the *déesse*…the goddess…'" She chewed her lip. "The ink has smeared here. *Demande,* maybe?" She shook her head. "I'm not sure that's right. But the next is 'seed.' 'The seed of the…' I can't make out this word, but then it's 'of the first.'" She studied the illegible word again. "*Armure?*"

"Armor?"

"I'm not sure. Her handwriting is so stylized."

"So we've got 'The harvest will come to fruition when the goddess demands. To the seed of the armor of the first must the seventh son be bound to be free.'"

They both shook their heads. It didn't make any sense.

"Wait." Fran looked closely at the text again. "*Arbre*, not *armure*. Tree."

"The seed of the tree of the first… The family tree? Maybe the first is Madeleine. So the seed of Madeleine would be…" She glanced up at Fran as the meaning came clear.

"Madeleine's descendant." Fran set the phone down. "I've heard this before. Phrased a little differently, as a daughter of Lilith. It used to make Edgar pink with rage. No son of the house of Smok was going to be bound to a daughter of Lilith, as long as he was alive."

So a daughter of Lilith had to willingly bind herself to Lucien. Theia didn't have a problem with that. If it meant legally, well…that might take a little more convincing.

"But there's one more line," Fran pointed out. Theia had mistaken the stylized, repeating letters for the signature. "*Lié à l'enfant et lié à l'enfer.* 'Bound to the child and bound to hell.'"

That wasn't quite so promising. If she freed Lucien, it seemed to be saying, she'd end up pregnant and in hell.

Chapter 30

Theia waited until morning when Fran closed up the cabin to face the drive home. She had no plan for finding Lucien, and even if she found him, the loophole might not be a loophole at all. It might be a death sentence.

She responded to anxious texts from Rhea once she was back in range of a cell tower. That she'd found Lucien but lost him again was all she was willing to tell her. She wasn't about to go into the whole night. Rhea probably wouldn't tease her about it at a time like this, but she just wasn't ready to talk about the fact that she'd finally gotten laid. And she'd never hear the end of it if any of her sisters even suspected that she'd turned a guy into a dragon and sent him to hell the first time she ever had sex. That topped Ione's first time with Dev and Phoebe's sex tape combined.

There was also a message from Laurel. Once again, she was the only sister Theia could talk to. After checking in with the TA who'd subbed for her biology final, she met Laurel for lunch downtown.

"I have news," Laurel said before Theia could bring up hers. "I got in touch with Rowan and Rosemary."

"You did? That's terrific." But Laurel's face wasn't saying "terrific."

"We met for lunch, and they seemed really happy to see me. There was hugging and reminiscing, and it was all great until I told them I'd been in touch with Dad's other daughters."

"Oh. No."

"Yeah, it didn't go well. They think I've joined up with 'the enemy.'"

"I'm sorry, Laurel. I know it's not the same, but you have us. Ione's open to getting to know you, and Rhea will come around."

Laurel laughed. "I'm not holding my breath, but thanks. Anyway, it's not like it's any big loss. I hadn't seen them since I was little. I barely remember them. But it was just one more childhood fiction bubble popped, you know? I used to imagine they'd come rescue me and we'd all be a happy family again."

Theia reached across the table and squeezed Laurel's hand, but Laurel laughed and brushed it off. "Really, I'm okay. It's you I'm a little worried about."

"Me?" Theia swallowed. "What did you see?"

"Carter's up to his old tricks, isn't he?"

"Oh." Theia breathed a little sigh of relief that it wasn't something horrible about Lucien. "Yeah, you could say that. He convinced Lucien's father to sign half the company over to him—they own Smok International—in exchange for an extra dozen years of life, and then he killed the guy."

"Oh my God."

"He was dying anyway, but Carter never misses an opportunity to make a bad situation worse." She wasn't sure how much she should say about Lucien's problem.

"And Lucien—sounds like you decided which way you were going to go with that."

"Yeah, I guess both our visions came true there." Theia concentrated on her food to keep from blushing furiously, which she knew she would if she saw Laurel's face. "That's what I wanted to talk to you about, actually. It turns out—"

"He's turning into a dragon?"

Theia's head shot up. "Shit. You do see everything, don't you?"

"To be fair, it's not much of a leap, considering the rest of your family."

"Ha. Yeah. I just didn't think… I mean, I figured I'd

end up with the Prince of Darkness, not a full-on dragon who happened to *be* the Prince of Darkness. And here's the kicker—I think I can save him from being permanently damned to hell. But it might mean damning myself."

"By signing the contract."

Theia nodded. "Figuratively speaking."

"No, not figuratively. I saw an actual contract."

"But where would I get a contract that would involve selling my soul?"

"From Smok Biotech, I suppose."

"Smok…" Theia dropped her fork, and it clattered loudly on the ceramic-tile floor of the outdoor patio. "The fine print."

There was something to be said for being a monster. Lucien didn't have to care anymore whether what he was doing was right or wrong. He might not be able to pick up a pen and write a check from the bottomless Smok account to get what he wanted, but he could take what he wanted, when he wanted. And who cared if anyone saw him do it? They pissed themselves and ran away—or simply told themselves it wasn't real. Amazing what humans were willing to just *not see*.

The area around Heber-Overgaard in the White Mountains was known for UFO sightings—the *Fire in the Sky* abduction had allegedly taken place there in the '70s. So, really, what was one naked half man, half dragon breaking into the general market stockroom in the middle of the night and stealing a cheap pair of jeans, an oversized plaid flannel shirt—to wear over his tucked wings when he wasn't flying—and work boots? When they reviewed the security camera footage the next day, they'd probably find some way to explain it. Just another out-of-work logger on a bender. He'd grabbed a red ball cap for good measure.

Lucien had stayed close to the cabin, worried that he'd

left Theia vulnerable. He'd seen Fran show up, and he'd seen the two of them leave in the morning. Who knew what misguided plan they were hatching together? Fran must have already known what had happened to him after talking to Lucy. But it didn't matter what they were planning. He was beyond helping. And he didn't give a damn how they felt about it.

Except that he couldn't stop smelling Theia on his skin. And every time he closed his eyes, he saw her perched in his lap, head thrown back in ecstasy, that one bead of sweat trickling between her pink-tipped breasts as she came.

Great time to have a pair of gnarled forelimbs for hands.

It was also infuriating that the transformation hadn't progressed any further. Hell needed to get it over with and open up and swallow him already.

He waited for nightfall again and kept to the forested mountain terrain as he flew until he reached the stunning red hills and zeroed in on Lucy's villa in Sedona. As much as he'd relegated himself to the realm of monsters and as little as he was sure he cared about what happened to anyone else, he'd shared a womb with Lucy. And she'd inherited his stupid curse by mistake.

He perched like a gargoyle on the rooftop of the building opposite and watched for any sign of her. But nothing moved inside. If it had, he'd have seen it. His eyesight was excellent. He could have used this when he was hunting things like him.

So if Lucy wasn't inside, where the hell was she?

A little while later, he spotted her car pulling into the lot. She'd driven somewhere? Looking like a freak? Except when Lucy got out of the car, she wasn't a freak at all. She was just Lucy. No horns. No claws. No wings. No scaly anything.

Lucien swooped down and climbed through the window

of the kitchenette—shockingly easy to jimmy with a good pair of claws—and sat waiting for her in the dark.

She opened the door dressed in one of her tailored suits—nowhere to hide wings in that—and jumped when he moved in the dark. She didn't have his eyesight. Instead of turning on the light, Lucy dropped into a defensive posture, ready to kick his ass. And she probably still could, enhanced strength or not.

"Lu, it's me." The growl managed to sound like words.

She lowered her fists and straightened. "Lucien?"

"Don't turn on the light. I just wanted to see if you were okay. Looks like you're doing much better than I am." He moved in front of the window where she could see his silhouette against the streetlamp.

"Fran told me. Why did you take off again? Why not stay there?"

"And do what? I can't be with Theia." The words were ragged in his throat. "Her blood did this to me." It hurt that Theia had been the cause of it. Even though she hadn't known for certain it would happen, it felt like a betrayal.

Lucy interrupted his thoughts. "It wasn't Theia. Edgar's dead."

"He's…" Lucien blinked. "How?"

"Someone took the amulet during the night. He suffered total organ failure almost immediately."

He ought to feel bad about it. He *did* feel bad about it. But on a level so deep he didn't know how to touch it. Lucien was floating above it. Stoic. Monster. Whatever.

"That's why you're back to normal. The curse fully transferred to me."

"Sort of. Not entirely. If you hadn't run off, Fran and I could have helped you get the serum. She got some for me last night. It works, Lucien. It suppressed my symptoms."

"But it's too late for me now."

"I think it might be, yes."

"Why am I still here? Why hasn't my damn soul been harvested?" It occurred to him that maybe it had. Not having a soul would explain why he couldn't feel anything.

"I don't know. You haven't fully transformed yet."

"Maybe there's a backlog in hell."

She smiled in spite of herself. He'd always been able to make Lucy smile when she didn't want to.

"You know Edgar set up the trust to transfer to you on our twenty-fifth birthday. Maybe there was a reason for that. Maybe whatever effect Hamilton's meddling has had on the curse, it can't fully manifest until the time is right."

Lucien nodded. It made sense. Their birthday was in a few hours. It gave him a sense of finality even as it terrified him. He couldn't go on like this indefinitely. If he were his former self, he'd have hunted his new self down by now. But there were other things he could hunt down in the meantime.

"I'm glad the serum helped you, Lu. Take good care of the company. And don't be too quick to send me new souls." He smiled even though she wouldn't see it and turned away.

"Lucien, wait." Lucy crossed the room, holding something out to him. His phone. "At least take this with you so I can contact you if something changes."

He shook his head. "What could possibly change that matters?"

"Just take it, goddammit."

He showed her his claws. "How would I even use it?"

"I disabled your password and the thumbprint recognition. You can use your knuckles. I tried."

Lucien sighed and snatched it from her to avoid an argument. "Happy birthday, Lu." He leaped through the window before she could say anything else. He hated long goodbyes.

He went through his list mentally—rogue creatures and deserving half humans he'd kept in his sights. He supposed he didn't need the crossbow now, even if he could have wielded it.

There was a certain priest in the Phoenix area who'd been transferred from one parish to another for years to hush up scandals. The harm he'd caused to the young boys entrusted to his spiritual care had been bad enough while he was mortal. Now he fed on his victims as well after having been turned by a former parishioner in an act of revenge. He ought to have died, but he'd managed to summon Smok Consulting in time to save his pathetic life and allow him to continue it as a closeted bloodsucker.

Maybe that phone would come in handy after all.

It didn't take long to nail down the priest's current location. Lucien took to the air and soared over the desert with the night birds. They viewed him with idle curiosity. He had a good sense of direction, and he'd memorized the map on his phone. The grid of the metropolitan area was laid out for him in lights.

At the church, his heightened senses led him to the scent of blood. He found the priest in the darkened chapel. Far too late for mass, he was cloistered in "confession" with a child he must have kept after. Lucien tore the roof off the confessional, exposing the monster. He hadn't really thought about the standard problem with eradicating vamps. Wooden stakes were a Hollywood cliché, and burning them—with sunlight or fire—just made them angry. Though it did have the satisfying effect of making them experience a great deal of pain while they grew new skin.

But it turned out that Lucien's enhanced abilities included being able to bite a vamp's throat in two, taking the head clean off. Tasted disgusting, but it did the trick. The boy cowered on the floor of the confessional as Lucien tossed the priest's corpse aside. What could he possibly do to allay the child's fear? Nothing, he realized. He was the devil, and the devil had just killed a priest.

A familiar chill rushed into the church, the thundering of horses' hooves and raucous calls accompanying a hunting horn in the distance. Through the open chapel doors, Lucien could see the approach of the Wild Hunt. He straightened to face the chieftain.

Leo Ström swung off his spectral mount, sword drawn, taking in the bloody scene with cold calculation. He approached Lucien with his sword raised, his brown leather duster scattering the flurry of ice that seemed to emanate from the Hunt itself—ice in May.

"So this is how I get to hell," said Lucien. "Makes sense."

Leo drew up short. "Lucien?"

His growl was still mostly intelligible, but he was surprised that Leo recognized him. "You have a good eye."

"Just a good nose."

He wasn't sure how to take that. He imagined he wasn't smelling too good about now, and he didn't think he'd had a body odor problem before turning into a monster.

"Fair warning," said Lucien. "I can more than beat you in a fight now, and I don't intend to go easily."

"Go? I'm not here for you. I came for this piece of garbage." He kicked at the head and it rolled under a pew. Leo studied Lucien's condition. "Slept with Theia, did you?"

Lucien burst out laughing—though it probably sounded more like a roar. It felt good for a moment to have a genuine laugh.

Leo sheathed his sword inside the duster. "I could use someone like you in my hunting party."

"That's a generous offer coming from a man I tried to kill, but I won't be around much longer. Just waiting for my soul to be collected."

"Sorry to hear that." And he actually did seem sorry. "But it won't be collected by me."

Lucien nodded and turned toward the shattered stained-glass window he'd climbed through. "Do me a favor," he said as he jumped onto the sill. "There's a very frightened boy in the booth over there. If you could get him some help, I'd appreciate it. He's lost a lot of blood, and he'll need some antivenin therapy from Smok Biotech. Give Lucy a call. She'll know what to do."

Leo nodded and tipped his hat. "Farewell, my friend."

Lucien hadn't expected that. Maybe he did have some capacity for emotion left in him, because it made him blink his eyes rapidly as he took flight. Maybe it was just the force of the wind.

As he pondered his next target, his phone vibrated in his pocket. Lucien ignored it. For all he knew, Lucy might have told Theia he had the phone, and he couldn't afford to let himself indulge in any communication from her. When it buzzed again, he decided to set down on a rooftop and turn off all notifications before he took a moment to figure out where he was headed next.

A message from Lucy showed on the screen, just Hamilton.

Well, that was a thought. He could take out that piece of shit as a gift to both Lucy and Theia.

But the next message was just as brief and cryptic. Daisy.

Daisy? The shade that had possessed Lucy?

Painstakingly, he texted her back. Where are you?

He could see her typing, but there was a long pause before the answer came—in three distinct texts.

Holy C
Holy holy holy
Holy shit, you are both so stupid. Enjoy rotting in hell.

Lucien let out a roar and shot into the air, his blood boiling—and it didn't feel like a metaphor. He'd been right about the incident with the shade. Carter Hamilton was controlling it, and he was using it to control Lucy. But what had all that "Holy" stuff been about? She'd started typing Holy C— but seemed unable to finish whatever word started with *C*. Holy Cow? Holy Christ?

It could be the name of a church. *Holy Cross.* The Chapel of the Holy Cross was a well-known landmark in Sedona. Lucy had been trying to answer his question: "Where are you?"

He arrived at the darkened church nestled between a pair of Sedona's ubiquitous red buttes to find Lucy alone in front of the chapel. She faced outward atop the short brick wall that served as a tourist lookout point for the desert valley.

Lucy turned at the sound of his approach and grimaced. "God, she was right. You really do look like hell." Something glittered in the darkness, nestled in her cleavage. She saw him zero in on it and looked down, fingering the gemstone. "Pretty, isn't it? They let me in any time of day or night to visit Edgar. All I had to do was give him a little Judas kiss and take this with me."

Lucien chose not to respond to the taunt. "I offered to help you the other day. I could have freed you from the one who's controlling you. Lucy still can."

A hooded figure stepped out of the shadows beside the chapel. "Lucy will do nothing but join you in hell." The figure drew back the hood, and Lucien wasn't the least bit surprised to see that it was Carter Hamilton.

He took a menacing step toward the necromancer. "Lucy is stronger than you think. And I'm about to end you."

"Are you really? I highly doubt that."

Hamilton made no move to block him or even evade his attack as Lucien charged with demon speed—and nearly tumbled off the edge of the wall behind the spot where Hamilton had been standing. Just like at the reception, it was only a projection.

"Coward."

Hamilton smirked. "This from a privileged scion who didn't even have the guts to take his place at the table of one of the most prestigious and influential firms in the world. So now that place is mine." He glanced at Lucy. "And it can be your sister's as well if I choose to keep her in her body." He stroked his phantom hand over Lucy's breasts. Her face had gone blank. Daisy's autonomy within the body had apparently been suspended.

The idea of what Hamilton might do to Lucy when he was gone turned Lucien's stomach and made his blood heat with rage. "You keep your damn hands off Lucy's body. If you think I can't find you wherever you're hiding and tear your head off with my bare hands, just try me."

"And how are you going to manage that while you're fending off my friends?" Hamilton nodded over Lucien's shoulder. Something in the desert night smelled even worse than Lucien.

He turned to find half a dozen shuffling revenants crawling over the rocks. But these weren't just revenants. They were *draugr*, resurrected in putrefying bodies to serve their master.

"I understand they find living women irresistible," said Hamilton. "Like a drug habit or a sweet tooth they can no longer satisfy while in their graves—and then, suddenly, they're presented with candy."

"You piece of shit," Lucien growled and turned, snarling, to face the advancing *draugr*.

Chapter 31

Lucy wasn't answering her phone. Theia had found her copy of the Smok Biotech contract, and she needed a legal interpretation of the fine print. If only Phoebe were back from the Yucatán. She'd stopped practicing, but corporate law had been her specialty in school before she'd gone to work for the public defender. Of course, this was more like infernal law.

While Theia was pondering what to do next, she got a call from a number she didn't recognize. With all that was going on right now, she figured she shouldn't ignore anything.

"Polly would like to have a word with you." The voice was oddly thick, as though it was coming from a larynx not built for human speech.

"Oh, really? And just who is this?"

"Hello, Theia." The caller had evidently handed off the phone.

"Polly."

"I've been alerted to a situation I thought you ought to be aware of."

"Oh?"

"Normally, I wouldn't discuss one patron's business with another, but when a patron betrays my trust, all bets are off. I thought you'd want to know that Carter Hamilton is currently employing necromantic means to put Lucien's sister at risk. And when Lucy is threatened, Lucien responds."

So that was why Lucy wasn't answering. Goddamn Carter, up to his old tricks.

"Do you know where they are?"

"The Chapel of the Holy Cross. You're likely to need reinforcement against Hamilton's magic. That's all I can tell you. It's all I know."

"Thank you, Polly. I won't forget this."

"I know."

Theia tried to reach Rhea on the way to Holy Cross but got no answer. Ione was equally unresponsive. What was going on? The clock on her dash said it was almost midnight. She hadn't realized how late it was. Maybe they were in bed.

She arrived at the road to the chapel with a sense of foreboding. The last time she'd been here had been under the hypnotic control of a century-old Nazi bent on stealing Leo's soul. She had zero memory of the experience, but Rhea had told her enough that she counted herself lucky.

A gray, bloated form scrabbled across the road in front of her. Theia swerved to miss it, but it was already gone. A terrible stench, worse than Mrs. Ramirez, seemed to seep in through the vents as she drove through the space it had occupied. Theia's stomach lurched. Rhea had described the undead thing that had been unleashed on them by the Nazi, Brock Dressler, and Theia was certain she'd just seen one. Another skulked in the bushes ahead.

As Theia parked the car in the lot at the top of the hill, it occurred to her that Polly might have been setting her up. Why should Theia believe she was betraying a confidence and not just helping Carter further his agenda?

An inhuman, gut-churning bellow came from the walkway to her left, followed by a slightly more human snarl and a thick sound, like something punching through gelatin. As she came around the corner of the lot, she tried to make sense of what she was seeing. The remains of several of the things were strewn across the rocks, but the severed parts were inching back toward one another, and in the center of the melee what looked like a reptilian lumberjack was ripping one of the things in half.

Theia blinked, holding her hand over her mouth and nose against the awful stench. "Lucien?"

The glowing eyes fixed on her for a moment, and he growled. "Dammit, Theia. What are you doing here?"

Trying not to vomit. Theia swallowed against the urge. "Polly told me you needed help."

"Of course she did." He tore the arm off the *draugr* advancing on him and hurled it into the brush. "Start grabbing up these things before they reassemble and toss them as far as you can."

Theia swallowed again. "Grabbing?" There was no time to be squeamish. Steeling herself, she plucked up a—God, she didn't know *what* it was—and flung it over the low wall into a clump of cactus before grabbing another and hurling it into the parking lot below. "Isn't there any way to kill them?"

"Not unless you're a necromancer or you know where their graves are. Best I can do at the moment is keep them in pieces."

Theia was pitching the things at a fairly even pace, keeping up with the ones creeping toward each other while Lucien battled the already reassembled. She tried not to look as he tore them to pieces. At least she'd forgotten to eat today, because she'd seriously be losing her lunch.

At a lull in the festivities, she realized someone was standing motionless on the top of the wall beside the chapel, facing out toward the valley. "Is that Lucy?"

Lucien hurled a bloated head up into the rocks, and it burst like a melon. Theia steadied herself against the wall, trying not to succumb to a convulsion of dry heaves.

"She's being controlled by a shade. Waiting for Carter to come back and give her the order to jump. I've been too busy fending off these foul things to try to get her down from the wall."

"A step-in?" If only Phoebe or Rafe were here. Phoebe was a talented evocator who'd been channeling step-ins most of her life, and Rafe, of course, had the power to command the dead. "Maybe I can get the shade to talk to me."

"Be my guest. Her name is Daisy." Lucien punched a *draugr* that had crawled over the parking lot wall, having apparently found all—or most, anyway—of its parts, and beheaded it with a kick to the jaw. "Wish I had that Viking sword of Leo's. Would make this work a lot quicker."

Theia approached Lucy carefully, sitting on the wall beside her and swinging her legs over the edge. The side of the butte below wasn't a sheer drop—more like a wide, sloping ledge. Lucy would have to take a running leap to fling herself over it.

"Daisy, can I talk to you?"

Lucy didn't move, but after a moment, she broke her silence. "What for?"

"I was just wondering if you could communicate with Lucy. Can she hear me when I talk to you? Can you hear what she's thinking?"

"She's asleep." Daisy gave her a quick sideways peek as if she was curious about this new person addressing her. "I can wake her up. But she won't be able to answer you."

"Would you, please?"

Daisy shrugged Lucy's shoulders, and her posture changed, becoming more tense and alert.

"Lucy, I don't know if you can hear me—"

"She hears you."

"Fran told me she'd given you something to control those symptoms you were having. Do you know if Carter is aware of your…condition?"

"I told you, she can't answer."

"Well, you can. Does she know?"

Daisy sighed and pondered for a moment. "She doesn't think so."

"And how long do you think the medication lasts? When do you need to take it again to keep the condition under control?"

Lucy's brow wrinkled—clearly not an expression that was natural to her—as Daisy tried to understand the answer. "Not long? I think that's what she said." Daisy turned to look at Theia. "Why? What are you trying to do?"

"I don't think you really want to do what Carter's telling you. I think Lucy can help you defy him."

"You don't know anything about it. *He* said he's got one of my bones." She threw a glance at Lucien, who was flinging the lower part of a *draugr* torso over the wall.

"And we can get it back and release you. I've done this before with my sisters. We bound the necromancer so he couldn't hurt anyone."

Daisy laughed, making Lucy sound hoarse. "Yeah. I see how well that worked out."

Theia shrugged in acknowledgment. "Well, we still have to find the source of his power, but we could certainly help you."

"The ugly one over there said the same thing. It's bullshit. You just want me to step out because all you care about is your friend. But even if I could, I wouldn't. Why should I? You'd just double-cross me as soon as I did. And then he'd make me pay."

"My brother-in-law is Rafael Diamante. Have you heard of him?"

Lucy's brows drew together in suspicion. "The Lord of the Dead? I don't believe you."

"What does Lucy say? Can you tell if she tries to lie to you?"

Lucy frowned. "I can hear what she's really thinking.

She says it's true. She also says he's in the Yucatán. So how's that going to help me?"

"He can be here in just minutes using his *nagual*—his animal form." She hoped that was true. God, Phoebe was going to kill Theia if she interrupted her honeymoon. "His power trumps Carter Hamilton's."

Someone else spoke behind her. "That's what you think."

Theia whirled to see Carter looking overly dramatic in a hooded cloak.

"He's not really here," Lucien growled. "He's a projection."

"Am I?" Carter smiled. "Try me."

Lucien stalked toward him and flung the rotting forearm of a *draugr* in his direction as if he expected it to go through him, but a look of consternation crossed his face when Carter snatched it out of the air.

"You'd be wise not to underestimate me." Carter tossed the forearm aside and glanced at Lucy with a nod. "Daisy."

Lucy's face fell, and she looked up at Theia. "You see? You couldn't help me at all." Before Theia could stop her, she'd turned and stepped off the wall, tumbling onto the rock ledge below. Lucien's roar drowned out Theia's shout. Lucy was still crouched on the ledge, arms and legs scraped up but otherwise apparently unhurt, staring down at the sheer drop as though trying to psych herself up to jump.

Lucien had charged toward them, but Carter threw him back with some kind of necromantic spell. Whatever magic he'd tapped into this time was definitely stronger than before. It was up to Theia to stop Daisy from finishing what she'd been ordered to do.

While Carter was occupied with Lucien, she climbed over the wall and skidded down the rock face, digging her fingers into a crevice for purchase as she slid toward Lucy. With her fingers firmly in the handhold, she stretched out her other hand.

"Daisy, don't do it. Just take my hand."

Lucy turned halfway and glared at her. "You said the Lord of the Dead would come."

"I can call him right now if you promise to stay put for a moment." She put her hand in her pocket and took out her phone, selecting Phoebe's name one-handed. Rafe's cell phone number was third on the list under Phoebe's and her landline. Might as well go straight to the source and save time. Phoebe was going to murder her either way. It rang three times, and Theia was afraid it was going to voice mail when Rafe answered.

"Well, hello, Tweedledee. Phoebe says this better be good…" He paused. "And also 'why the hell is she calling you, Rafe, are you having an affair with my baby sister?'" Rafe laughed. "Just relaying the message. What's up?"

"I need your particular skills to stop a shade from killing someone."

Rafe's voice turned serious. "Of course. How can I help from here?"

Theia hit FaceTime and held out the phone. "Rafe, this is Daisy. Carter's controlling her, and he wants her to throw Lucy Smok off a cliff. I was hoping you could talk her down."

Rafe spoke from the video. "Daisy, can you hear me?"

Lucy's eyes went wide as she straightened. "It's really him."

"Listen to me, Daisy. The necromancer who's bound you has usurped my authority. I know it will be difficult for you to obey, but you must ignore the pull of his magic and do as I tell you. Come away from the edge."

The struggle was visible on Lucy's face. "I can't."

"Yes, you can. Come to me." He held out his hand as if he were actually standing there and she could take it. Maybe as a shade, she could.

Daisy took a halting step forward, looking as though the

effort caused her physical pain. Theia inched toward her, pondering how to grab Daisy's hand and hold the phone at the same time without letting go of the crevice in the rock.

"That's it," Rafe encouraged her. "You can resist him."

Lucy was just a foot away from Theia now. Above them on the walkway, the sounds of conflict between Lucien and Carter were ramping up, rocks shattering and crashing. She let go of her handhold. What mattered right now was keeping Daisy from jumping. She could worry about getting back up once Lucy was safe.

Rafe continued to speak in a calm, authoritative voice. "Come to me. Take Theia's hand and let her help you."

As Lucy reached for Theia's outstretched hand, her face suddenly contorted. "No. No, it doesn't matter. You can't help me. He's taken my body away from me. What's the difference?"

"Daisy, don't," Theia pleaded, but in an instant, Lucy had taken two broad steps back. Theia lunged toward her with a shout as Lucy plummeted from the cliff. The phone tumbled from Theia's grip as she grabbed for a handhold once more, and it bounced on the rocks and skittered off to follow Lucy.

Chapter 32

Theia nearly skidded off the rock ledge with them, managing to catch herself with a sneaker wedged into a crack. She closed her eyes, in shock, feeling the currents of the brisk spring wind swirling around her in eddies. It was quiet in the chapel courtyard above. Crickets were serenading as though it were an ordinary May night. What had happened to Lucien?

Carter's treacly voice echoed down to her. "It's pointless to go against me, Theia. You and your sisters should have learned that by now. My devoted, if somewhat pungent, foot soldiers have defeated all of them. You can come back up here and face me like an adult, or you can follow Lucy. The choice is yours. But know that either way, I own you. You signed an oath of fealty to Smok International and its leadership. And that leadership is now me. The house of Smok is no more. I own it all."

Which meant Lucien was dead. Despair fell over her like a black cloak. Like darkness must feel if you could touch it. What was the point of resisting? Carter had won.

Theia worked her shoe out of the crack that kept her from sliding farther, resigned to letting gravity finish what it had started. As her feet dangled over the empty air, something stirred it, whipping her hair around her face. Out of the darkness, crimson wings swooped toward her, and a pair of talons grabbed her by the shoulders, carrying her up and over the wall and dropping her onto her feet.

Beside her, Lucy brushed off her suit as she folded her wings over the torn jacket, glaring at Carter, who stood speechless before her. "Wrong again, asshole. You forgot to wish me a happy birthday."

"So you inherited the curse as well." Carter's pale brows drew together in irritation. "But not fully. Not enough to open the gates of hell, as your brother has done. And not enough to cast out my little helper. Daisy, close her mouth."

Lucy had taken a menacing step toward him, but she stopped and stared blankly as Daisy took over her conscious functions once more. The unexpected shift had apparently only bought Lucy momentary control.

At the perimeter of the courtyard, the reassembled host of *draugr* hovered as if awaiting Carter's command. And against the rocks behind Carter lay an object that at first glance appeared to be a large, blue, crumpled tarp. But Theia knew what it was. It was the wyvern from her dreams. It was Lucien. She ran to the dragon and knelt beside it. It was still taking shallow breaths.

"He lives, for the moment," said Carter. "His transformation was very helpful in unlocking a source of power I've been seeking to acquire for some time. 'When the heir to the infernal throne rises, the gates of hell are opened, and when the heir descends, the gates are closed again for seven generations.' A little something I learned from Madeleine Marchant."

Stroking the dragon's neck, Theia was barely paying attention to him, but the last words sank in, and she raised her head. "You've been around since the *fifteenth century*? I'd have thought you'd be better at this by now. But I guess practice makes perfect, you fucking psychopath."

Carter laughed, though his eyes weren't smiling. "I didn't learn it from Madeleine directly. I learned it from the elder Rafael Diamante. He was quite the magical history buff."

"So where are these open gates you're so fond of? I don't see anything."

"It's not a visible manifestation. At least not for someone of your limited vision. It flows through the heir—*H-E-I-R*. In essence, he *is* the gate. I can't keep it open indefinitely, of course, but the longer it remains open, the greater the power I can absorb."

The wyvern stirred beneath her hand, its gem-like blue eye opening. Theia scrambled back as it struggled to rise. As dragons went, it was fairly small, but it was still easily twice as large as a man. The wyvern rose onto its jointed wings, using the forward joint like the forelimbs it no longer had to walk on the stone like a bat. The right wing was clearly broken, and it dragged beside the wyvern as the dragon hobbled forward, eyes fixed on Carter as though sizing his throat for its teeth.

"Still trying to win." Carter shook his head. "You can't win, Lucien. You lost before you were born—the moment Edgar sold your soul. You should know better than anyone that a soul price will always be paid, no matter how you attempt to avoid it."

A soul price.

Theia narrowed her eyes at him. "You killed that poor old woman. It was your people who gave Rosa Campos the overdose when Lucien went to take it back."

"*Lucien* killed the old woman when he tried to circumvent his own corporate contract. I didn't feel it was good business." Carter raised his arm and held up his palm toward the wyvern as if signaling "stop."

"I'd rather not strike you again. It would most likely hasten your death. The way I see it, I have at least another five or ten minutes of energy transfer from the gates if you just stay put." The wyvern continued moving toward him, and he shook his head. "Have it your way, then. I've gotten plenty."

As Carter lifted his arm, Theia darted forward and put herself between him and Lucien. "Over my dead body."

Carter observed her with amusement. "If you insist."

Theia threw her arms out at her sides as if to block Carter's attack from the wyvern and closed her eyes, bracing for impact, but as she did so, she seemed to feel her sisters' hands taking hers and the Lilith bond forming. They'd pooled their strength before, but never without physical contact. Maybe she was just imagining it. Or maybe Carter had been over-confident about the success of his *draugr* minions.

She closed her fists around the invisible hands, taking strength from them, and willed Carter's attack to be inert. Theia felt the strike, but a field of energy rushed out of her at the same moment, and the space between the two opposing forces seemed to warp for an instant, rippling like gelatin as her energy absorbed the blow.

She opened her eyes to find Carter's blazing.

"Stop wasting my time. You're only going to exhaust yourself, and Lucien is in no condition to take me on. I have endless reserves of energy as long as the gates remain open, and you have the finite potency of demon blood."

He was trying to wear her down emotionally before he wore her down physically, but it was true. She wasn't going to be able to hold him off for long, even with the Lilith bond. Maybe if she had a binding spell from Ione, but without her sisters physically here, there was no hope of that.

As she repelled a second attack, the aura of a vision wavered at the perimeter of her sight. Theia clenched her teeth. What good was a vision now? It would only detract from her concentration. Lightning flashed in the distance, and thunder rolled around the edges of the surrounding mountains, circling the butte, echoing from rock to rock. The air began to ripple with the electrified energy of a monsoon storm, though it was too early in the season.

Theia watched the lightning fork beneath the clouds again, horizontal, a bolt of brilliant blue turning the night sky to daylight for an instant. A loud crack split the air directly over their heads, almost deafening her. The strike had been just feet away. She seemed to be floating within herself, unanchored but full of power—the power of the demon goddess.

She shouted something at Carter as he struck out at her once more, a word she didn't even recognize, old French. Carter jerked backward as if she'd stunned him. Behind her, the dragon was moving once more, taking a running leap into the air. Despite its broken wing, the wyvern barreled into Carter like another flash of lightning and toppled him to the ground. Carter lashed out, not with magic, but with a short blade. He slashed the leathery blue scales and drew blood.

The dragon stumbled, and Theia shouted again, more words she didn't consciously know, and this time she could see her feet actually floating inches off the ground. Carter made a noise of pain, as if her words were hurting him, but lashed out once again with the desperation of a cornered animal. The dragon was limping as it tried to evade the blade, and it sank into scaly flesh.

Noise and chaos seemed to have risen up around the valley, stones and cactus undulating, as if the ground were fluid. And then Theia heard the unmistakable thunder and whinny of horses and the blast of a hunting horn.

Leo, in a cowboy hat and duster, led the party charging toward them across the sky. "For Freyja!" he shouted—or was it "For Rhea"?—and leaped from his mount with his sword drawn.

Theia was still muttering foreign words, and they trailed out in front of her like pieces of gold rope, forming unfamiliar curly letters she knew instinctively only she could see, and surrounding Carter Hamilton.

The wyvern pinned Carter against the stone with the thick joint of its good wing and roared. Fire blasted from its nostrils and curled around the hand that held the weapon, burning it until Carter shrieked and let the blade fall.

Leo stood over him, sword point at Carter's throat, and nodded to the wyvern. "I've got this, brother."

Electrical energy was still pulsing through Theia, but the Lilith bond was receding, and she stumbled as her feet touched the ground. She grabbed for Lucy's arm, and a startled noise escaped Lucy as Daisy's shade stepped out of her, visible to Theia somehow, looking as shocked as Theia felt. Both Theia and Daisy hit the ground, and Lucy turned as if waking from a trance.

"Theia? Are you all right?" She reached down and touched Theia's shoulder but recoiled, gripping her arm, as the dissipating energy snaked toward her in a visible static spark. "Shit. I think you've been struck by lightning."

Daisy seemed to look through them both, eyes wide, and Theia turned in the direction of her gaze to see an unusually large crow alight on the top of the wall. As it lowered its wings, the crow became a man—Rafe Diamante, his iridescent blue-green-and-violet-feathered wings half folded at his sides.

"The Lord of the Dead," Daisy whispered.

Rafe, wearing nothing but a pair of rather thin white linen pants, stepped down from the wall and came toward them, eyes taking in the entire chaotic scene.

He reached a hand down to Daisy and touched her lightly on the head in an almost fatherly gesture. "You're free, Daisy. Go where you will."

The shade, tears pouring down her cheeks, nodded and dissipated.

"Theia." Rafe sank onto his haunches. "Thank God. I thought you'd gone over the edge with..." He paused and looked at Lucy. "I thought you'd both—oh, I see." He nodded with approval. "Nice wings."

Lucy smirked. "Same to you." She glanced at Theia.

"Theia's a bit…electrified. I think lightning struck her. I'll leave her in your hands. I need to see to Lucien."

"I'm fine," Theia insisted as Rafe looked her over with concern. "Although I could see Daisy. I thought for a minute I might have crossed over without realizing it."

"You saw her shade?"

Her head was starting to throb. "I think I was channeling my sisters. Maybe it was Phoebe's gift."

"Phoebe can't see them."

Theia shrugged. "I don't know. But really, I'm okay. Stop fussing." Around them, the *draugr* minions still hulked on the perimeter. "Maybe you can do something with them, though."

Rafe stood and nodded. "We had some in Cancún as well. I sent them packing."

"I think he sent them to Rhea and Ione, too," she said as Rafe helped her up.

"They seem to have lost their power." Rafe threw a smug look toward where Carter still cowered under the point of Leo's blade. He threw his arms out wide and stretched his wings. "Return to your graves, unnatural *muertos*. Your master is defeated."

The nasty things recoiled and shuffled backward, whining, and disappeared into the dirt as if they'd sunk into the ground.

In the corner, by the chapel doors, Lucy was engaged in an earnest discussion with the wyvern. As Theia approached them, Lucy turned and shook her head in warning.

The wyvern's blue eyes met Theia's for a moment, heavy with sorrow, before it turned and limped toward Carter. Leo stepped back as the wyvern grabbed hold of Carter by its foreclaws. It leaped into the air, taking Carter with it, and flew away.

Lucy blinked back tears. "The gates couldn't stay open

any longer. I'm sorry. He can't survive in this realm. He had to go."

Madeleine's loophole no longer mattered. Lucien was gone.

Chapter 33

Theia rode back to Phoebe's place with Rafe—who had expended too much energy in translocation to return to Phoebe the same way—letting him take the wheel. In her lap were the torn garments Lucien had cast off with his transformation, including the stupid red cap.

After a few minutes of respectful silence, Rafe glanced over at her. "Those Lucien's?"

Theia nodded. "I suppose you think I'm an idiot for falling for him anyway after your warning. After reading your father's archives."

"Of course I don't. Nobody's an idiot for loving someone. And from what I saw, it seems I misjudged Lucien and his sister without even knowing them."

"They were both entangled in the darker side of Smok's business," said Theia. "But Lucien was trying to do the right thing. And I think, in her way, Lucy is, too. Of course, it's all hers now. Lucien inherited the *other* end of it."

"I'm sorry, Theia."

"Me, too."

He turned onto the semiprivate drive that led to Phoebe's place. Lined up on the side of the road in front of the house were two cars besides Rhea's Mini in the driveway. Among them was Ione's motorcycle, her not-so-secret secret.

"What's going on?"

Rafe shrugged. "I haven't been in contact with anyone. I left my phone in Cancún. Phoebe's probably going insane right now."

"Yeah, sorry about that."

He parked behind what looked like Dev's Mercedes. "Seems like the gang's all here."

Rhea threw open the screen door and ran out as Theia stepped from the car, and Dev darted after her to catch the speeding ball of Puddleglum fluff making a break for it.

Rhea bear-hugged her. "Why haven't you called or answered your texts?"

"I lost my phone."

Rhea glanced at Rafe. "So you did make it here. Phoebe's on the phone, and you're in big trouble."

Rafe grinned. "What's new?"

"Ouch. Trouble in paradise already?"

"Nothing but good trouble."

Rhea linked arms with Theia, turning her toward the house. "You're not going to believe who else is here."

Inside, Laurel was seated in Phoebe's living room, with Ione next to her. They looked remarkably civil.

"We pooled our resources," said Rhea. "Did you feel it?"

"I… The three of you? Together?" Theia shook her head in amazement. "I certainly did. I just didn't realize— I thought maybe Phoebe had somehow joined remotely."

"It was Laurel's idea." Ione rose. "She came to find me. Said you were in trouble. She'd seen it, but she couldn't reach you. So we formed the bond."

So it was Laurel's ability she'd been channeling when she'd seen Daisy's shade.

Phoebe's exasperated voice came from the cell phone sitting on the coffee table. "Is that Theia? Goddammit, you guys! What's going on?"

Rafe picked up the phone. "I'll take care of her," he said with a wink and headed for the bedroom.

Rhea snorted. "I'll bet you will."

Theia tucked her hands into her pockets, feeling awkward. "Carter said he'd sent *draugr* after all of you."

Dev nodded. "We handled it."

Rafe popped his head out before closing the bedroom door. "He's finished, by the way. He won't be bothering anyone anymore."

Rhea glanced at Theia. "Leo took him to Náströnd?"

Theia shook her head. "Lucien took him." She sank onto the couch. "And he's not coming back."

"Oh, sweetie." Rhea enfolded her in her arms. "I'm so sorry."

They stayed up talking until Leo arrived just after dawn. Dev and Ione headed home, giving Rafe a ride to his place, while Laurel headed back to Flagstaff despite Rhea's insistence that she was welcome to sleep there. Theia finally got to crash.

When she woke after noon, Rhea and Leo were gone. Rhea had left her a box of her favorite sugared cereal. Theia curled up in the papasan chair with the entire box, eating it by the handful. She'd finished her finals, so she had the whole day to just wallow and be disgusting.

But someone was heading up the drive as she glanced out the window. Theia sighed and set the box aside as Lucy pulled up in front of the house. How had she gotten this address? She supposed Smok's database had everyone's information. She locked Puddleglum in the bedroom and opened the door.

"Theia." Lucy took off the dark shades that made her look like one of the Men in Black. "I wanted to thank you for what you did for me last night."

Theia shrugged. "You would have done the same." She held the door open. "Did you want to come in?"

"Actually, I came by because I knew I couldn't reach you by phone." Lucy held out a brand-new smartphone. "It's from Smok."

"Oh." Theia took it reluctantly. "I guess I'm still bound by the contract."

"It's not that kind of phone." Lucy made an attempt at a warm smile. "It's just a gift. The contract, well…that's what I wanted to talk to you about."

"Did you come to wipe my memory? Because I think you're going to have to use your flashy thingy on my entire family if that's what you have in mind."

"Flashy thingy?"

"*Men in Black.* Never mind."

Lucy shrugged. "I don't watch television. But, no, I didn't come here to make you forget. I talked to Fran this morning, and she mentioned the text you and she translated."

"It's kind of a moot point now. He's gone."

"It's not as if he's dead."

"Well, it's not as if I can just go to hell, either. Unless you came for my soul."

Lucy made her scoffing version of a laugh. "Not today." Well, that was encouraging. "I received a call from Polly. She said you should go see her."

Theia sighed. "What, do I owe her more blood for her help last night?"

"I think she has something for you, actually."

Polly might have saved Lucien's skin last night, but there was no way she didn't want something else for her trouble. Theia might as well get it over with. The sooner all of this was over, the sooner she could get back on track with her program and her classes. She hadn't even looked at the outline for her thesis in over a week.

Business was apparently already in full swing for the evening when she arrived at Polly's place. The bouncer seemed to recognize her, even though she was sure she hadn't seen him before. Maybe there was something about Polly's gammon that gave them away. Maybe he could smell it on her; he was big and bearded, and he looked like a werewolf. On second thought, maybe he was just a bear.

A waiter escorted her to Polly's table without asking who she was, and Polly, mercifully, was alone.

"You wanted to see me?"

Polly smiled, aqua-blue hair flowing in waves over her shoulders to rest on a teal gown that sparkled with red where her fingers brushed the nap. "Theia, darling. Have a seat."

Theia scooted into the booth reluctantly.

"Lucy told me what happened with Lucien, and I understand there was some prophecy about the two of you? That only one of your line can break the Smok curse?"

"I could have, but it's too late."

"Not necessarily. I know the words. I heard them many years ago. And the key begins with the descent of the goddess."

Theia wrinkled her nose. "I don't even know what that means."

"It means, sweetie, that you couldn't have broken the curse before it came to pass, before Lucien's transformation was complete. It means you have to journey to the underworld to complete your 'quest.' It's one of the oldest myths. You can find it in many cultures."

"And how the heck am I supposed to journey to the underworld?" She'd already asked Rafe and Dev and even Leo about the possibility. Even if they'd been willing to help her enter it, there was no telling if Lucien shared a common underworld with them. It was all about perception—his. "The gates have to be opened, and only Lucien can do that. And I can't contact him."

"The thing about Polly's is that it exists in many dimensions at once, in many places and many times. If I choose, the doors can open virtually anywhere." Polly smiled darkly. "Even in hell."

It took Theia a moment to understand the significance. "Wait...are you saying you can get me into hell?"

"That's exactly what I'm saying."

"What would I have to give you?"

"Nothing at all, darling."

"You don't strike me as the altruistic type."

Polly laughed. "No, indeed. But Lucien is special to me, and I'd prefer for him to be able to travel in this plane and not be trapped in hell being miserable. Besides, I owe him one, and I don't like owing people. So if you'll agree to go in and get him, I'll open the door for you. It's as simple as that."

"And will you open the door for me to come back, or is this a one-way ticket?"

"Such a smart question. Two-way door. No strings attached."

She didn't need to think about it. "I'm in."

As busy as the Grotto was, she couldn't imagine how Polly was going to manage having a door that opened into hell, but Polly, of course, had a separate, private door. When she opened it, it was impossible to see what lay on the other side.

Theia took a deep breath and stepped through. But she was still in Sedona, golden-orange setting sun glinting off the red rocks encircling the little enclave where Polly's was tucked. The back door led to the alley. Polly was full of shit.

Theia turned around, but the door had disappeared. Great. She'd fallen for the dumbest trick in the book. She hoped the siren and her creepy friends were having a good laugh.

When she walked around to the front of the building, the parking lot was empty. The sign that said Polly's was still there, but the club looked dark inside. What was going on?

Theia yanked open the door, determined to give Polly a piece of her mind—and found Lucien, in his human form and looking absolutely devastating. He was seated in front of a fireplace in a leather chair with his feet up on a matching ottoman, intent on reading some leather volume.

Theia breathed in sharply, intending to say his name, but only a squeak came out as she choked on her own saliva. He'd taken her breath away. Again.

Chapter 34

Lucien glanced up at the sound, and his mind couldn't make sense of what his eyes were seeing.

"Theia?" He jumped up from the chair, scattering the delicate pages as he let the ledger fall to the floor. Maybe he was starting to hallucinate. She couldn't be here.

He crossed swiftly to her and peered into her eyes, hands at her shoulders, and Theia sputtered, eyes welling up as if she'd swallowed wrong and couldn't catch her breath.

Lucien pounded her on the back awkwardly. "Are you okay?"

Theia nodded, the moisture in her eyes a little brighter as she gazed up at him.

"What are you doing here? You haven't…"

"No." She shook her head. "I haven't crossed over. Polly opened a door for me."

"Polly?"

"She said she owed you one. When I went through the door, I thought she was pulling my leg. It looks just like home out there."

Lucien nodded. "It's merely a different plane. It's all about perception. Which is why you perceive me as myself, as you knew me."

"Stop talking like you're dead."

"I am, to the plane above. I can't come back, Theia." He tucked her hair behind her ear, pained by her understated beauty. "God knows, I wish I could." The irony of his choice of words wasn't lost on him.

"But you can. Fran and I deciphered Madeleine's message. The curse can be broken."

"Theia, it's too late. I'm not human anymore. If I went back, I'd be a monster. And I have a job to do here. It's all very bureaucratic and dull, actually. You can't even imagine. Nobody burning in a lake of eternal fire, no demons prodding people with hot pokers. Just a lot of people doing ordinary jobs. And a lot of creatures that have to be cataloged and managed in their proper zones to keep order. There are lower levels, of course. Personal hells. Like where Carter Hamilton will spend eternity feeling powerless and bitter."

"Lucien, listen to me. There's a way for you to return with me—at least part of the time. If you're willing to be bound to me."

"Bound to you?"

"Fran said it was a blood bond." Theia's cheeks went pink. "We might…have to have…offspring together."

"*Offspring?*" Lucien's hands fell away from her shoulders and rested at her hips. "Are you telling me you'd have my child?"

"Well, not right away. I mean, I have my master's to finish, and I was hoping to get my PhD—"

"You realize you're certifiable."

"Maybe a little." Her mouth curved up in a slight, mischievous smile. "All it means for the moment is that we'd agree to be bound by blood. Always. It would break the curse that keeps you from being able to retain your human form in the earthly plane—and it would tie me to hell along with you."

Lucien frowned, the little flicker of hope she'd ignited extinguishing. "I can't tie you to hell, Theia."

The flush of pink in Theia's cheeks took on the redder hue of anger. "You don't get to make decisions for me, Lucien. If I want to tie myself to hell, I damn well will."

Despite his misgivings, Lucien couldn't help smiling. "*Damn* well, huh?"

"Oh, shut up." Theia slipped her arms around his neck as he let his hands travel around her waist. "Just say you'll do it and kiss me."

Lucien did the latter, just to silence her, but their mouths together felt right—everything about her felt right. He'd forgotten how not touching her felt like he was deprived of air. And the idea of having a baby with her wasn't, as he'd always imagined, an unthinkable prospect. It wasn't anything he wanted any time soon, but he wouldn't mind the practice involved.

"This binding…how would it work?"

"Fran said it could be a finger prick and a vow. Or…other physical contact involving…fluid exchange."

Lucien laughed. "You're saying if we have unprotected sex, I can walk out that door with you and end up in the earthly Polly's."

Theia smirked. "That's the idea. And there's no rule that says we can't use the morning-after pill. I've got some at home, in fact."

Lucien lifted an eyebrow. "Do you, now?"

"You never know when you're going to need it—or a friend or sister is."

He trailed his fingers down her arm, enjoying the little shiver the touch elicited. "I suppose they're all waiting for you now."

She shook her head. "They have no idea I'm here. Polly's offer took me by surprise."

Polly was *full* of surprises, it seemed. She never did anything without expecting something in return. But Lucien was thinking too much again. There would be plenty of time to find out what she wanted later. Right now, Theia was here, and he was flesh and bone, and he wanted her so badly his chest ached.

Theia was watching him intently, as though cataloging his emotions as he cycled through them. "So what do you think? Should a son of Smok and a daughter of Lilith be eternally bound by blood?"

"Is that a proposal?"

Theia colored. "I didn't mean… That's not exactly…"

Lucien laughed and kissed her, pulling her into his arms. "Doesn't matter, darling. For you? Whatever it is, the answer's yes."

Despite thoroughly enjoying the necessary ritual, Lucien maintained his skepticism until he walked through the back door with Theia, prepared at any moment to do a quick about-face and return to his den. But when the door opened into Polly's suite, he was still himself. Polly was nowhere to be found, and Lucien walked out the private door with Theia into the spring Sedona evening, and nothing changed. Crickets were chirping, Oak Creek was still running over its polished slabs of sandstone, and the full moon was unabashedly gorgeous.

Lucien drew Theia into the circle of his arms. "No claws or wings. It seems Madeleine's loophole works after all."

"Fran said you should come see her. There might be a time limit to how long you can stay, but the Smok Biotech serum might still be useful in setting your own schedule."

"Time enough to figure that out, though, I suppose. Right now, I just want to go home with you and do some more bonding."

Phoebe arrived home from Cancún the following morning, still a little cranky about having been abandoned on her honeymoon and a bit put out to discover that Ione and Dev had beaten her and Rafe to the altar. Rhea had conspired with Dev to throw Ione a surprise reception, and Theia helped distract Ione, taking her shopping and bringing her back to her house to find the entire place festooned with cream satin ribbon and balloons.

Lucien showed up looking gorgeous in a buff-colored silk suit. "You didn't tell me what you'd learned about Fran," he murmured as he wrapped his arms around her from behind.

"I didn't think it was my place."

"Lucy knew. For years, apparently. I asked her why she didn't tell me, and she said it wasn't her fault I was born stupid."

Theia laughed. "Yeah, I get that kind of thing from Rhea a lot. There's an evil twin in every set, I guess. So did she have any insight into how long you can stay?"

"She thinks it may be tied to the phases of the moon."

Theia turned in his arms and smirked. "So I guess we'll have to wait and see if we get PMS together."

Lucien grinned, but then his expression turned serious. "I also talked to Polly. Her comment about owing me one was evidently in regard to my circumstances solving a rather vexing problem for her. It turns out Carter Hamilton was actively trying to turn her patrons against her in his bid to control the unnatural world. That stopped, of course, the moment I took him with me through the gates. But what she said she owed me wasn't the opportunity to let you complete your rescue mission." Lucien winked. "That was for her own selfish purposes. What she wanted was to return this."

He reached into his pocket and pulled out a small, hinged red velvet box. Theia's hand flew to her mouth as he opened it to show her the most perfect, flawless diamond nestled inside.

"It was the price she asked of me that day you drove me to the Grotto. A tear. You showed me I could express them without shame. So I think it should be yours. It's just the stone, of course, at the moment. We can shop for a setting together."

Theia couldn't speak as Lucien dropped to one knee in his exquisite suit among the tea roses in Ione's garden.

"Theia Dawn, will you do me the honor of becoming *officially* eternally bound to the reluctant Prince of Darkness?"

All she could do was nod, happily. As usual, he'd taken her breath away.

* * * * *

Lucy Smok's story,
KINDLING THE DARKNESS,
will be available in August 2018
from Harlequin Nocturne!

For more passionate stories from Jane Kindred,
be sure to check out the rest of the
SISTERS IN SIN *series:*

THE DRAGON'S HUNT
BEWITCHING THE DRAGON
WAKING THE SERPENT

Available now!